HIGHLANDER
REDEEMED

ALSO BY LAURIN WITTIG

HIGHLANDER REDEEMED

GUARDIANS OF THE TARGE

BOOK 3

LAURIN WITTIG

Montlake
Romance

Text copyright © 2015 Laurin Wittig

Published by Montlake Romance, Seattle

www.apub.com

Amazon, the Amazon logo, and Montlake are trademarks of Amazon.com, Inc., or its affiliates.

ISBN-13: 9781477829769
ISBN-10: 1477829768

Cover design by Regina Wamba

Printed in the United States of America

For all the amazing, strong, talented women in my life—
each one of you inspires me!

CHAPTER ONE

Southwestern Scottish Highlands, 1307

SCOTIA MACALPIN PUSHED HER DARK HAIR OUT OF HER FACE
with the back of her water-wrinkled hand, then looked up from
the huge iron pot she was scouring as she had every morning and
every evening for what seemed her entire lifetime, though it had
only been a fortnight or a little more. The sun was barely peeking
over the ben into the Glen of Caves as she glanced down the
length of the narrow clearing outside the caves that for weeks
now had been home to the MacAlpins of Dunlairig. Mud puddles
from last night's rain had collected in those places her kinsmen
trod most—around the cookfire, on the path to the privies, and
here, where she squatted, as she did twice a day, scouring pots.

A breeze, soft with damp and scented with the earthy aromas
of the forest floor and the sharp freshness of pine and balsam,
drifted across her face, shoving away the less pleasant odors of
too many people living in too close quarters for too long. She gave
thanks for the momentary respite and tried to ignore the beckoning of the forest that had of late become her refuge, her sanctuary.

She closed her eyes and tried to remember her life before this
place. Before her mother died, before the castle's curtain wall
had fallen and the great hall burned, before her entire life had
been ripped from her, leaving her alone amidst her clan—bitterly,
silently, alone.

Scotia fisted her hands, ignoring the sting where the sand had scoured them as well as it did the pots, and reminded herself that this was war, as she did many, many times each day.

She opened her eyes and forced herself to look at the women huddled over their tasks, worried expressions drawing down every face she saw. Even the bairns and weans were unnaturally quiet. The few warriors about seemed to sag, as if the very ground pulled too hard upon them and they had not the strength to resist it much longer. If she was tired, she knew they were fatigued beyond measure from constant rounds of training, scouting, watching, planning, and back to training. Most of the warriors were deployed outside this glen, searching and watching for the next wave of English to arrive—her sister, Jeanette, the newest Guardian of the Highland Targe, had seen the arrival in a vision. Everyone was touchy, snapping at each other, the caves filled each night with the echoes of uncomfortable dreams.

Waiting was far worse than fighting.

This was war.

She kept saying that to herself, trying to make sense of the words. She had known war raged in Scotland most of her life, sometimes with the English, sometimes between factions of Scots, or even clan against clan, but never had it been this close, this personal. And this was personal. The English king had sent spies into her home—one had killed her mother, the other was now their chief and the husband of her cousin Rowan, also a Guardian of the Targe.

"Pay attention to those pots, Scotia," Peigi, the elder who acted as chatelaine in this terrible excuse for a home, chided her, as she did every day of late. At least Peigi spoke to her . . . sometimes.

Scotia drifted through her kinsmen these days like a ghost everyone knew lived amongst them but no one wanted to acknowledge. After the clan's success at the Battle of the Story Stone, a brief euphoria had swept through everyone but her. At first she had been too shocked at how close she had come to losing her life to join in the celebration—she ran her fingers along the healed, but still raised line along her throat where the gap-toothed soldier had cut her before she could free herself—but then the clan's mood had swiftly changed to anger at Scotia. They blamed her for causing both the battle and the death of the young warrior, Myles. Once the shouting stopped, she was left with averted gazes and silence even from her sister, Jeanette, and her cousin, Rowan. Her father scowled at her and said nothing. Even Duncan, who always seemed to champion her, often at the same time he chided her for whatever scrape she had gotten herself into, refused to look at her.

"Scotia, the pots!" Peigi barked at her. "They do not clean themselves."

"Aye, Peigi, I ken that all too well. Leave me be." She scowled at the old woman and scooped up a fresh handful of sand from the battered bucket at her side, and returned to scouring the large iron pot that was still crusted with bits of porridge from the morning meal.

"That I cannot do, lest you hare off after some new scheme that will get more of us killed without cause."

"I did not—"

"You did." Her voice quavered, but was still strong enough to carry to all who worked near them. "We all ken it, as you should."

Scotia sighed, scooped up another handful of sand, hardening herself against the humiliation she knew the old woman was going to throw at her again, railing at Scotia for something that was not her fault though Scotia seemed to be the only one who understood that.

"You went against your chief's orders and forced Myles into a position he should not have been in, and for that he paid with his life." Peigi glared at Scotia, something she had never done before Myles's death. "We have all coddled you too long. 'Tis beyond time for you to grow up and take responsibility for your actions." Peigi banged a long wooden spoon against the rim of another iron pot that hung over the cookfire, then replaced the lid and turned her full attention back to Scotia, her gnarled hands fisted on her hips, one still clenching the spoon. "You are a woman now, Scotia, but still you act a child. It is unbecoming of the daughter of a chief, the daughter of anyone, to be so thoughtless with the lives of others."

Scotia peeked through her lashes as several other women working near the cook circle stared up at her. The momentary acknowledgment that she still existed among them almost made up for the glints of distrust and disappointment she saw in their eyes. She looked away from them all. It was not her fault that the English had killed Myles. Aye, he would not have left his perch high in a tree for the ground if she had not passed by his lookout position, but she was not the one to pull the blade and kill him.

She turned her attention back to her task, blocking out the sideways looks, the shaking heads, and the heat on her cheeks that she knew gave away her humiliation at Peigi's groundless blame. She could shun them just as much as they shunned her. Besides, if the clan had taken up the task to fight the English who had made their way into the MacAlpins' glen, rather than just watch for them, she never would have taken it upon herself to search them out to deliver justice. If the clan had attacked, she never would have been taken hostage, never would have had a knife held at her throat. It was not her fault they had a chief who did not ken how to lead. 'Twas Rowan's fault for falling in love with the spy, then declaring him her Protector, displacing Scotia's da from a position he had held with honor for many years.

But then again, if the clan had attacked, as it should have, she never would have had reason to train herself in the art of weaponry so she would never again be at the mercy, if one could call it that, of the English bastards.

A bloodthirstiness she had not thought herself capable of until recently took over her mind, loosing all the hatred she had for the English to burn through her veins, gathering all the grief she had endured at their hands into a writhing ball of pain where her heart used to beat, and in her belly . . . she did not ken what that sensation was, but it roiled, dark and oily, demanding release. She had to be ready when this new and larger invasion of English soldiers arrived, and she did not have long if Jeanette's visions were correct—and they had been so far.

She kept scrubbing at the already clean pot while glancing around the clearing again, taking note that once more no one was looking at her. The council was huddled in their circle on the far end of the clearing arguing, though they kept their voices low enough she could not make out what the topic of dissension was today. She feared Nicholas would allow them to argue forever without ever stepping up and declaring what they would do, as was his right as chief and Protector of the Guardians. The women were all busy at their tasks, preparing food for the evening meal, spinning the wool that had been shorn from a few sheep before sending them off to hide with some of the older lads in the bens, or minding the wee ones. Peigi had sent the lads to gather wood, and the lasses to haul water. The warriors had disappeared to whatever duty they had for this day. Peigi was muttering to herself as she laid more fuel on the fire. She looked over at Scotia and wagged a finger at her, which Scotia knew was the woman's admonishment to stay put, then she stomped off toward the main cave as if she marched into battle.

The forest ran right up the benside to the edge of this narrow clearing. The sweet scented breeze once more washed over her. The trills of small birds and the rustle of leaves called to her to slip into the cool, welcoming quiet of its arms, an enticing escape from all the averted eyes and thunderous silence that was her only company amongst her kin. She was tired of pretending she didn't care how they treated her. She was tired of Peigi's constant barrage of blame. She could not bear to waste another minute doing things that did not matter. *This was war,* she reminded herself again, and she was not about to be left behind scrubbing pots when the next battle was engaged. Next time, one way or another, it would be she who cut down their foes.

She took one more look about, satisfied for the moment that no one was paying her any attention, and slipped away into the refuge of the trees.

DUNCAN OF DUNLAIRIG SHIFTED ON THE COLD STONE THAT served as a seat in the makeshift council "chamber," a circle of downed tree trunks and large stones set up at the far end of the clearing from the cook circle. Though it had only been a little more than a fortnight since Malcolm returned with his kin, it seemed every morn of Duncan's life had been spent in this circle listening to plans being debated and adjusted that had only been set in place the day before. He had nothing to add to what had already been said. He had no specific role on this council now that Malcolm MacKenzie had been named the chief's champion, along with being an unprecedented second Protector of the Guardians once he and Jeanette had married. There was nothing special required of Duncan that the Guardians and other council members couldn't provide now that Nicholas had settled into his role as chief.

Duncan tried to pay attention, but found it hard to stay focused on the debate as it bounced from person to person around him. Nicholas and Rowan, the chief and a Guardian, seemed always in accord with each other, though Rowan would at times defer to her uncle, Kenneth, the previous chief who now served as an advisor. Jeanette, also a Guardian, and her warrior husband, Malcolm, each held strong opinions about what the clan should do to prepare for the impending English push into Glen Lairig, hers based on the abilities and lore of the Guardians, his on firsthand experience fighting the English in King Robert's army. Uilliam sat next to Duncan, no doubt feeling every bit as useless as Duncan did now that Uilliam was no longer Kenneth's champion. He grunted his agreement or dissent periodically, and it was only because Duncan had known the great bear of a man most of Duncan's five-and-twenty years that he could discern the difference.

"The warriors are well prepared, would you agree, Duncan?"

Malcolm's question drew Duncan back to the conversation, though he was surprised Malcolm asked for his opinion.

"Aye." He sat up a little straighter and tried not to look startled. "The younger lads still need to train daily, but the men are very well prepared. Malcolm's experience with English hand-to-hand tactics has been very useful. I have learned much from him so far."

Uilliam grunted his agreement just as Peigi's voice rang out from the mouth of the main cave. "Och, that wee devil." Everyone looked in her direction as she strode as fast as her aged legs would carry her to the council circle. She started talking before she was halfway across the clearing. "She's gone again, Kenneth! That daughter of yours will not do as she is told, and I am mightily vexed. Something must be done!" she declared as she came to a stop between Rowan and Jeanette, her knobby finger wagging in the air at Kenneth across the circle.

Rowan and Jeanette shared the same scowl, but it was Jeanette who said, "She promised me she would not slip away again. I vow, if she were a wean I would beat her."

"Or we could just truss her up and tie her to a tree," Rowan said.

"I'll not see her tied up"—Kenneth actually glared at Rowan—"but I agree something must be done."

"Aye," Uilliam said. "None of the lads I've set to watching her can find her once she gets into the forest. 'Tis Duncan's fault for teaching her how to track when they were weans."

Duncan started to defend himself when Peigi started to laugh, or maybe *cackle* was a better term for the sound that wheezed out of the old woman.

"He did, did he not?" Her head was bobbing up and down hard, and a disturbing glint was in her eyes. She turned to Nicholas, who sat on the other side of Rowan. "It seems Duncan has little to do here at this time." To hear his own thoughts from her mouth made him wince. "Why not set him to minding Scotia, at least until she can be trusted to keep her word?"

"Do you think that will really happen?" Rowan asked Peigi.

"Aye, my lassie, I do, but it will take some time . . . and the right kind of patience, which it seems is in short supply from all of us of late. But Duncan has always had more patience with her antics than the rest of us, even if he scowls over them."

Duncan realized he was scowling now. 'Twas bad enough that he had no particular role in the clan, but 'twas worse that Peigi wished to set him to minding Scotia, as if she were a bairn in need of a nursemaid.

Duncan watched as Nicholas polled everyone but him with only a look. Each one nodded.

"Very well. Duncan, I know it seems I ask you to take up a menial task, but we cannot allow her to get away with this sort of behavior any longer. Already she has caused one death by slipping away. The lads have been instructed to follow her but to keep a good distance so they would not fall into the same fate as Myles, but she clearly uses that distance to her advantage to evade them. We cannot risk that she is putting the clan in danger"—Rowan started to interrupt him, but he took her hand in his and rested them on her thigh. "I ken she does not mean to put us in danger, but she has, and she may do so again if we are not careful with her."

Rowan sighed but did not argue.

"As you wish," Duncan said, rising from his stone seat, the old adage *be careful what you wish for* whispering through his head. He'd wanted to be useful, to have a role in the clan's preparations, and now he did. Scotia's mood would not be improved when she discovered he was her new shadow.

Lord Sherwood, commander in King Edward of England's army, dragged himself up the ladder as waves crashed on the deck above then sluiced down over him and into the bowels of the pitching ship. It took all the fortitude he could call upon not to humiliate himself by vomiting as he struggled to pull himself onto the deck of the storm-battered vessel. It was one thing for the men he commanded to spend their days and nights retching into a bucket in the fetid cargo area below, but it would not do for the son of the Earl of Walesby and the leader of this expedition to show such weakness. He grabbed for a rope and braced himself as another of the unending waves broke over the side and tried to wash him out to sea.

"Release that line afore I slice yer hand from yer arm!"

Sherwood glared through the dim light and frigid rain that sliced at him like tiny, icy knives. A sailor with the squinty eyes of a rat was making his way toward him.

"I said let go of that line!" he said, grabbing Sherwood's wrist and wrenching it as if he thought that would be enough to make Sherwood release his hold on the one thing that was keeping him from washing overboard.

Sherwood swallowed bile as the ship pitched hard, and he was surprised that the man who gripped his arm seemed to need no other help to keep his feet.

"I said, let go and get yer arse back below where it belongs—"

"Release me," he said, trying to hold on to his dignity as the ship's deck bucked and tried to toss him into the sea again.

Sherwood had put up with too much disrespect from the crew of this ship already, spending days and nights shut in the dark below with his men when the captain should have had them to Scotland a full week past. This latest storm was more than anyone should have to bear, and he was in no mood for further excuses. The king had sent him to find the Highland Targe, take the head of the spy who had betrayed the king by keeping the Targe for himself, and retrieve the red-haired witch who, if the stories were true, controlled the damn relic. The stakes were high if he succeeded, and he'd not let the captain's fears of storms and roving Scottish and Irish ships keep him from his destiny any longer.

Perhaps a purse filled with silver would get the captain to finish this journey with alacrity where strong words and threats had not.

"You will release me and take me to the captain this minute," Sherwood said, letting all his years of command lend gravitas to his voice.

"I'd sooner toss meself into the drink than take ye anywhere. Get below afore you cost someone his life!"

Sherwood shook his head at the belligerent jackanape, drew his dagger and sank it deep into the man's gut before the sailor knew what he was about.

He leaned in close but still had to shout over the gale, "I give you my word, I shall see that you make it into the 'drink.'" He was pleased at the mix of surprise and pain that suddenly glazed the sailor's eyes as his grip weakened. "I am on the king's business, and none of you shall keep me from it any longer." It was past time he took control of this poor excuse of an armada.

Sherwood quickly looked about to see who else he might have to deal with, but there were only a few sailors on the deck, and those who weren't struggling up on the yardarm to lash down a loose sail were focused on the fight. He pulled his dagger from the sailor and watched as the man crumpled, one hand to his gut, the other reaching as if he searched for something to hang on to just as another wave crashed over them, swamping the deck. Sherwood barely kept his feet. When the water fled back into the sea, the sailor lay where the deck met the railing, either stunned or dead. Sherwood didn't care. He took one more look about to make sure none of the others were bearing down on him, intent to send him back below, then took advantage of the relative calm between the crashing waves to move toward the quarterdeck. He made slow progress though it was not far, stopping every few steps to hold on as a wave broke over the ship and swept off the deck. The third time he looked back the sailor's body was no longer to be seen.

Sherwood always kept his word.

CHAPTER TWO

DUNCAN MOVED THROUGH THE FOREST LIKE A DEER, QUICKLY and silently, stopping only to examine Scotia's tracks when he could find them. The wily lass had doubled back on her own trail, then veered off through a burn a short way, then out on the same bank and down the ben. He did not know whether to be irritated that she worked so hard to hide from her own kin, or proud of her for making it difficult to track her. Instead of debating his own feelings he braced himself for an argument as he continued to follow her obscure trail down the ben.

Scotia would not come back to the caves just because he told her to. Nay, he'd likely have to carry her back over his shoulder or drag her back, hissing and scratching like a cat. He did not look forward to it. He did not like the idea of humiliating her that way, but she gave him little choice since she had once more put her own selfish desires before those of the clan, and if that meant he had to treat her like a wean to get her attention, then that was what he would do.

After more back tracks and false trails than he had anticipated, he heard an odd sound, along with quiet muttering, and knew he'd found his quarry. He crept up to the edge of a bright area in the wood, too small to be called a clearing, and discovered Scotia standing in a narrow beam of sunlight. It glinted off her night-black hair, reflecting iridescence, like the sun on a raven's wing. She held a stick in her hand like a child's play sword. A real targe, a round shield, was strapped to her left arm, and she gripped a dirk in that hand. Irritation sizzled through him. He knew she had to have pilfered the targe and dirk from somewhere, perhaps denying them to someone who needed those weapons. He touched the dirk at his hip, just to make sure she had not taken his. If only he could convince her to think of someone other than herself for a change, then he might be able to help her redeem her past behavior. He might be able to convince the clan to forgive her.

If he could not, he feared the clan might choose to take more extreme steps than shunning her in their midst. They might banish her altogether. Such an action, though justified, would tear her family apart and put Scotia's life at risk. The Highlands was no place for a woman alone. It was no place for anyone alone. Duncan might not have the role he wished in the clan, but if he could avert the need to send her away, 'twould serve the clan well.

He braced himself for the verbal battle to come, but before he could make himself known, Scotia began to move, hesitantly and without her usual grace, but so focused on her task he could almost taste her determination. She watched her feet, letting her weapons go slack in her hands. Even so, he quickly recognized the exercise Malcolm had been teaching the lads a few days ago. She shook her head, then started the series of moves again, talking to herself just under her breath. She repeated the process over and over until, all of a sudden, she flew through the short exercise as if it were a dance she had known her entire life, thrusting, parrying, spinning, attacking the dirt-clad roots of a toppled tree. The sharp sound of wood on wood reverberated through the forest like a woodpecker hammering on a hollow log.

His breath caught in his chest. She was magnificent. Beautiful. Strong.

She fought as if demons threatened her life.

And Duncan could not take his eyes off her. She was everything he would expect her to be if he did not know her so well. That thought stopped him.

Each time Scotia did the exercise she moved a little quicker, until suddenly her feet tangled in her skirts and she landed hard on the ground.

"Blast and damnation!"

Her curse resounded through the wood. Duncan noted that even as she fell she was wise enough to hold her weapons away from her. Clearly she had been carefully watching Malcolm work with the lads, and even without the hands-on guidance of a trained warrior she was remarkably adept at mastering the moves.

She got to her feet quickly and untangled her skirts, revealing well-worn brogues and shapely, strong calves as she did. She took her starting position and began again, repeating the exercise as she had before, faster and faster, until her sides heaved and she stopped, pushing damp hair away from her flushed face with the back of her sword hand.

"Take that, you damned Sassenachs," she said as she stared at the tree roots, her stick once more held at the ready. "I have killed each and every one of you this day and you shall not harry my home and my family again."

Duncan's breath hitched and his mind raced. If this was what she wanted, to be trained as a warrior—and he did not doubt for even a moment that was her intention—he had the weapon he needed to keep her close. If she wanted to be treated like the adult she must become, if she truly wanted to learn to fight for her home and family, he would give her a reason to behave like a woman worthy of her lineage. He would give her a reason to be reasonable. And he did not care if Nicholas or Kenneth or any of the others agreed with his plan. They had given her over to his keeping.

Duncan would teach Scotia to be a warrior.

The lass was immune to any negative reactions such training might instigate in the clan, as evidenced by her behavior past and present. She could train herself with anger and selfish goals—for he knew she still sought her own vengeance against the English no matter what Nicholas and his council planned. That way would likely end up being even more dangerous to her own kin.

Or he could convince her to let him train her properly, not just physically, but to fight without anger, to fight with the keen intellect he knew her to have, and to fight with the natural talent she appeared to hold. He could train her to be an asset to her clan, something no one thought she could ever be after the last few weeks.

He was certain everyone would be safer if Scotia knew how to fight, how to defend herself and those who fell within her realm of troublemaking. If she'd known how to fight, Myles might yet be among the living.

He held his ground as she once more paced herself through the exercise slowly, just as Malcolm had the lads do, muttering each move as she did so. But this time, when she flew through it, he watched her with new eyes, with the eyes of a teacher, assessing her weaknesses and her strengths—making a plan for her training.

SCOTIA TRIED TO IGNORE THE PAIN IN HER SIDE WHERE SHE'D landed on a large stone. She must remember to bring the trews she'd "borrowed" from one of the lads and hide them with her training gear. Skirts clearly did not mix with battle.

She shoved loose tendrils of hair out of her face, reset her stance, and prepared to do the exercise yet again. She refused to stop until she had it perfect. She gripped the stick hard, pulled the targe up to guard her torso, took a deep breath—

"If you turn a bit more to the side, you shall present a smaller target to your foe."

The calm focus she'd been cultivating shattered with the first startling word. She'd spun around to face the intruder, her poor excuse for a weapon gripped hard and held high to defend herself, before she even realized 'twas Duncan.

He leaned his long, lanky frame against a young oak tree, his thumbs casually hooked in the belt that held his faded green, brown, and the palest yellow plaid about narrow hips, as if he'd been standing there watching her for some time. A fitful breeze ruffled the unruly curls of his shoulder-length, dark-brown hair, and the errant thought that he should braid it at his temples as her da did destroyed what remained of her battle focus. His posture spoke of relaxed indifference but she knew him too well to be fooled. His intense curiosity, a curiosity that easily matched her own, lit his dark eyes, giving the lie to his guise. Damn the interfering man!

"I thought you were at the council meeting," she said, turning back to the exercise as if she cared nothing that he had discovered her secret. She hoped he would leave now that he had found her, now that he knew she was not haring off across the bens to kill any English soldier she could find, though she knew the tenacious man would not.

But her mind was no longer sharply focused on the exercise. Instead, though she took the starting stance, she prepared herself for another of Duncan's lectures on her disrespect for the safety of others, or on her disrespect for the rules laid down for her behavior by Nicholas, Kenneth, Uilliam, Jeanette, Rowan, auld Peigi, and even himself.

"Surely they are not done rehashing their plan so soon this morn." She did not bother to hide the disdain she felt for the blethering that went on and on in that circle day after day.

"Nay, they are not."

She took the first step in the exercise, determined to irritate him further by ignoring him, hoping he would, as he sometimes did, stomp off muttering about how childish she was. But then the words that had startled her came back to her as if Duncan said them only now. She turned her torso a little more sideways, shifting her forward foot a little closer to her center for balance, surprised at how those small changes increased her reach, protected her torso more easily, and strengthened her balance. She began once more.

"Put more of your weight on your back foot when defending and loosen your grip on the stick just a little," he said as she moved into the exercise. "You do not want to strangle it, for that hinders your arm's flexibility and strength."

She did as he said, though it felt awkward. She stumbled as she concentrated on keeping her body turned and her grip relaxed.

"Damn skirts."

"Why do you not kilt them up?" Duncan asked.

She glanced at him, sure she would see disappointment and scorn in his dark eyes, but was surprised to see a calm gaze, thoughtful, not judging. He tilted his head and narrowed his eyes, and she knew from long experience that his sharp mind was working on a problem.

"Never mind," he said. "'Tis good to train in skirts since that is likely what you will be wearing if ever you are ambushed."

She waited for him to say *again*, but he did not, and she found herself distracted by his change in behavior. He was not attacking her, or treating her like a child, and that alone was remarkable, for nothing about her had changed, so in theory his opinion of her should not have changed either, but it seemed it had, at least for the moment.

Even though she agreed with him about fighting in skirts, she could not let him know that. Scotia set her weapons and targe down and kilted her skirts, tucking the ends, still damp from the mud puddles at the caves, up into the wide leather belt she wore, just as she had when she'd waded into the burn to throw off the lads who usually trailed after her. But Duncan had not been thrown off her trail. Duncan was the best tracker in the clan and had taught her all she knew of tracking both beasts and people.

On her own, she had turned the lessons around and, over the years, become quite adept at hiding her own tracks when she did not wish to be found. Clearly she must work harder if she wished to hide her trail from Duncan in the future.

She waited for him to say something, but he was silent as she settled her weapons. She started, as she always did, by closing her eyes and moving through each step of the exercise slowly in her mind, fixing it there. Next she opened her eyes, turned her torso, set her feet, checking both balance and that the weight was more to the back foot, relaxed her grip on the stick, and then moved through the exercise slowly, making sure each step was precisely as she'd seen Malcolm doing it when he taught the lads.

"Good," Duncan said, circling around to her other side. "Now faster."

"I do not need your commands," she said, still wishing the man would leave her, though his suggestions did seem to help. She brought the face of the gap-toothed English soldier who had held her captive into her mind, then put the memory of his blade to her throat there as well. That was all it took to bring into her heart all the rage and helplessness he had made her live with. She imagined he stood in front of her, that smirk on his face as he'd told her what he would do to her after he and his fellow soldiers had slaughtered her family, what they would each do to her, and when the rage lived within her like a beast she flew through the exercise, repeating it without pause. Exhilaration spilled through her, as it had the last few days as she'd practiced, as if she'd finally, finally found the thing she was meant to do. After nine or ten repetitions her breath burned in her lungs and throat, and sweat dripped from her face. She stopped, resting her hands on her knees as she gulped in the cool air of the wood, damping down the burning.

"You really are quite good at this," Duncan said, as if he truly was surprised by what he saw. "But—"

"But nothing," she snapped, standing up to face him before he could ruin the subtle warmth that flirted over her skin at his compliment by telling her everything wrong with her, by telling her this was a foolish thing to do, a foolish thing to want. She did not want to hear any of it.

"But," he said again, his voice remarkably patient, "you need a proper teacher if you mean to continue." He held up a hand to stop her next retort.

But it did not come.

Scotia knew her mouth was agape, but she was powerless to close it.

"And I do think you should continue to train," he added.

He looked a little too pleased with himself so she pressed her lips together hard enough to close her mouth, and tried to understand what he had just said.

"You cannot mean to let me train with the lads. What are you about, Duncan? Surely you mean only to trick me into letting my guard down before you dive in to tear me apart with sharp, mean words."

He nodded. "I do not blame you for thinking that, and indeed, that was my intention when I was searching for your trail."

"Searching?"

"Aye. It took far more work than I expected to discover where you had gone. It would seem you are a good student when the subject serves your purposes."

She couldn't decide if that was a compliment or a complaint, but she did not care. She clearly had more work to do to slip the sharp-eyed Duncan, but she had at least made it difficult for him to find her and that was an accomplishment she could be proud of.

"I do not think you should train with the lads. 'Twill demoralize them to see a lass who is far more skilled than they are."

Pride and surprised satisfaction warmed her.

"Nay," he continued, "but *I* can train you in the ways of a warrior, if you agree to my terms."

Scotia realized she still held her weapons at the ready, as if she protected herself from Duncan, which was daft, for though his words had always had the power to sting, he'd never physically hurt her.

But now Duncan was asking her to allow him to help her.

Could she do that? Could she trust him?

"If I agree," she said slowly, "I get to train with a bossy instructor? What do you gain by helping me in this?" Ingrained wariness held her back from jumping at his proposal.

"I get to make sure you are properly trained so that you may be an asset to this clan, so that I can be assured that you are able to protect yourself and those you fight with." The words were almost soft, as if he sought to lull her into accepting his oversight, but they hit her like a slap, a rebuke.

Irritation sizzled in her gut, but there was too much at stake to give it voice. She raised her chin and squared her shoulders, meeting his gaze with her own. "If I accept, will you promise that I will join the warriors in battle when the English return? Will you promise not to force me to stay at the caves, no matter what any of the others say?"

"If you accept, and if"—he held up his hand to stop her from interrupting him—"*if* you prove yourself an able warrior, then I promise to do everything I can to make sure you get the chance to fight our enemies."

She realized she was breathing fast and shallow. He offered everything she wanted, and she knew him well enough to know he would not lie to her.

"You will not go easy on me because I am female." She did not ask, but demanded. She needed to be every bit as skilled as any warrior if she was to avenge the horrors that had befallen her clan. If that meant submitting to Duncan's training then she would do it. "And I have one more requirement," she said, now thinking how all the others would react when they found out she was being trained to fight. "This must remain a secret between the two of us until I say otherwise."

Duncan considered her terms, his arms lightly crossed. "If I agree to your terms, you must agree to train with me every single day, no matter how tired or sore you may be, *and* that you will not go off alone, ever. As long as you do this, I will keep the secret."

"Done," she said before he could add more requirements.

"Done."

Scotia wanted to throw her practice stick at him when she realized that even when she thought she was in control, Duncan had maneuvered her into doing as he wished. What was she thinking?

She was thinking of vengeance.

She took her fighting stance, facing him instead of the exposed tree roots. "We begin now."

CHAPTER THREE

DUNCAN STARTED SCOTIA WITH THE MOST BASIC OF INSTRUCTION but quickly found she had mastered the simple exercises on her own.

"Show me the exercise you were doing when I found you," he said, circling around her to check her stance and her arm positions. Once more he watched as she closed her eyes. Her lips moved without sound, and then she moved through the combination as if it were a dance, lightly, and with grace, but without any power behind the strikes and parries. That would have to change, but not just yet. He had her show him the other two exercises the lads had been working on for weeks, and again, she moved lightly and with grace, but no power, and he suspected her balance would not be strong enough when clashing swords were involved.

"Now, do all three exercises in order without stopping," Duncan instructed as he circled around to stand behind her, then picked up a stout stick about the length of his sword but far lighter. "No hesitation. No thinking. Just let your body do what you are training it to do."

She stilled, and he knew she had closed her eyes and that her lips were moving without sound. He lunged toward her and poked her hard in the ribs.

She spun, ire spitting from her emerald-green eyes. "What—"

He held his position, ready for her attack, but he had not managed to goad her into motion.

"'Tis clear as day I said no hesitation," he said. "No thinking." He aimed the thick stick at her belly and lunged, as if with a sword.

Scotia didn't have time to think, so she did as he hoped, she simply reacted, letting the training she'd had so far carry her into battle with him, parrying his first lunge, then flying through the rest of the exercises just as he'd said, one after the other, blocking every blow and thrust he aimed at her without thought, taking the advantage when she had it, but attacking him without power or conviction.

"You are fighting like a lass, Scotia. Are you so weak? You will kill no English unless you put some strength behind your sword."

She spun and brought her stick around in a hard, sure arc parallel to the ground, as if she would take his head off with one swipe. He blocked her, and the impact of his stick and hers almost made her drop her weapon, but she managed to hold on to it and dropped back, as the exercise dictated. She drew in a huge lungful of air, and with her next attack let out a loud shout as she drove him back. It was all he could to do keep from grinning at her ferocity. He dared not let her know how well she was doing, how fast she was learning, as if she'd always known the skills of a warrior and he was but reminding her. Telling her how well she did might encourage her to revert to her cocksure ways. He must keep her attention. He must make sure that she knew she had much more to learn so he could ensure she kept to their bargain. 'Twas imperative that he keep her close so she caused no more harm to her clan.

He sped up, in an effort to throw her off what she had trained into her body already, but he could see the moment everything changed for her.

A calm came over her, and her focus was absolute. He knew she had reached that place where time slowed and reactions seemed to speed. He could see it as her movements became more sure, fluid still but with strength and power as if she understood exactly what each step of the exercise was for, what it taught.

She battled him right through his final blow, and her final block with her targe.

For a long moment they just stood there, breathing hard, staring at each other, their weapons held in the final clash as if frozen in time.

Exhilaration filled Scotia's eyes and lit her face with a radiance he had never seen there before. It transformed her from the fiercely angry lass she had been for weeks, since her mother's murder, to a woman who had suddenly learned her own strength. The change was startling, kicking him in the gut with an awareness of her that had nothing to do with weapons and battle, and everything to do with the confidence shining in the sparkling green eyes of the woman who stood before him.

He smiled and stepped away, putting some distance between them.

"That was amazing!" She grinned at him, and all he could do was nod. He turned away, needing to look elsewhere in an attempt to gather his thoughts and calm the heat that gathered within him.

"'Twas a good start," he said as he forcefully turned his attention back to her training.

"A good start? Aye, it was. But that is the easy part, aye, the beginning lessons?"

"Easy?" He turned back to her, his mind focused back on her training. "It takes more than learning the moves of a lesson to be prepared for battle. You must also develop the mind of a warrior, and that is often more difficult than mastering the physical. But we start with the physical skills." She had found that calm, that singular focus he only found in hard training and battle, but there was still much to be learned in this lesson. "Do it again. All three without thought or hesitation."

He could see the argument gathering within her so he raised his brows at her, daring her with a look that he knew would spur her to respond, but she surprised him. Instead of a sharp retort, she pressed her lips together, trapping whatever she had been preparing to say in her mouth, and took up her beginning stance once more.

'Twas time for another lesson.

"Hold there," he said before she could move. He walked around her slowly, assessing her position, then came up behind, so close he could feel the heat of her body on his though he tried, and failed, to ignore it. He put both hands on her shapely hips, turning her just a little more to the side, then cupped her shoulders and lined them up with her hips. He slid his hand along the underside of her sword arm, working hard not to think about how soft her skin might be beneath the sleeve of her kirtle, as he adjusted the angle upward, touching the inside of her elbow with his fingertips so she would soften it. He moved her targe arm just a little more to the left so it would still protect but not hamper the swing of her sword.

"Do not drop your sword arm," he said quietly as he circled around her once more. He stepped close again, though he had not meant to, and tucked that ever-errant tendril of her hair behind her ear. He told himself to leave it, to step away, even as he remembered tucking that same silky tendril behind her ear when she was a wee lass with hair that was always tangled, no matter how often her mother tried to contain it in a braid.

"You should get back in the habit of braiding your hair as you did when you were little, or at least secure the sides like the warriors sometimes do," he said, finally stepping away. He wondered when he had ceased breathing.

"That would only serve to draw attention to what we do here," she said, her voice unusually whispery. Her breath was as fast as it had been during their duel but now it was shallow. "Everyone kens I hate braiding my hair." Her voice was a little stronger, with a familiar snap in it.

"Aye, you always have, but now it might serve you well. You have never avoided changing your mind about things before. 'Twould be a believable explanation." And it would keep him from being tempted to touch it again. "Your sword arm . . ." He made a lifting motion with his hand, and she raised it back to where he had positioned it. "Do not let anything distract you from your purpose in a battle. The mind and the body must stay focused at all times, aware of what goes on around you, but focused on the immediate danger whether 'tis in front of you, behind you, or charging at you on a caparisoned courser from across the battlefield."

He watched and waited until her arm, still firmly in the position he had required, started to tremble. She gripped the stick tighter, her knuckles going white and the blue veins in the back of her hand standing out starkly against her pale skin, but to his surprise, she did not complain. An unexpected and unfamiliar respect for her tenacity took hold within him. She was serious about this training and that was a very good thing.

"Loosen your grip, Scotia. The trembling is from muscle fatigue. I can see we have more than swordplay and a battle-ready mind to master. Now, move!"

He lifted his stick and lunged for her, fast and agile, moving out of the way of her offensive moves before she could even finish them, moving in on her, poking her in the ribs when she forgot and let her targe drop, smacking her across the upper back when she did not spin quickly enough to defend herself. A little pain and bruising often reinforced a lesson, though he hated the thought of doing that to her. But he had promised not to go easy on her, to train her as the lads were trained, and so he did.

Again and again he attacked, running her through the exercises over and over and over until her breath rasped and her arms surely screamed for rest.

"Enough," he said. "'Tis enough for our first day."

"You do not look the least fatigued," she said to him, still struggling to hold her weapons up.

"Scotia, lassie, we are finished for this day. Lower your weapons. Give your arms a rest. You did well."

Still she did not drop her guard. Stubborn, untrusting lass.

"I am serious. We are done. Put your weapons away. We do not want your da sending out a search party for both of us."

"He would not—" Her stomach rumbled loudly enough to interrupt her. Puzzled, she looked up at the small circle of sky above them. "How long have we been at this?"

Duncan judged the change from where the sun hit the forest floor when he had arrived and now and was surprised to find the sun must be low in the western sky.

"Most of the day, 'twould seem. It cannot be long before the evening meal is ready."

"The whole of the day? Nay, 'tis not possible." She did finally let her arms drop limply to her side, the heavy wooden shield staying in place only because of the sweat-soaked leather straps.

"We will meet here again tomorrow," he said, letting his stick drop to the ground. He waited for a complaint, a grumble, even an irritated stare, but none of that came.

"Good. I will be ready." She stashed her weapons in the bole of a hollowed-out tree and left without so much as a hand raised in farewell.

Duncan stared after her, pleased that she had passed every test he had set her this day. He was equally pleased that he had kept her from causing any trouble to vex her family. If he was any judge, she would return to the caves, eat a larger than usual meal, then sleep the sleep of the dead. She would rise tomorrow stiff and sore, with bruises from blows she wouldn't remember receiving. Even so, he rather thought she would return to train with him, out of sheer stubbornness if nothing else.

The true test of her pledge lay not in the physical training, though. He had witnessed her determination to perfect that today. The true test was to see if she could change her way of acting and thinking, to see if she could change her heart and her mind from those of a selfish lass to those of a battle-ready warrior.

He had his doubts, but he also had his hopes. If she could master this and prove the change was real and lasting, she might be welcomed back into the clan with open arms. She might be able to redeem herself.

DUNCAN FOLLOWED SCOTIA AS SHE MADE HER WAY FIRST TO A burn where she drank and washed her hands and face. She brushed dirt and bits of leaves and twigs from her clothes, then headed back to the caves. The closer she got the more he could see the change in her. Her stride grew stiffer, her shoulders drew up, and her pace slowed.

He let her enter the clearing outside the caves first, giving her a few moments before he entered so that the council, and anyone else nosy enough to pay close attention, would think he only followed her. He did not know how any of them would react to the promise he had made to her, but it did not really matter since he had also promised to keep her training a secret for now.

When he stepped into the gloaming of the clearing Peigi was already berating Scotia for leaving her duties behind for a full day. All the women and lasses who were nearby preparing the evening meal were averting their eyes, or even turning their backs, as if they did not want to so much as look at Scotia.

The brittle anger he could see clearly in the way Scotia held herself was such a contrast to the easy, dare he say happy, lassie he had spent the day with, that it made him all the more aware of how the clan subtly shunned her. Each dismissive gesture seemed to push Scotia deeper and deeper into that pit of anger she had lived in since the day of the fire, the day her mother was slain. Did he shun her, too? Aye, he did, when he wasn't tracking her like an escaped prisoner.

He had thought 'twas Scotia isolating herself in her anger and grief, but he realized 'twas more than that. The lassie who everyone for so long had shaken their heads over and smiled at her antics when she landed in yet another bucket of trouble was now treated as if she did not exist, except by Peigi, who condemned her to forever scrubbing pots.

That Scotia had not lashed out with more than angry words of late, that she had slipped away to the forest instead, was interesting, though he did not understand why she did that . . . but he would.

Not long after they returned, Duncan sat in the gloom of the darkening evening eating the stew that somehow Peigi and the other women had managed to make savory in spite of the small number of rabbits the lads had managed to trap this day. Scotia also sat in the gloom, upon the flat-topped boulder just outside the main cave. She was as far away from the clan as she could get without retreating into the cave itself.

He was glad she had gone back for a second bowl of stew. She had earned it with her hard training. Though his stomach still felt hollow, he had not gone back for more, letting her take his share. There was little enough to go around thanks to the fire that had destroyed most everything in the storage areas under the great hall. And the game was nearly hunted out in this small glen after just a few weeks of hunting and trapping. The lads would need to extend their trapping into other glens soon. It did not bode well for the clan if they had to remain here into the winter.

Out of the corner of his eye he saw Scotia rise and take her bowl to the wash station, then she quickly made for the cave. Peigi started to call out to her, one hand in the air, but then cocked her head as she watched the shadow that was Scotia in the gathering gloom, and let her hand drop.

Duncan placed his bowl on a towering pile by the washbasins. He wished he could sit quietly near the fire with a cup of ale or a dram of whiskey, though they had neither after the great hall burned. But even if they did, he could feel Rowan and Jeanette watching him, and he did not want to have to walk that fine line between keeping Scotia's secret as he had pledged and not lying to them. They were the Guardians. He would never lie to them.

He gathered his bedding and carried it toward the council circle where he slept when there were still people gathered near the cookfire. He only slept in one of the caves when it rained, and then near the mouth. He slept far better in the open than in the dank confines of their temporary shelters. At least he hoped it was temporary.

As he crossed the clearing, skirting the circle of light thrown by the cookfire into the darkness that rapidly deepened to night, he could feel Jeanette and Rowan's eyes upon him. They had yet to come right out and ask him anything about Scotia, but he could feel their need to gathering strength within them, and he found himself reluctant to tell them anything of the determined, driven, dare he say compliant lass he had spent the day with.

Before he had laid his bedding out Rowan appeared at his left elbow, Jeanette at the right.

"Where did she go?" Rowan asked, pitching her voice low.

"Aye, where did she go and what was she about?" Jeanette added.

"She was wandering the wood," Duncan said. "She's angry, and grieving, and embarrassed." He wasn't so sure about that last one, but she should be. "Can you blame her for wanting to get away from all the judging looks and whispers?"

"Aye," Rowan said, "I can. She was told to stay near the caves. She kens well that every time she hares off into the wood someone has to follow her. Today it was you and we could have used your counsel. It is high time she grew up and took responsibility for her actions like the rest of us."

Rowan's tone and accusation irritated Duncan, and though he did all he could not to show it, he wasn't entirely successful.

"How is she to do that? How is she to take responsibility, to grow up, when no one here—not even me"—until this day, he realized suddenly—"treats her like anything other than an overgrown child?"

Both women were silent then, and Duncan thought perhaps he had overstepped.

"He is right, Rowan," Jeanette said, and Duncan let out a quiet sigh of relief. "It is difficult not to treat her as if she is always about to cause trouble." The three of them stood there in silence for long moments, the murmur of those clan folk still awake and the occasional pop of the fire the only sounds.

"Duncan," Jeanette said, settling a hand on his arm, "you have always been the one to understand her, to watch out for her far better than any of the rest of us. What do you think we need to do to help her make this change?"

The image of Scotia whirling through her exercise this morning, fierce, determined, focused entirely on what she meant to master, flashed through him. She was so intent on her quest that she had even agreed to his deal.

"You need to let her roam," he said, trying to answer their questions without lying, and without revealing Scotia's secrets, for he knew if he let on what she was really up to, Rowan, Jeanette, and pretty much everyone else would hobble Scotia like a horse and throw her into the back of a cave until she came to her senses . . . which would be never. "She is unhappy, and here she is surrounded by disapproval and your happiness."

"Happiness? Here where we hide in the bens, driven from our home by the English?" He could see the silhouette of Rowan's curly auburn hair tremble with each angry word.

"Aye," Duncan replied, letting his own anger lend weight to his words. "You accuse her of selfishness, yet the two of you flaunt your newfound happiness, your husbands, and your places as Guardians, in front of her, without a thought to how it makes her feel." *Or the rest of us*, he thought. He did not mean to tarnish the joy these two women had managed to find in spite of the trials that had overtaken the clan of late, but he knew he found it difficult to watch their happiness when he had none of his own. He could only imagine Scotia felt the same. "She is grieving and she needs time and understanding to move through that. She does not have a Nicholas or a Malcolm to teach her that happiness and grief can go hand-in-hand, nor does she have the responsibilities of a new Guardian to distract her from it, so she will have to learn how to grieve on her own. I will do what I can to keep her safe and out of trouble, but I think only she can figure out how to move past the hurts and betrayals."

When neither Rowan nor Jeanette spoke he said, "I am sorry. I did not mean to make you feel discomfited because you are happy. I would not take that from either of you. I only meant to show you how you look to Scotia."

"And you have done that very well," Rowan said, but he could tell he had offended her from the flatness of her voice, even though he could not see her face well in the dark.

Duncan looked down at the plaid clutched hard in his fists. He did not like hurting these women. They had lost so much, but they had gained much, too, in these last weeks, and he was genuinely happy for them.

But for now Scotia was his priority.

Jeanette sighed. "You seem to see her more clearly than either of us can. Will you continue to watch over her, Duncan? I ken you would rather be out keeping watch for the English, or preparing battle plans with the council, but right now watching over Scotia is every bit as important. Rowan and I can only concentrate on our training and preparations for the coming battle if we know she is both safe and not endangering the clan."

Duncan's mind raced. Of course he would agree, but was there anything that might help him keep Scotia's secret while he kept his promise to the Guardians, even if 'twould not be in exactly the way they expected?

"I will continue to watch over her safety, as I did today, but I must ask for two things from you," he said, choosing his words with exquisite care.

CHAPTER FOUR

Scotia sat just inside the mouth of the main cave, wrapped in her blanket, but unable to sleep after the eventful and surprising day, when she watched first Jeanette, then Rowan, casually leave their places by their husbands and follow Duncan into the council circle.

She knew what was happening even though she could not hear their voices, and could barely make them out against the dark forest background. She knew Rowan and Jeanette were about to interrogate Duncan on what he had learned of Scotia's activities this day. Doubt sprang alive in her, gnawing at her confidence and whispering betrayal in her heart. Rowan and Jeanette always got their way, and Duncan would be no match for the two of them if they really wanted to make him tell Scotia's secrets. She knew better than to believe anyone would be on her side, an ally in her quest for vengeance. Even Duncan, the one person she could always depend upon to defend her, even when he was himself chiding her for whatever her latest debacle was, couldn't stand up to the clan's Guardians. She wouldn't be surprised if, when the women were done with him, she ended up in shackles, taking away her freedom and leaving her helpless to defend herself or anyone else, on top of all the other losses she had suffered.

Scotia rose slowly and made her way out of the cave, slipping almost silently through the night-black shadows at the edge of the clearing and into the wood, heading carefully through the darkness for her cache of weapons, as if a beacon lit her way. If they came for her with shackles, at least she'd be ready to defend herself, even if it meant fighting off those she loved.

She hadn't made it far when a man jumped out of the wood not far in front of her. She stopped, tried to make out who it was in the near total lack of light, then took a few steps backward, the memory of just such an ambush with Myles fresh in her mind. At least this time there was no one else with her to be murdered.

She almost tripped over a thick dead branch. Quickly she caught her balance, then dropped her blanket and picked up the branch, brandishing it in front of her, though it was so heavy it wobbled in her grasp.

"Put that down, Scotia."

The voice disoriented her for a moment. It wasn't English, as her mind had been prepared for. 'Twas familiar.

"Put it down, Scotia. If I meant you harm, running and hiding would serve you far better than standing to fight with that. I can see we have a lot of training to do."

"Duncan?"

"Of course."

She threw down the branch, barely missing her toes when it bounced unexpectedly back toward her. She stomped down the barely there trail to where the man stood his ground.

"You told them, did you not?" It was both question and statement.

"I did not."

She was ready to throw insults at him about his manhood, his integrity, his . . . wait. "What?"

"I did not tell them of your secret, and instead I secured their promise not to demand to know where you are going when you leave the cave site, and also that they no longer send lads, or anyone other than me, to follow you."

"And they agreed to that?" She tried to quash the hope that surged within her.

"They did."

She took a step closer to him. "And you believe them?"

"I do," he said without hesitation.

Scotia tried to understand what he'd done. He'd stood up to the Guardians and he'd gotten promises from them.

"You did not trust me to keep your secret, did you?" he said, and she could hear the disappointment in his voice.

She considered telling him she was only going for a walk, but he would know it for a lie, and she did not want to repay his good faith with anything less than her own. "I did not think you were strong enough to stand against both Rowan and Jeanette."

"Then we have both learned something new of the other this day. Where were you going?" he asked.

"I thought they would throw me in shackles to keep me from my training."

"So you meant to fetch your weapons and fight your own kin?"

When he said it like that she realized how shameful that would be. She did not want to fight her family. She wanted them to take her seriously, to respect her. Fighting them would never gain her that.

She rubbed her face with both hands, as if she could scrub the daft idea right out of her head. Where did these ideas come from? And why did she never question her own thoughts before she acted upon them?

"Scotia?"

"You will make me admit yet another mistake in judgment?"

"Nay, I only want you to recognize it so that the next time your fears and anger drive you to action, you might take a moment and think through the consequences, or talk to me so that I might help you see them, before you take action. Can you do that?"

She closed her eyes and sighed. "This is part of my training, aye?"

"An important part. A warrior cannot fight with emotion. A warrior must fight with clear eyes and a calculating mind. I am confident, if you really want to be a warrior, that you can learn to do that."

"And if I do not?" She stepped closer, looking him in the eye, searching for his doubt, his disappointment, his belief that she would fail in this training. But she saw only determination.

"Then I will not allow you into any battle of any sort, for an emotional warrior is a dead warrior, and I do not want your death upon my conscience. Can you agree?"

She closed her eyes again and knew that what he asked was for the best, though her pride ached at the admission. "More than anything, I want to fight with my kinsmen, so aye, I agree."

Duncan's fingers grazed her cheek, startling her with his warm touch in the chill night air. "And now you surprise me again." His voice was soft and for a moment she thought he leaned closer. For a moment she thought he meant to kiss her, but then he dropped his hand, and the moment was gone.

"'Tis time we both got some sleep." He scooped up her discarded blanket and headed back up the trail toward the caves.

Scotia watched him disappear into the darkness of the forest. She looked over her shoulder in the direction of her weapons and sighed. Becoming a warrior was a trickier business than she had imagined.

THE NEXT FEW DAYS WERE CHALLENGING, TO SAY THE LEAST, both for Duncan and for Scotia, but they fell quickly into a pattern. Scotia would rise early, though Duncan was usually already at the cookfire, eating his morning porridge, when she made her way out of the main cave. She ate, and then took off into the wood. Duncan would give her a few minutes' start, then quietly slip out of the cave site, as if he were only trailing after her, keeping an eye on her. Every day she took a different route to her stash of weapons, Duncan keeping a discreet distance, ready to lead anyone astray who might decide to follow them. Duncan was all too aware that he had received promises from Rowan and Jeanette, but not from the men who led the clan. Still, no one gainsaid a Guardian, and now there were two to stand between Duncan and his charge and the leaders.

But he would not allow the sudden truce between him and Scotia to be threatened by someone taking it upon him or herself to follow them, so he was even more vigilant than usual as they made their way to her weapons cache.

They worked on swordplay, but they also worked on strengthening her body. He devised obstacle courses for her in the wood that tested her speed, agility, and her endurance. In the afternoons they had taken to exploring the glen, with Scotia showing him places she had discovered over the past weeks: passes, other caves, a lochan halfway down the ben at the foot of a waterfall—a wee loch just big enough to bathe in. While they trekked up and down the ben he began to teach her the art of strategy, the art of reading her opponent and the terrain. He also challenged her tracking skills by having her follow animal tracks, teaching her things he had learned in the years since he'd first shared his tracking lessons with her. The parallel was not lost on him—he had taught her tracking to keep her from wandering off on her own and getting herself and the other weans, who inevitably tagged along with the charming and fearless lass, into trouble. She might be ten and eight now, but her fearless streak remained, and unfortunately that still got others into trouble with her . . . only now that trouble included loss of life.

Each day with Scotia made Duncan see her with fresh eyes. She was fierce, determined, focused, as he'd never seen her before. She was driven by something other than the next lad she fancied. And she was turning out to be a talented warrior.

"Once more," Duncan said, knowing he was pushing Scotia past her endurance, expecting her to snap and turn on him, wagging a finger in his face and calling him names only Scotia could devise.

But she didn't.

Her breath was ragged, and sweat streamed down her face. Her hair, once neatly contained in a thick braid, wafted about her face in strings. She pushed it out of her way and took a few slow, deep breaths as he'd taught her to calm her heart and steady her mind. She swallowed, pushed her sleeves back above her elbows, made sure her skirts were kilted up securely, and went back to the beginning of the line of obstacles he'd set up in the wood to challenge her.

Duncan tried to hide a smile, but from the glare Scotia sent him he didn't think he was successful.

"You are enjoying torturing me all too much," she said, then she took off, sprinting for the first downed tree. She scrambled up onto it, not as gracefully as the first four times she'd done this, but she got there. She ran down the length of the trunk, leapt off it, easily missing the wide mud puddle that was in her way. She dodged under the branch of another downed tree, swung up onto its trunk, drew her stick sword from a loop of rope at her waist, and danced through the intricate steps of one of the exercises he'd taught her just yesterday, resheathed her stick sword, and hurtled through another five obstacles and tasks he'd set up. Skidding to a stop just in front of him, she bent over at the waist, bracing herself with her hands upon her thighs, her sides heaving.

"You are a beast," she said without looking up at him, but there was no heat to her words. She sat back, hard, her breath whooshing out with a very unladylike grunt.

"And you are getting stronger and faster every day. I do not think there is a lad in the clan who could manage that as fast." He was not flattering her, just telling her the truth. She was remarkable at these physical tests of endurance and agility.

She peered up at him. All of her hair had escaped her braid now and it cascaded around her narrow face in sheets of ebony, accentuating her icy green eyes. The doubt in her eyes bothered him.

"'Tis the truth, Scotia." He reached out a hand to help her up, and was a little surprised when she took it. He pulled her up, and for no reason he could think of he did not immediately release her hand, enjoying the heat of it against his and the feel of the calluses beginning to form on her soft skin.

She met his gaze and for a moment he saw confusion, then a glint of irritation as she pulled her hand out of his and stepped back, putting a little distance between them. "I told you not to treat me like a lass. Do you help the lads up when they are tired?"

"Sometimes, aye, but I will not help you again, unless you ask it of me." He was irritated by her reaction for some reason, though he knew 'twas nothing out of the usual for Scotia. "We are done for the day. Tomorrow we shall spar and see if you can take the exercises you have learned and turn them to use."

Her eyes lit. "Finally." He shook his head at the intensity of that one word.

"It has only been five days since we began. I did not think you would be prepared so soon, but you have worked hard. In truth, I did not think you would." He picked up a waterskin and handed it to her. "You have surprised me, Scotia."

"Then you seriously underestimated my determination to kill my enemies."

He nodded, the irritation disappearing as he once more saw her in a new light.

"I did. You are not the same girl you were before the English took you. In an odd way, they have given you a purpose, a focus that you have never had before. I like it."

She took another long draw from the waterskin. When she lowered it she met his gaze. "I like it, too." She quirked an eyebrow at him, a teasing gesture he remembered well but had not seen in many years. "But that does not mean I like you or this arrangement any better."

He could not help but grin at her, glad that somehow her new-found passion for fighting had also resurrected the teasing lass he'd known when she was a child. "I would not expect you to." Though he suspected she did.

He certainly enjoyed his time with her, far more than he would have thought possible. Here in the wood she was a fierce warrior, sure of herself, capable, with her eyes fixed on her goal. Inevitably, when they returned to the cave site, she would revert to the sullen, angry lass she'd been of late.

"When are you going to let the rest of the clan know who you are becoming?" he asked.

"Not until I can kick their arses when they treat me like a child."

"If you stopped acting like a child around them, you would not need to kick anyone's arse." He knew he should have kept his mouth shut even as the words spilled out of it.

She handed him the waterskin, her eyes gone hard and her pink lips tightened over what he knew were clenched teeth. "You have worked me so hard I cannot go back to the caves like this lest someone ask me why I am such a mess. I am going to the lochan to wash up, and you have my word I shall return directly to camp. You may not follow me." She wagged her finger at him. "Do you understand?"

"You ken I cannot leave you alone away from the caves, aye? I will give you privacy, but I will await you near the lochan—" She started to interrupt, but he kept going. "I promise to keep my distance so you can bathe in private."

"I will not—"

"'Tis the only deal I can make, Scotia. You have done an admirable job in gaining my trust, though my trust is not unshakeable yet. The rest of the clan, though? They do not trust you at all, which is why I was tasked to keep an eye on you in the first place. I will not break my word to the Guardians. 'Twould be a terribly unwarriorlike thing to do, and it would shame me greatly. Would you break your word to me: me with you at all times in exchange for training you to be a warrior?"

He knew how to get her attention when he had to.

"I—"

He looked at her, his own eyebrows raised in question as he watched her start to argue, then stop herself one, two, three times.

"I do not have a say in this, do I?" she finally said.

"Nay, lass, you do not." He looped the waterskin over his shoulder and picked up a small sack that held their midday meal. "Let us put your weapons away . . . unless you'd like to run the obstacles again?"

She scowled at him and turned to make her way back to her cache. He smiled as he followed her. 'Twas good to see Scotia finally growing up, but 'twas also good to see she hadn't lost the spark of the troublesome lass she'd been.

SCOTIA'S HEART WAS BEATING HARD AND FAST AS SHE LAID HER targe, dagger, and the stick that had become her practice sword inside a hollow tree. She kept her back to Duncan as she strode off toward the lochan she had shown him a few days ago. She dared not look at him lest he see how he had unsettled her.

She had put her hand in his without thinking. Shivers ran over her skin again, just at the brief memory of the touch of his strong hand clasped in hers. There should have been nothing unusual in his gesture. Despite what she had said, she'd seen him help up lads and grown men alike in the training yard, but something about it was different.

There was no teasing of besting and beating an opponent as she often saw amongst the warriors as they trained. A sudden, inexplicable tightness in her chest and an inability to look away from him had caught her off guard.

She had always taken Duncan for granted. He was simply always there with his dark hair, and deep brown scowling eyes.

At least they were scowling whenever he looked at her these last few years, as if she were a great disappointment to him.

But today there had been something different. He had touched her, held her hand in his. His eyes had been soft, happy, smiling even, and she could swear she saw pride, too. He had transformed right before her eyes, as if she had never seen him before.

When had he gone from the gangly lad she had trailed around after when she was small to the handsome, assured man he was now? How had she not noticed?

And now that she had noticed, did that change anything? Did it change her feelings about him? Did it change her training?

Nay. It changed nothing. Her training was the most important thing. If she lost her focus on that, she would not be prepared for battle when the time came, and she knew that time was coming quickly.

Nothing would change between them. He had said he liked her new purpose, her focus, her passion for her training, as did she. She would stay firmly fixed on that.

Nothing would change.

DUNCAN KEPT HIS WORD, SETTLING IN AT THE BASE OF AN OAK tree. He was close enough to the lochan to hear the splash of the small waterfall as it tumbled over the stony face of the ben, but he could not hear Scotia. Part of him wished to make sure she was still there, but she had given her word that she would bathe and then join him, and he had to admit that he found both her word, and the lass herself, surprisingly trustworthy over the last few days. He smiled, pleased with his plan and with himself. He had tamed the headstrong lass. Well, he had worn her out at least.

Perhaps they had all had it wrong when it came to Scotia. The lass seemed to need a purpose, and the more physically taxing the purpose, the better. If she had been a lad they would have seen that, but 'twas not the normal way of a lassie.

Of course, Scotia was not a normal lass, so he really should not be surprised. Willful, stubborn, angry more often than not did not hold up well against the gentle, quiet intelligence of Jeanette, or against the cheery good nature and industriousness of Rowan.

Scotia had always gotten herself in trouble, and it was only now that he could see 'twas because she needed activity in order to stave off boredom. He chuckled. He'd certainly found the answer to that in the last few days. A whisper of a thought of other ways to keep a lass physically active had him leaping to his feet and pacing away from the lochan as if he could leave it behind.

But he couldn't.

His whole idea of who Scotia was had changed in the last few days. She wasn't a child anymore, at least not when she was with him, but she was still Scotia, and he was still in charge of her. He'd always known she was a beauty—the dark hair and green eyes had marked her as one from birth.

But he'd thought himself immune from the effect she had on lads . . . until today. He had not been able to keep himself from holding her hand, from enjoying the warmth of her skin against his. The tenderness that had drifted over him had been as much a surprise to him as it appeared to be to her.

He was not daft enough to think she hadn't seen it. Her retreat back into her prickly self had been evidence that the moment had made her uncomfortable.

He needed to remember his task, for if he spooked her with an errant soft feeling he'd never keep her trust. He would not let it happen again.

He paced back toward the lochan, then away, forbidding himself to think of what she was doing in that icy water. As he paced back a shout came from her, and he sprinted through the trees only to find her pulling on her kirtle as he arrived, water droplets still sparkling in the sunlight on her thighs. He turned his back quickly, his heart thrumming in his ears at the sight of her milky skin.

"What is it?" His words were harsher than he'd intended, but the lass tested him sorely.

"We are needed back at the caves." She drew up close to him then, fully clothed and braiding her wet hair.

"The caves?"

"Aye. I cannot say why, but I am sure of it." She hurried back the way they'd come, heading to the caves. "Come on, ye sluggard!"

The familiar teasing tone in her voice was a welcome clue that she had let the awkward moment pass far more easily than he had. He hurried after her, curious to find out if her instinct was right.

CHAPTER FIVE

Scotia skidded to a stop as she cleared the forest. Only auld Peigi was there, huddled near the cookfire as if 'twas the middle of winter rather than early summer.

"Where is everyone?" Duncan asked as he passed Scotia.

"Och, there ye be," Peigi said, pushing herself to her feet. "Ceit's wee lassie has wandered away. She thought the bairn was napping in the cave, but when she went to take a keek, the child was nowhere to be found. Everyone is out looking for her."

"Maisie?" As Scotia said the child's name she suddenly knew where the tow-headed toddler was, as if someone had placed the knowledge in her brain without her awareness. "Come with me," she said, grabbing Duncan's hand and pulling him after her. She kept saying the name over and over in her head, as if it were a lodestone drawing her toward the child.

"Where are we going?" Duncan asked, pulling free of her hold before her touch distracted him from their search. "Slow down, Scotia, we need to look for sign if we are to be of any help finding the child."

"I ken where she is, Duncan." She did not slow down, nor look back at him. She just kept climbing straight up the steep side of the ben, though her breath was already growing ragged.

"How do you ken?" he asked, right on her heels.

"That I do not understand, but when I said her name, I knew she was above the caves. She is caught in some brambles."

They hurried up the steep benside as fast as they could. Duncan called out the toddler's name every now and then, but they heard nothing.

"If you are wrong about this, Scotia, then we are wasting valuable daylight when we could be looking for her in a more methodical, less . . . strange . . . way."

"I am not wrong. She is—" She stopped then, closed her eyes, and said the name again in her mind. "She is . . ." She turned a little to her left and looked into a bramble patch, and there, just at the base of a large stone she must have fallen from, far enough into the prickly dense arching stems to be hard to see, slept the child, her thumb in her cherub mouth. Her gown was caught on the thorns, and her face and chubby little arms were scratched in many places, as if she'd tried to extricate herself from the brambles.

Duncan slipped his dirk free of its sheath and began cutting away the bramble canes just as the child's eyes opened wide. She let out a piercing wail and reached for Scotia, then the cry changed to one of pain and she recoiled from the thorns, once more plugging her thumb into her mouth.

Scotia knelt down, and reached in as far as she could, though the thorns dug into her arm and pulled at her gown, to let Maisie grip her finger with her free hand. Her eyes were big and blue, and the tracks of dried tears stained her fat cheeks. "'Twill be all right with you, soon, Maisie. You ken braw Duncan, aye?" She saw the girl's gaze shift from Scotia's face to Duncan's then back again. "He has come to free you, and I will be right here until he does."

"Just a few more," Duncan said as he cut another long cane, only to find it was tangled in Maisie's gown.

"Hold still, sweetling," Scotia said, cooing at the child to keep the increasingly fretful wean calm as Duncan freed the last of the thorns from her ripped clothing. "Ah, there now," she said as Duncan lifted the toddler out of her nest of brambles, and handed her out to Scotia. Settled on Scotia's hip, Maisie looked up at her, shoved her thumb back in her mouth, then burst into loud, heart-rending wails. Fat tears streamed down her face, and no matter how much Scotia swayed and patted her back, the child would not calm.

"Maisie? Maisie!" A woman's frantic voice came from below them.

"'Tis her mother, Ceit," Scotia said.

"We have her," Duncan called. "She is safe. Stay there and we will bring her to you!" He took the child from Scotia and began the tricky descent down the crumbly rock face of the ben, stopping here and there to hold a hand out to Scotia to help her down. Normally Scotia would not have accepted such help, for she feared it would make her look weak, but after their morning of training followed by the fast ascent up the ben and the effort to get the girl free of the brambles, she was beginning to stumble over things she shouldn't, and really didn't want to lose her footing and descend the ben face first in the scree. But each time she took his help, her awareness grew of him, of his strength, of the way the child hugged his neck with both arms—not entirely calm yet but enough so that she hiccupped instead of screamed—creating an unfamiliar heaviness in her gut that rivaled the strange tightness in her chest.

As they slid down a particularly steep bit on their bums, Ceit came into sight not much further down the ben. She cried out, and called the child's name, which only served to rouse the girl enough to take up her ear-splitting howls of fear and pain again. They hurried down the next tricky bit of the path and had barely stopped before the mother pulled her child out of Duncan's arms and hugged her tight.

"I was so worried, *mo ghaol*. You are a naughty lass to wander away like that." The child hiccupped and gave her mother a sweet open-mouth baby kiss, and Scotia could not help but smile. Not yet two summers old, and already Maisie knew how to make her mother forgive her naughtiness.

"I cannot thank you enough, Duncan," Ceit said, as she hugged her child tight. "I thought she was gone for good." She gave Duncan a quick kiss on his cheek. "I thank you with all my heart."

"You should thank Scotia, she—" But before he could get the words out Ceit threw a doubting look at Scotia, then quickly looked away, once more shunning Scotia as Ceit rejoined her friends who stood down the slope a little way, and hurried back toward the caves.

As Duncan said her name, Scotia had felt a blush of pride start. He was trying to give credit to her, but the look on Ceit's face quelled any pride she might deign to feel and replaced it with anger.

"Of all the ungrateful—" She stopped, not sure what to call the woman.

"I am sure she wants to get Maisie to Jeanette to make sure there is nothing more than scratches and a bump on her head to worry over." He looked back at Scotia. "I shall make sure they ken 'twas you who found the wee thing, not me."

"Nay." She felt her nails bite into her palms and was oddly happy for the physical pain to distract her from the less visible hurt the woman had dealt her. "They will not believe I found her, not even coming from you. We found the scamp—"

"*You* found her," he said, stepping close enough to take her shoulders in his big hands. Scotia was so startled by the comforting weight of his hands, she did not shrug them off. "And now there is time for me to ask how you knew where we would find her."

"How?" His question startled her out of both her pique and the distraction of his touch. "I—" How did she ken where to find the child? "I just knew. I said her name, and I knew."

Duncan let his hands slide down her arms, leaving a trail of pleasant tingles in their wake. "You just knew?"

"Aye." She looked up at him, as she mulled over the sequence of events. "I just knew. It was suddenly there, in my head, almost like someone whispered it to me, but I did not hear a voice," she added quickly, not wanting him to think she was going daft. "I just *knew*."

His brow furrowed, and she searched his deep brown eyes for any trace of doubt. But there was none, only that look of complete concentration that came over him when he was pondering something he did not understand. He and Jeanette shared that expression.

"Has it happened before, this knowing?"

"Aye. Do you not ken things in this way?"

"Nay. What other things have you *known*?"

"I *knew* we were needed back at the caves. 'Tis also how I knew . . ."

She looked down, damning the man for making her forget that she wanted no one to know her greatest shame, and berating herself for telling him anything about the strange knowings. She let anger wrap around her, obliterating any softness Duncan's nearness had created. She felt his finger under her chin as he urged her to look back up at him.

"What, lass?" His voice was soft. He did not move his finger from her chin, forcing her to look deeply into his eyes. "You can tell me. Whatever it is 'twill go no further."

But she couldn't. She could not bear to even speak the words. She wrenched free of his touch and fled.

DUNCAN STARED AFTER THE RAPIDLY DISAPPEARING SCOTIA, dumbfounded. The lass always, always stood her ground, fighting with cutting words and looks sharp enough to cut the strongest warrior to his knees, fighting with every bit of passion and skill she brought to her training with stick and targe.

But this time she didn't. This time she fled.

He drummed his fingers against his thighs, trying to figure out what had happened. What had he said? She was opening up to him, telling him of this amazing skill she had kept secret even from him. She had been about to tell him of another knowing . . . but instead she had run from him, or from whatever she had been about to say.

Scotia never ran.

Duncan scrambled down the steep ben as quickly as he dared, worry tangling his guts. If Scotia ran, she wasn't thinking, just reacting, and that was never good for anyone, but especially not for Scotia. There was no telling what the lass might do if she let her emotions get the best of her. And 'twas Duncan's task to keep her safe, even from herself.

As soon as he hit the relatively flat trail, he checked to see which direction she had taken—away from the caves—and took off after her. It was only another minute or two before he caught up with her, grabbing her arm and spinning her to a stop.

"Release me!" She struggled to get free of his grip, but he was ready for her this time.

"Nay, not until you tell me what is wrong."

She swung at him, and relief swept through him. This was the Scotia he knew. He blocked her hand, locking his around her wrist and pulling her against his chest. She kicked him in the shin, and he switched his hold, wrapping both arms around her, one around her shoulders, the other around her waist, so she could not get far enough away to kick him again.

"Nothing. Is. Wrong." Each word was emphasized by a wiggling attempt to free herself. She narrowed her eyes and glared up at him. "Let me go, you—"

Now it was Duncan who didn't think. He silenced her with his lips.

CHAPTER SIX

Shock froze Scotia the moment Duncan's lips met hers. Their eyes met. The battle enjoined. It wasn't a soft kiss, not a tentative first kiss, not a passion-filled kiss between lovers, but a kiss meant to control, a kiss meant to stop her from telling him exactly what she thought of him. A kiss meant to distract her from . . .

And then he tilted his head a little, closed his eyes, and let his lips go soft against hers, and she knew she had won . . . or would. She played along, knowing that now he was not thinking with his head but letting lust lead his actions. Lust surprised her in the normally quiet and thoughtful Duncan. She had not known he had lust within him, but he was not the first lad she had manipulated with his own lust. Lust she could work with. Lust she could use as a weapon against him.

She let her lips go soft and parted them, just enough to let him think she had given up her will to him. She pretended to welcome his tongue as it swept over her own, leaning her weight against him, waiting for the right moment to bite him and gain her release as his lust-fogged brain took time to understand.

But the longer she waited, the less she wanted to . . .

Her eyes drifted closed and she gave herself over to the taste of him, the feel of his lips against hers, the arousing press of his hard chest against her breasts, the feel of his fingers threaded into her hair, tilting her head so he could gain better access to her mouth, to her jaw where he nibbled, to her ear and the spot just behind it that was so sensitive when he nuzzled it before returning to her lips.

Desire burned in her, brighter and hotter with every kiss until she did not know why she had run from him. She threaded her fingers into his hair, prepared to . . .

Nay. She would not let herself be distracted. Not by Duncan's soft kisses, or anything else. She could not let herself be distracted. There were English on their way here, a battle to be fought, and she would not let Duncan of Dunlairig distract her from her goal: to kill as many English as she could, to avenge her mother's death, and Myles's.

She stilled, her breath coming harsh and ragged, even as he continued to nibble at her lips, to pull her hard against the evidence of his own desire.

"Stop," she said against his mouth. "Duncan"—she turned her head away—"I said, stop."

DUNCAN HEARD HER SPEAKING BUT THE WORDS DID NOT CUT through the sharp desire that drove him. Her mouth was like nectar, sweet, making him greedy for her taste. Her body, something he had known had grown softer with a woman's curves, was a revelation: soft where she pressed against him, warm, with a scent that told him his was not the only desire between them.

And then the word *stop* filtered into his brain, and he realized with it she had gone still.

Duncan released her so fast she almost stumbled as she immediately put distance between them, the soft mountain air cooling his blood just enough for him to make sense of what had just happened. "I am sorry, Scotia. I did not mean to kiss you."

She swallowed and he saw her fingers tremble ever so slightly. He was gratified to see the glaze of desire still in her eyes even as he was surprised at the passion that had burst to life between them. But now was not the time to wonder how or why that passion existed.

"It cannot happen again. I do not want that to ever happen again. There will be no trysting, Duncan, not with you. Not with anyone. I'll not be distracted by . . ." She swallowed and raised her chin. "Do you understand?"

He nodded. "Aye, and I agree. Nothing good can come of it." He ran a hand through his hair, viciously scraping it back from his face. "Shall I find another to train you?"

She looked at him. "Nay. I do not want anyone else knowing of my training until I am ready to fight. Can you train me without . . ."—she waved a hand back and forth between them—"this?"

"I can. I will. But to be clear, 'twas not me doing all the kissing."

Scotia's face blushed a becoming dark pink, and for a moment he thought she meant to deny that she had kissed him back with a fervor to match his own, but then she gave a quick nod and looked him in the eye. Pride that she accepted her part in the kiss mingled with his cooling desire, heating it up once more.

"You were not," she said, her voice cool and controlled though the tremble was still in her fingers, "at least not at the end. I will not kiss you again, either."

They stood facing each other in awkward silence until at last he could stand it no more. "We should return to the caves. Nicholas needs to ken how you found the child. This *knowing* of yours might be of use to the clan."

"Nicholas will not believe me," she said, licking her lower lip and reminding him of the softness of it against his own.

He closed his eyes so he could not see her and silently berated himself for wanting to kiss her again.

"I will make him," he said. "I will tell him how you found Maisie, how you *knew* where she was, and that you have had other *knowings*."

The look on her face when she had been about to speak of one of those *knowings* returned to his mind. What could she know that would make her run away from him or, more likely, run from herself? Whatever it was that had spooked her, she seemed to have put it away wherever she put things she did not wish to think about. So perhaps kissing her had been the right thing to do after all, distracting her from harsh memories by rousing her desires.

His kiss had roused her desires? 'Twas something to ponder later, for now they needed to tell Nicholas of her skill.

"What are you smiling about?" she demanded.

"You and your secret skill." He hadn't realized he was smiling, but since he was he let it grow. "Let us away to the caves. There is a chief to convince that we have a powerful new weapon in our coming battle."

"Me? I am no weapon."

"Och aye, lassie, you are, in more ways than you ken."

She narrowed her eyes, and settled her fists on her hips. "What do you mean by that?"

He wiped the smile off his face and set off for the caves, letting her trail behind him. She had skill as a warrior, nascent, but growing. She had an uncanny *knowing* that made her a far better tracker than he was, and he still did not ken the breadth and depth of that particular skill—'twould add a facet to their training that he had not anticipated. And she had befuddled his mind with her vulnerability and her strength.

But the lassie had pride enough for ten warriors, and he feared, if he said all of that to her, that fierce pride might overtake the lessons in humility and honor he had been trying to subtly instill in her. He did not wish to stoke that particular fire.

"Duncan," she said, "what is your hurry? Tell me what you mean."

She grabbed his sleeve and deftly turned him so he came to an immediate stop facing her. The familiar snap in her eyes was softened by . . . doubt? Uncertainty?

He sighed, knowing he could not lie to her. He chose his words with great care. "I mean only that you are proving yourself equal to the task of becoming a warrior, and now you have revealed a skill that no one else has."

"No one? Surely you ken things just as I do."

"Nay, I do not. Do you think it would have taken me so long to find you as you trained if I had this *knowing*? Do you think I would depend upon tracks and bits of broken plants and overturned moss when I must find someone?" He cocked one straight dark eyebrow at her since over the ten-and-eight years of her life she was often the one he tracked. "If I could but *know* where my prey was, the way you kent where Maisie lay hidden, I would have need of none of those clues."

He could see his words sinking in, and then she grinned. For a moment he thought she meant to kiss him again, too, but instead she strode past him.

"Well, haste ye on, then, sluggard! This is my way into the battle. We've a chief to convince!"

He shook his head, knowing he had not succeeded in keeping her pride out of it. He could only hope that Nicholas would not tarnish it too badly if he did not believe them.

SHOUTS AND WAR CRIES ECHOED THROUGH THE MOONLESS night, raising Lord Sherwood's hackles as he crouched in the dark with his men. How could the barbarian Scots see to attack the English camp in the inky darkness? He'd forbidden any fires, any lanterns, any candles after last night's attack when the ghastly Highlanders had managed to kill several of his detachment and injure several more, somehow sneaking past the doubled guard keeping watch.

A Highlander pelted toward Sherwood in the dark, seeming to form out of nothing, screaming and shrieking like a banshee as he wheeled his two-handed sword to the left and the right around him as he ran, then disappearing into the night again without engaging. He could not tell if it was one man who did this or many, for they seemed to come from all directions, though not all at once. It was as if the Highlanders sought to confuse and rile more than to kill. The craven bastards had kept up this odd attack for hours, sometimes waiting so long between forays that the English were sure they had abandoned the game, only to rampage around the English encampment again, keeping them all awake, letting the fatigue grow.

Weariness from their rough passage on the ships had already slowed the detachment's progress into the Highlands. The arguing amongst his detachment was rapidly getting beyond his control. Sleep-deprived tempers grew more and more combustible as bellies went empty, or nearly so, yet another day, for the few crofts they had come across had been abandoned, all food and drink missing with the crofters. As the Highlanders withdrew before the sky even began to lighten, as if they knew the exact moment the first wan light of day would break the night sky and turn it a leaden grey, Sherwood made his decision.

"Set the watches about the encampment," he said to his second in command. "Bury any who have not survived the night, and have the cooks prepare anything they can. Anyone not on watch is to sleep. We shall meet the Highlanders here again tonight, rested and ready for them, and on the morrow we shall continue on for Glen Lairig."

His second strode into the camp bellowing orders while Sherwood climbed up on a large boulder and scanned the countryside around him, planning his own surprises for the Highlanders.

Tonight he would turn the darkness to his advantage.

CHAPTER SEVEN

SCOTIA DID NOT SLOW DOWN AS SHE MADE HER WAY TO THE caves. In spite of the aches and fatigue settling into her body, 'twas all she could do not to sprint back.

Her mind raced with the implications if her ability really could be used as a weapon. If she and Duncan could convince Nicholas that her *knowing*, something that she had not understood was unique to her, was of use in the coming battle, it would not matter if she had time to complete her training as a warrior. It would not matter that she was not a Guardian. The chief and the Guardians would need her to be part of the battle to rid them of the English. 'Twould still be up to the Guardians to figure out how to keep the rest of the English out of the Highlands, but this latest force would be done for.

She tripped over a tree root, letting loose an epithet worthy of a warrior as she fought to keep her feet. Duncan caught her arm, righting her just before she fell.

"Slow down. 'Twill help nothing if you kill yourself tumbling down the ben."

Scotia pulled her arm out of his grip and slowed her pace just enough to mind where she put her feet. It irritated her that he was right, and that his touch, his nearness, pulled her attention back to their kiss. She had meant to ask him why he kissed her, but she didn't really want to know. Just as she didn't want to know why she had reacted as she had, kissing him back when she had intended to bite him and free herself. She did not need answers to either question because it would never happen again. She would not be distracted from her goal by anyone.

No more kissing, she admonished herself. No lads to distract her, especially not Duncan, who had always been like an annoying older brother to her. Though she had to admit there had been nothing remotely brotherly about that kiss. Heat started to gather low in her stomach again.

Nay, she must focus. She could not think of Duncan that way. 'Twould be of no purpose, for he was clearly as caught by surprise at the intensity of their kiss as she was. Neither of them wanted to see where that path might lead.

He was her teacher, nothing more. He would train her. He would help her convince Nicholas that she was of use in the coming battle.

"Do you truly believe Nicholas and the council will let me go into battle because of this *knowing*?" She threw the question at him over her shoulder, but before he could respond a flash of *knowing* stopped her cold, and he almost ran into her. Her first thought was that her imagination was busy today, but then she realized this was another *knowing*, and if it was true, their allies needed help. As soon as she'd accepted what she *knew* another flash sped her feet again.

"Scotia?" Duncan called from behind her. "What is it?" But she did not have breath enough to spare to answer him.

"Nicholas?" she yelled as she skidded to a stop in the clearing near the largest of the cookfires. "Rowan, Jeanette! Where are you?"

Rowan stepped out of the dark maw of the main cave, wiping her hands on her skirts. "You bellowed, cousin? Jeanette is tending to the bairn. I've sent lads and lasses out to let the other searchers know the bairn was found. They should be back soon . . ." She was smiling until she really looked at Scotia, then at Duncan. Rowan turned back to the cave and summoned Jeanette immediately.

Jeanette came out, blinking in the soft light of the late afternoon. "Maisie will be fine, if that is what you are wanting to know," she said. "You made quick work of finding her, Duncan."

"'Twas Scotia who found her," Duncan said, looking around the clearing.

"Scotia?"

Scotia waved a hand to silence everyone. "Where is Nicholas? I have news that he will need."

"News? What news?" Jeanette asked. Several women, including Ceit with Maisie still sniffling in her arms, stepped up behind Jeanette, their faces unwelcoming but curious.

"'Tis news for the chief and Guardians," Scotia said, scowling at the other women.

Jeanette looked behind her and must have said something, for the women melted back into the darkness of the cave. She led the way to the council circle, Rowan behind her with Scotia and Duncan bringing up the rear. 'Twas as far away as one could get from the main cave and still be in the clearing.

"Nicholas is still out searching for Maisie. What news have you, sister?" Jeanette asked.

Scotia stood mute, once more doubting the knowledge she had. She was sure Jeanette and Rowan would scoff at her *knowings*.

"Whatever it is, Scotia, tell us," Duncan said quietly. "Tell us what you *know*." The subtle emphasis on the last word was lost on Rowan and Jeanette, but she heard it and took courage from his belief.

"Lord Sherwood, the English soldier with the white lock of hair Jeanette saw, the one Nicholas said he knows, is setting up a trap for our allies who have been harrying his detachment as they travel here from the shore. They must be warned before they attack again tonight."

Rowan and Jeanette simultaneously asked, "What?" and "How do you ken this?".

"Where?" Duncan asked. "Do you *know* where?"

She closed her eyes and concentrated on the flash of *knowing* she had received. "Nay, not exactly, but they are not yet in the mountains."

"And 'tis tonight the trap will be sprung?" he asked.

She nodded, carefully examining the *knowing* again. "Aye, tonight. 'Tis as if I know Sherwood's thoughts . . . at least this thought. Do you think I really do?"

Duncan shook his head. "I dinna ken, but I think anything is possible. They are not in the mountains? Can you tell if they are coming by river or over land?"

She closed her eyes and groped for more information but found none. "I cannot say, but if the English were traveling on the river, they would not encamp on the shore each night, would they? Our allies would have little chance to attack them in the night if they stayed aboard boats. Besides, it would take too many boats to bring so many to Glen Lairig by water, if they could even navigate upstream and over rapids and falls."

Duncan looked surprised at her analysis, but he was nodding slowly as his fingers drummed on his thighs. "You are right. They come overland. If they have not entered the bens yet, then they are too far away for any of us to travel, even on a fast horse, before nightfall. Then there is naught we can do to help our allies."

"Nay, we ken this will happen. We must do something, else what is the use of this gift?" she demanded, her gut twisting painfully at the idea that even with her knowledge they were powerless to do anything.

"What do you mean, you ken this will happen?" Rowan asked. Scotia looked at her cousin and realized the woman was staring at her as if she'd grown another head.

"I ken it . . . I *know* it."

"Are you getting visions like Jeanette?"

"Nay. I . . ." Scotia looked over at Duncan, unsure how to present this to them.

"She *knows*, Scotia does," he said. "She kens things none of us do."

Rowan started to speak but Jeanette cut her off before she got a single word out.

"'Tis an odd way to phrase this: She kens things none of us do." She stepped in front of Scotia and took her hands. "What sorts of things do you ken that we do not, my sister?" Her voice was quiet, but as intense as her iron grip, and Scotia was grateful that Jeanette, with her incredible thirst for knowledge, was not scoffing at her but seemed genuinely curious.

"She kent where Maisie was. I did not track her. Scotia just *knew* where to find her."

"I do not understand," Rowan said, rubbing her forehead with the heel of her hand as she often did when wrestling with a problem.

Scotia did not even have to look at Duncan to know he was still drumming his fingers on his thighs.

"Perhaps we should summon Nicholas and the others of the council to join us so we only have to explain this once," he said.

Jeanette squeezed Scotia's hands and nodded slowly. "Aye, 'tis a good idea. Rowan, I need to finish tending the cuts on Maisie so her mum will stop fretting over them. Perhaps the three of you can collect cups and make sure there is ale"—she stopped and shook her head, for they all knew the ale had burned up in the great hall fire—"water for the men when they arrive."

"We shall need to prepare drink and food for ten . . . nay, thirteen allies who are arriving, too," Scotia said.

Jeanette, Rowan, and Duncan all stared at her. "What?" Jeanette asked.

Just then they heard the sound of the lookout's horn—one blast. Friend.

Scotia looked at Duncan. "Perhaps that is them now," he said, his eyebrows raised.

"Allies?" Rowan asked. "'Tis probably just last night's watch making their way home. What makes you think 'tis allies?"

"Aye, what makes you think 'tis allies?" Jeanette echoed.

"Another *knowing* that came to me right after the information about Lord Sherwood. Thirteen men. I dinna ken what clan they are from, though."

They all looked at each other.

"We shall know soon enough if 'tis allies or the night's watch," Duncan said.

"Aye, we will. Jamie," Rowan called to a lad who was bringing a load of wood into the clearing, "leave that. I need you to go down the ben toward the training area. That is where Nicholas and Malcolm were going to search. If they are not already on their way back here, fetch them immediately."

"And any other warriors you see," Scotia called after the retreating lad. "They will all want to be here when our allies arrive," she said to her companions, trying to sound confident, though she was anything but.

As Jeanette finished tending Maisie, the rest gathered waterskins and cups, then waited restlessly in the council circle.

It was not long before Nicholas and Malcolm, trailed by Kenneth, Uilliam, and a few other warriors and lads who had been searching for the bairn, began flooding into the clearing, their voices, for the most part, loud and happy. Peigi, who must have been in the cave, was now waiting in the shade of the cavern's mouth. She quickly sent the lads off on other tasks as the chief's council gathered in their accustomed circle of logs and stones.

"What news?" Nicholas asked.

Rowan tugged on his hand as she took a seat, pulling him down to sit beside her. "Duncan? Scotia?" She raised her brows at them across the small circle. "Who shall start?"

Duncan quickly filled in Nicholas, Malcolm, Uilliam, and Kenneth on what they knew of Lord Sherwood's plans.

"I know not how you ken this," Kenneth said, "but it sounds like they are in Clan Campbell territory. Angus Dubh, their chief, is a wily man. I doubt not that he has eyes on the English even during the day and kens exactly what they are about, just as we would be . . . will be."

"There are also allies on their way into this glen," Scotia said, not waiting for Duncan.

The circle was quiet, then Kenneth spoke. "How do you ken this, child?"

At the word *child*, all the tiny hairs on Scotia's body rose like the hackles on a dog. "I just ken it," she said.

"She *knows* things, Kenneth," Duncan said, leaning forward and resting his elbows on his knees. "'Tis Scotia who learned of the English trap this night. 'Twas Scotia who found the wee lassie, not me. She *knew* exactly where to look for her."

"How?" Nicholas asked. "She did not track the wee lass?" He directed this question to Duncan, who shook his head but said nothing. "How did you find her, Scotia?"

Scotia's ire rose at the doubt in her chief's voice, and in preparation for a battle, for she knew already they would not believe her. But before she could spring to her feet Duncan reached back and laid a hand on her arm, holding her in place. He glanced over his shoulder at her and subtly shook his head as if he could hear her thoughts.

"Just tell them how it happened." He sat back, stretching his long legs out in front of him, crossing them at the ankles, as he slowly looked each person in the circle in the eyes, but he never took his hand off her arm. "They will listen without judging."

It was as if they all took a long breath as tension eased.

Duncan looked over at her, his eyes filled with what she could only call encouragement and support, and gave her arm a small squeeze before he let it go.

"Just tell them."

She pulled the warmth of his belief around her like plate armor, focusing on it instead of the disbelief she expected from everyone else. "When I said her name, the child's, I just . . . *knew*. I knew where she was and how to get there. I know not where the knowledge came from, nor why it came to me. Later, after we found her and her mum had brought her back here, Duncan and I were . . . talking." For a moment the taste and unexpected passion of that kiss tried to overtake her senses again, but she forced her mind to stay on the trouble at hand, not the man sitting beside her. "And all of a sudden, I *knew*, first that the English lord planned a surprise attack for our allies and that they had not made their way into the bens yet, and then, almost immediately, I knew a small contingent of our allies neared this glen."

Nicholas looked at Jeanette, and Scotia knew he was asking her, without speaking, if she thought Scotia spoke the truth.

Jeanette got that look that was both far away and inward that signaled she was searching through the things she had learned before rendering an opinion.

"There are records of some Guardians," Jeanette said, her voice dreamy, almost as if she were reading directly from the scrolls that held the Chronicles of the Guardians as she spoke, "who had this sort of gift."

Scotia held her breath. A Guardian gift? She had hoped, but only now realized she had not thought it possible.

"But Scotia is not a Guardian," Kenneth said, "is she?"

Jeanette and Rowan looked at each other, Rowan's auburn brows raised as if she, too, questioned Jeanette without words.

"Perhaps," Jeanette said. "We did not ken there could be two Guardians at the same time. Who are we to say there could not be three?"

"Truly?" Scotia said. "You think this is a Guardian gift?" She hated the way her voice almost squeaked with the hope that engulfed her.

"I think we need to speak to Scotia alone, if you will all excuse us," Rowan said, and she and Jeanette rose.

"But the allies," Scotia said, also rising to her feet, unsure of whether she wanted more to know if she was right or if she was a Guardian. "Should we not wait to find out if I am right, if my *knowing* in this is true? There is no point in testing me if it is not."

"We do not intend to test you, cousin," Rowan said. "There is no test to pass to become a Guardian. The Targe stone either strengthens your gift, or it does not. There is nothing we can do to influence it one way or the other. And I do not doubt that it is a gift. You found Maisie, aye?"

"Aye."

"And she has had other *knowings* as well," Duncan said. "Scotia, you should go with them now. When our allies arrive, which should be any moment judging by when the horn sounded, it will take time to settle them, feed them after their journey, and to ascertain what strengths they each bring to bear. And if it is only the watch returning, then it will not matter that you have gone off with Rowan and Jeanette—but I do not believe 'tis the watch." He grabbed her hand and tugged her back down by it, giving it a squeeze before he released her. "If this *knowing* is a Guardian gift, then the Targe stone will make it more powerful, perhaps even letting you direct it to the things we most need to ken in order to overcome the English force. That alone would be more useful to us than all the information the watchers and scouts we've sent out can gather." He dropped his voice and caught her gaze with his. "That alone would make you a part of the battle as you so wish. Patience, careful planning, and knowledge of our enemy's weakness comes first. Remember? This gift might make all of those things easier, which means we would be able to protect our home and our people much better than we can now."

Scotia started to object, though she did not know why. If she was a Guardian then the clan would have to stop shunning her, and she would be part of the battle, as he said. So why were her hands icy at the thought of facing the Targe stone?

He touched her once more, this time letting his hand rest lightly on her forearm while he finished.

"For now, 'tis the best use of our time if you, Rowan, and Jeanette can determine if this is a Guardian gift while we assess these allies you ken will join us soon. Remember, though, even if it is not, 'twill be of use in protecting the clan."

In her head she still argued to wait, to put off what was surely a test even though Rowan and Jeanette said 'twas not, but the gentle pressure on her arm, and the reminder of her lessons had her modulating her voice, bringing it down from a demand to a statement. "Very well, but I want to be part of the battle, whether or no I have a Guardian gift."

Duncan looked around, and it was only then that Scotia realized the two of them had been talking solely to each other while the others watched the exchange, some with surprise, others with a smile. Only her father glowered.

"I promise, when the time comes, if you are ready, you will fight," Duncan whispered, and she realized he was doing his best to keep her secret, so she nodded.

"I shall put myself in Jeanette's and Rowan's hands—for now," she said, more loudly so everyone was once more included in the conversation.

"Let us see what we can learn." Jeanette motioned for Scotia and Rowan to follow her out of the circle.

"I will hold you to your promise," Scotia said to Duncan quietly, as she stood.

"I did not make it lightly. Will you promise to remain calm and cooperate with your sister and your cousin?"

Scotia glanced at Jeanette and Rowan, who had stopped by the trail that led down the ben, waiting for her to catch up. She knew they were anxious to learn if Scotia would join them as

Guardians, and Scotia had to admit, in spite of her doubts, she was as well.

"I promise," she said.

"I shall hold you to that, ye ken?"

Scotia nodded her head. "I will patiently let Jeanette and Rowan do what they will to me." She started to follow Jeanette, then returned to Duncan once more. "I expect to hear everything about our allies when I return," she said only to him.

"I expected nothing less," he said, smiling at her.

She glanced once more at everyone else in the circle and still saw reactions that ranged from smiles to confusion to the even deeper frown on her father's face, but she did not care what they thought. Duncan believed her. Duncan was her ally. And if this gift she had not realized was a gift proved her to be a Guardian, they would all have to believe in her, too.

CHAPTER EIGHT

Scotia followed Jeanette and Rowan a short way down the ben from the caves, then along what had originally been a faint deer trail but which had over the last weeks quickly become a path, now that her sister and cousin came here daily to practice their Guardian skills. As they neared the burn—Jeanette needed water for her gift of visions—a strange tingling sensation washed over Scotia's skin, there and gone again in a single step. Rowan and Jeanette glanced at each other.

"What was that?" Scotia asked, their behavior telling her it was not her imagination.

"A barrier," Rowan said, with a bemused smile. "'Tis too small to be of much use, but we constructed it three days ago, and it still holds."

"But we walked right through it," Scotia said, looking behind her to see if she could tell where the barrier was. There was nothing to see.

"Aye, we can, because we have no ill intent." Jeanette was kneeling next to the burn. Rowan knelt facing her. She pulled the snow-white ermine sack from where it hung at her belt, laid it on the ground between them, and pulled it open until it lay in a flat circle.

The Highland Targe lay on it, a heavy grey stone the size of a warrior's fist, flattened on opposite sides so that it looked like a small, fat shield—a targe. Rowan turned the stone over, revealing the three swirls in a circle symbol that had been incised on it by some ancient Guardian forgotten by time. Rowan settled the stone in the center of the open sack, directly on top of the same swirls in a circle symbol that had been painted in a now-faded red dye on the amber-colored hide.

Jeanette rotated the sack until she seemed satisfied with the arrangement. Two of the three additional symbols painted on the sack around the central symbol were aligned with the two Guardians. A third, an arrow broken in two places, was arranged facing Scotia. Both Guardians sat back upon their heels and looked at Scotia expectantly.

"Have you actually tested the barrier with someone of 'ill intent'?" she asked as she slowly approached the two women and the stone.

"Nay," Rowan said, "but if you happen to anger someone enough to goad them into trying to harm you, you can lead them here and test it for us."

"Very funny." Scotia knelt down and sat back on her heels, facing the stone. The burn burbled happily opposite her, with Jeanette on her right and Rowan on her left.

"Tell us about this *knowing*," Rowan said.

"There is nothing to tell. I simply *know* things that I have no way of knowing. I do not ken how or why I know these things."

"How long has this been going on?" Rowan again.

Scotia had to think about that question. "I think . . . I think it has been going on my whole life." The two women said nothing. "I did not think 'twas anything unusual until today. I assumed it happened to everyone, but apparently it does not."

"Other than today, are there specific times this has happened?" Jeanette asked.

Scotia's first thought had her clenching her teeth, but her second thought she could share. "Remember how I went in after Ian when the great hall was afire? I knew he was in there, though I had not seen him go in, nor did anyone else seem to ken he was in there. I knew it. I knew he was in the kitchen. I knew that he was very afraid, and could not get himself out. I do not know how I knew it, but I did. Just like I knew where Maisie was today, and just as I know 'tis allies, not the watch, who are arriving."

"But you did not ken the curtain wall would fall, did you?" Rowan asked.

Scotia shook her head, remembering that day when Nicholas had come into their lives and everything had changed. She sighed. "Nay, I knew Conall was there waiting for me, but that was only because I heard his whistle when I went out for a walk. So how does this work?" She waved a hand at the Targe stone. "How do we tell if I am another Guardian?"

Both she and Rowan looked at Jeanette for guidance.

Jeanette shrugged. "Rowan and I were just taken by the power of the stone. We did not do anything to cause either of those events . . . at least nothing that we are aware of."

"Perhaps if she tries to use her gift with the stone?" Rowan asked. Her eyes narrowed and she cocked her head as she reached out and touched her symbol painted on the sack, an inverted V with three wavy lines under it. "I do not understand how any of this happens. I was first struck with my gift in the bailey, the night of Elspet's last blessing, but wasn't taken by the Targe until that night in Elspet's chamber. Jeanette was led to the grotto by the deer with the bent antler and then found the stone in the pool there with her symbol"—Rowan pointed at the mirror painted on the part of the sack closest to Jeanette—"when she was overtaken with the power of the Targe."

"There does not seem to be any similarity except that we were both overcome with the force of the power when we were claimed by it as Guardians. Have you felt such a force?" Jeanette asked.

Scotia shook her head slowly, then faster. "I would ken it if I had, would I not? I have not experienced anything like what I saw when Rowan was chosen. I would not forget such an event."

"Nay, you would not," Rowan said, and Jeanette silently agreed.

"So then what are we doing here? Just waiting for it to overtake me? That does not seem likely since it has never happened before," Scotia said, disappointment making her words harsher than she meant for them to be.

"We are still learning, Scotia. Clearly we do not understand all of what the Highland Targe can do, or how to use it," Rowan said, her voice was calm but tension showed in her rigid posture and furled brow.

"In truth, we ken little of how the Targe works, sister. Perhaps we should just see if you can use the Targe to direct your *knowing* to something you wish to ken, like exactly where the English are now, or when they will arrive in Glen Lairig?"

"I have already told you where they are today. As for when they will arrive, your gift is better than my guess. My *knowing* does not seem to deal with anything in the future as your visions do. In every case I can think of I *knew* something that was happening at that moment, but that I could not see or hear."

"Very well," Jeanette said, "let us simply see if you can use the Targe to direct your gift and work from there."

"But how will we determine if what I *know* is true?"

"'Tis a good question . . ." Jeanette looked about. "Does your knowing work with objects?"

Scotia immediately thought of the dagger that had been used to kill her mother, and later Myles. She always seemed to know exactly where it was of late, needing only to think of it to find it. "Aye, with some objects, if I ken what the object is and think of it."

Jeanette looked at her, surprise lighting her face. "'Tis how you always seemed to know where Mum had mislaid the hair combs Da had given her, isn't it?"

Scotia had to think back to the many times her mum had been scouring the castle looking for the combs she wore almost daily but inevitably took out somewhere other than her chamber and mislaid. "Aye. I never really thought about it like that. I didn't always *know* where her lost things were, but could always find those for her."

"Good." Jeanette pulled the sack of herbs and simples she always kept with her off her belt and held it up for Scotia to see. "I shall go and hide this somewhere. When I come back we shall see if you can tell us where it is."

Jeanette took the pouch and left by the path. The quiet noises of the restless wood settled over Scotia and Rowan, accentuated by the burbling stream as it flowed over its rocky bed. Scotia took the opportunity to look closely at the open ermine sack, noting the symbols that she had only fleetingly glimpsed in the past. The inverted V with three wavy lines under it was for Rowan's gift, the energy that comes from beneath the ground that she focused with the Targe to move things without touching them. The mirror symbol was aligned with Jeanette. The mirror, a scrying tool, was like the water in a cup that Jeanette used to tap into her gift of visions.

And in front of Scotia was an arrow, broken in two places so it formed a Z.

"What does this one mean?" Scotia said, lightly running the tip of her finger over the details of the arrow symbol painted in red on the hide.

"We do not ken. Not yet. If 'tis yours, then you will understand what it means when the Targe claims you."

Before Scotia could form another question Jeanette was back. As she settled into her spot, Rowan lifted the Targe stone and handed it to Scotia.

"You may or may not need to be touching the Targe to focus your gift through it. I must touch it to focus the energy I pull from the ground. Jeanette needs it near, but she must be touching or peering into water to control her visions. Water is the source of her gift. Do you ken the source of yours? It might help you to understand how you must use the Targe . . . if you are to be a Guardian."

Scotia's head was starting to ache. "I do not ken the source of my *knowing*," she said. "But if the arrow is for a third Guardian, perhaps air is the source? An arrow flies." She ran her finger along the Z-shaped broken arrow again. "Except this arrow will not fly." She sighed. "Can we get on with this?"

"We can. Do you remember the first blessing Mum taught us?" Jeanette asked, her voice pitched low and soothing, almost the same voice their mum had used to calm Scotia when she was little and angry.

"Of course I do."

"'Tis a good idea to start with that."

"And then what?"

Jeanette shrugged. "We shall have to wait and see."

Scotia took a deep breath, glad she could start with something familiar, something known to her. She held the Targe stone up, as she'd seen her mum do many times, moving it to her right, then to her left, then up over her head, and back down to the right. Next she held it in front of her, heart high, and whispered the simple blessing in a long-lost language. And then she tried to *know* where Jeanette's healer's bag was, though she really did not ken how to force the knowledge to her. When that didn't work, she waited for the *knowing* to come.

"Well?" Rowan asked.

"Well what?" Scotia replied.

"Can you feel the power of the Targe?"

"Nay. I feel nothing."

"Close your eyes and concentrate on Jeanette's healer bag."

Scotia did as instructed, though she was sure now 'twas a waste of time. The stone did not claim her as a Guardian. Power did not surge through her as she had witnessed when Rowan was made Guardian. Nothing happened. She could imagine where Jeanette might have hidden the bag, but she did not *know*. She opened her eyes. "Nothing. How does the stone work for you?" she asked, looking to Jeanette for guidance.

Jeanette chewed on her lower lip as she considered Scotia's question. "When I call my gift, I let my mind go blank as I stare into the water in my cup, and it just . . . comes. How do you do it, Rowan?"

"You mean you two have not figured this part out yet?" Scotia lowered the stone to her lap and glared at her companions.

"'Tis not like we have been at this over long," Rowan said, squaring her shoulders and straightening her spine. "For me, when I hold the Targe stone I can feel the energy moving up through me. I can pull on it with my thoughts, or push it through the stone the same way. If 'twas not so clear that I am actually doing something, I would think 'twas all in my imagination . . . but it is not. 'Tis very real."

Scotia pondered what they had said. "So you can feel it and manipulate the energy with your thoughts, aye?" She directed this question to Rowan, who nodded. "And you do nothing but stare into a cup of water and your gift finds you, aye?" she said to Jeanette, who also nodded.

"'Twas like what we could do before we became Guardians, but more so . . . much, much more so, and we do not have to wait for our gifts to come to us anymore, we can call our gifts with the Targe upon need," Rowan said.

"That is not very helpful," Scotia mumbled as she once more raised the stone so it was on the level with her heart. She closed her eyes again and tried to quiet her mind, taking long slow breaths as her mum had tried to teach her when she was bristling with anger or frustration, as Duncan had taught her more recently. After a few minutes she gave that up, for her mind was never quiet, and instead she pictured the bag once more and said the words "Jeanette's bag" in her mind, over and over, as she had done with the child's name earlier.

Still nothing.

"Jeanette." Rowan's voice broke through the drone in Scotia's mind. She opened her eyes and lowered the stone back to her lap, glaring at her cousin. "Jeanette," Rowan said, "do you remember how I helped you learn to use the Targe stone? I held it while you touched it and—"

"Aye, and my gift burst through me. And it hurt you."

"Only a little and not for long," Rowan said quickly, reaching for the stone in Scotia's lap. She held it up so it was over the open sack, but face-high this time. "Put your fingers on it," she said to Scotia, "then close your eyes and see if you can feel your gift. Try to pull it forward with your thoughts. Try to *know* where Jeanette's bag is."

Scotia did as she was bade, though she did not hold out much hope at this point. She felt a tingling in her fingers where they touched the stone, but nothing more.

No *knowing*.

No Guardian gift.

Sweat beaded on her forehead, and her palms went sticky with dampness as embarrassment and failure engulfed her. Just as everyone expected, she was not good enough to be a Guardian as her mother had been. She was not good enough to join her sister and cousin in protecting the clan with their gifts, and their barriers, and their proven success in battle. All the fatigue of the long, eventful day suddenly caught up with her, weighing her down, making her feel weak in body and soul.

"'Tis useless," she said, lurching to her feet and dusting the dirt and grit from her skirts. She would not give in to such feelings, at least not in front of anyone. "I am clearly not meant to be a Guardian." She notched up her chin and threw her shoulders back, reminding herself of the training Duncan had given her. If she could not be a Guardian, at least she might be able to aid the clan as a warrior. "I just *know* things from time to time, through no doing on my part. Whatever that broken arrow means, 'tis not for me."

Duncan paced the length of the cave site, both excited and anxious to see if Scotia's *knowing* was as true this time as it was with the child. He glanced toward the path where Scotia and the other two women had disappeared a few minutes before and couldn't help but wonder if his raven-haired troublemaker would return a Guardian. It could only help to have a third Guardian in these difficult days, but even if she was not a Guardian, this knowing could be nothing but helpful.

"Mind yersel'," Peigi snapped at him. "We've work to do here if you expect an evening meal, Duncan. You are in the way." She waved her gnarled hands at the dozen or so women hard at work in and around the cook circle. "Go and join Kenneth and Uilliam!" She pointed at the council circle where the two older men sat facing the direction their visitors would come from. Nicholas and Malcolm leaned against trees just behind the seated men, facing the same part of the clearing.

Duncan did as he was told, but did not sit. Instead he paced back and forth between the council area and the path Scotia had taken with the Guardians.

"Your pacing will not make the news come any faster," Nicholas said when Duncan drew near him. "'Twould be better to save your energy in case we need it when our visitors get here."

"I would cease if I could, Nicholas," he said, turning on his heel and making his way back to the path. A tiny selfish part of him hoped Scotia would not become another Guardian. If she did, their long days together would be done, and Jeanette and Rowan would take over with a completely different sort of training. 'Twould be a shame, in a way. Scotia showed promise with a sword, with strategy. She was lighter on her feet than any other warrior he'd ever met, and her mind was fast, sharp. Of course she'd only had him for an opponent so far, so perhaps she had just become very good at assessing Duncan. 'Twas something he had to address in her training, and he knew, if she were to progress in her fighting skills, they would soon need to reveal her secret—their secret.

But for all he knew, their days of training might be behind them already, and that opened up an unfamiliar melancholy in his chest. Frustrated, he paced toward the path the visitors would come by, friends by the single blast of the horn. He stopped. Listened. Nothing yet. Were they crawling down the ben?

He paced back to the other path and stopped. Listened. If anything was happening with Scotia he could not hear it.

"You are going to make a rut from one end of this clearing to the other, Duncan." Peigi's wavering voice came from behind him. He turned and found her settling herself on a stump near the cookfire. She beckoned him over and nodded to the log laid out next to her stump. "If you will not sit with the men, sit with me."

He sighed. Unable to naysay the old woman, he joined her, sitting beside her though his feet itched to keep moving.

"You ken you cannot change Scotia's fate, aye?" she asked him quietly.

"I ken that."

"But?"

"But I do not ken what will be better for her or for the clan—to become another Guardian, or to continue as she has with—" He stopped himself, realizing he was about to reveal Scotia's secret. "As she has."

"With you, you meant to say." Peigi patted his knee as if he were a wee fussy bairn. "You are enjoying your time with her. You did not expect to, but she has surprised you, delighted you even."

"I . . . She . . ." He shook his head a little too adamantly. "Nay."

"Dinna deny it, laddie. 'Tis clear you and Scotia both enjoy whatever it is ye get up to of a day." She winked at him, and he wondered what she really knew. "She is glowing when you return to camp, though that mood disappears fast enough, and you"—Peigi patted his knee again—"you sometimes look proud, often bemused, and your familiar scowl is seldom seen of late."

Duncan did not know how to respond, for that was exactly how he felt at the end of their days together, though he thought he had hidden his feelings better than that.

"Whatever happens," Peigi said, "you must be strong for her. She depends upon you. She trusts you as she does not anyone else, not even her da since he killed that spy in the bailey."

"She wanted to do that herself," he said.

"Aye. She is a bloodthirsty lassie," Peigi said with a quiet laugh. Duncan could not help but smile at the description.

"Do you think—" At that moment a shout came from the far end of the cave site.

Duncan leapt to his feet and went to stand next to Uilliam, just behind Nicholas, Malcolm, and Kenneth. They watched as a group of thirteen men, escorted by Brodie MacAlpin and surrounded by several other MacAlpin warriors and two of Malcolm's kin, entered the clearing. Kenneth started to step forward, but checked himself.

"Allies," Uilliam said, his voice tinged with awe. "Just like Scotia kent."

Duncan tried not to smile, but he had to admit he felt a bit of awe at Scotia's gift himself.

"They are MacGregors of Loch Awe," Kenneth said quietly to Nicholas. "Dermid MacGregor speaks for them."

Nicholas nodded, but never took his eyes off the new arrivals as he strode to meet them. Malcolm, his new champion, followed one step behind and on his left.

"We welcome you, MacGregors of Loch Awe, and thank you for joining us. We offer you the hospitality of Clan MacAlpin of Dunlairig, such as we can."

A growl came from Kenneth, and Duncan was surprised when Uilliam's deep voice came calm and quiet, "Hold, Kenneth. Hold. Let him finish first."

It was only then that Duncan noticed, first, Kenneth's clenched fists, and second, a familiar blond lad who liked to dally with

Scotia. Duncan must have made a noise of some sort when he recognized Conall, for Uilliam growled at him.

"Dinna move a muscle, lad, or say anything," Uilliam commanded. "Either of you." He directed this back at Kenneth. "We shall deal with Conall MacGregor once they show that Nicholas has their respect."

"Are there others behind you?" Nicholas asked.

"Nay," the one called Dermid said. "Others chose to engage the English as they came from the coast, harrying them in the hopes of whittling down their numbers before they could get here. There were at least two score of the Sassenach bastards that arrived by ship. They were hard upon our heels for a short while, but their pace has been sorely slowed." He grinned, clearly pleased that the English were not easily making their way across Scotland.

"You did not lead them here." It was a command, not something Duncan had heard from Nicholas before.

"We were careful, MacAlpin. I gathered those I could as I journeyed here, as Kenneth bade me do." He nodded at the old chief. "We are all that could be spared with English crawling across our lands."

Nicholas's head bobbed slowly up and down as he surveyed the far smaller contingent of allies than they had hoped would arrive. Just as the silence was drawing taut between Nicholas and Dermid, Nicholas stepped forward and surprised everyone.

"You," he said, clearly looking at Conall.

The young man looked Nicholas calmly in the eye, though he had noticeably not done the same with Kenneth. "Aye?"

"I have seen you before." Nicholas stopped, as if he were trying to remember, but Duncan knew the ex-spy well enough now to know 'twas for show, though he knew not where the two might have met. Nicholas forgot nothing, no matter how inconsequential. 'Twas a valuable skill in a spy and a chief. "Ah. I remember. You were below the curtain wall at Dunlairig Castle the day it fell."

Conall started to deny it, but Nicholas cocked his head and the young man went quiet. Duncan could only imagine the look Nicholas must be giving him, for Conall went even paler than he'd started.

"You were with Scotia MacAlpin, my wife's cousin. I searched for you in the rubble after the wall came down."

Kenneth growled this time, his words lost in the sound, but Uilliam had a hand clamped to his shoulder, holding him firmly in place.

Nicholas did not appear to notice Kenneth's reaction. "'Tis glad I am to see you hale and whole. Rowan was very concerned that you might have been caught in the wreckage." He cocked his head the other way, and Conall shifted on his feet, as if he could not decide whether to stand his ground or flee. "She also told me your life was forfeit if you were caught with Scotia again." Conall blanched so much his freckles stood out like spatters of crimson blood. "You were caught, by Rowan, and by me. As I am chief here now, 'tis my duty to take your life."

Duncan swallowed an oath. What was Nicholas thinking? They needed these men on their side in the coming battle. As much as he did not want Conall here—and the thought of the randy lad chasing after Scotia raised an ire he was not proud of— there were bigger troubles to consider, and Duncan would do as he'd always done, though clearly not always well. He would watch over Scotia like a hawk.

The other MacGregors bristled at Nicholas's statement, two of them going so far as to draw their dirks.

"Put your blades away," Nicholas said, though he did not take his eyes off Conall. "I have no intention of carrying out this sentence right now."

"Never!" one of the MacGregors said.

"That depends upon Conall"—he turned and looked back at Kenneth—"and Kenneth." He speared the auld chief with a look that shocked Duncan. He knew Nicholas was capable of anything—as a spy in King Edward's employ he would have had to do many things he might not choose to do in his new life as chief. So far at least. This look said Nicholas was in complete control, that he had stepped fully and confidently into his position as chief of this clan, and that he expected Kenneth to respect whatever Nicholas was up to with Conall. Kenneth glared at Nicholas, but gave him a slight nod and said nothing.

Nicholas returned his glare to Conall. "Do you give your word that you will do as I bid, putting the protection of this clan and indeed, the entire Highlands, first in your thoughts and your actions for as long as you bide here with us?"

To Conall's credit, he straightened his back, dropped his shoulders, and faced the chief like a warrior. "Of course I do. 'Tis why I am here. The MacAlpins have long been our allies, and we are joined by many common kinfolk. You have my word that I am here as a warrior in the service of the Targe and its Guardians."

The other allies nodded their agreement, as Nicholas stared into the eyes of each man. "I have the same oath from each of you?"

"Aye!" they all said at once.

"Then I welcome you and thank you for coming to our aid in this fight. You are invited to partake of our hospitality, as much as we can offer, and in return for your service you have my oath that should you ever require it, you have but to call upon us and we will come to your aid."

"And Conall's life?" Dermid demanded.

"Will depend upon his keeping his oath," Nicholas quickly answered. "If he does, he shall be free to leave here, with his head still upon his shoulders, when this business is done." Nicholas stared at Conall a long moment, clearly making the lad uncomfortable once more. "If he keeps his oath," Nicholas repeated.

Duncan forced himself to keep his face neutral, though he wanted to grin at Nicholas's masterful way of putting the lad on notice. Nicholas suddenly pivoted and led the small group of allies further into the camp. As Conall passed Duncan and the other two men, he put as many people between himself and Kenneth as he could, and only glanced quickly at Duncan, as he followed the other allies into the camp.

As Kenneth, Uilliam, and Duncan fell in behind the newcomers, the scant number of them sank in. Ten and three. Only ten and three had come to their aid, though Dermid said more skirmished with the English as they came, which, Duncan suddenly realized, gave proof to at least that part of what Scotia *knew* of the English force. The MacAlpins must pray those skirmishes whittled away many of the English soldiers. Fifteen dead would give the MacAlpins a slim advantage. Ten dead English would bring them close to even numbers. Anything less would make the MacAlpins' success in defending their home and the Highlands an uncertain undertaking at best.

Duncan realized that Nicholas had been about more than just putting Conall on notice that he had not emerged from the falling wall as unscathed as he might think. By making it clear he knew exactly who Conall was and what his position was with this clan, Nicholas had asserted his position as chief with the allies, with Conall, and with Kenneth, effectively telling Kenneth he could not touch the lad without the new chief's assent.

But Duncan knew, despite Nicholas's assertion of his position, if Conall so much as thought of breaking his oath, Duncan would make sure the young warrior never broke another one long before Kenneth could even raise a fist.

Duncan would make sure the lad never again touched Scotia.

CHAPTER NINE

Scotia was humiliated. She wasn't a Guardian. She would never be a Guardian.

Before today it had always been a possibility, slim but still there, that she might become one. Now it was a fact that she would not, and everyone, the entire clan and anyone she might meet in the future, would know of her failure. Everyone would know she would never be more than she was in this moment—the younger sister and cousin of two Guardians, one of whom wasn't even a MacAlpin by blood!

She stormed down the ben, knowing she needed time to get her emotions under control, as Duncan had been teaching her, doing her best to think before acting, lest she make her humiliation even worse. But it was hard to think when she wanted to scream, to strike, to hit something. If only there were a battle now, where she could loose her anger. But Duncan said she must never go into battle fueled by her emotions. A warrior needed a clear mind and a steady arm. She slowed as she remembered the exercise Duncan had her do at the beginning of every training session, and how it aided her in calming her emotions and focusing her mind on the matter at hand.

She didn't have her sword, but there were sticks aplenty all about her. She stepped into the wood and chose her weapon, then looked for an area open enough and relatively flat. When she found it, she took her position and slowly moved through the thrust, parry, turn, block, attack, fall back, parry, and thrust of the exercise. Then she did it again, this time concentrating on her breath as she repeated the sequence. And once more, making sure she had every move in sync with her breath.

And then she flew through the sequence, again and again and again until her sides were heaving with the effort, and her mind was focused only on the moment. This moment. This move. This breath. She dropped her stick and braced her hands on her knees, drawing the cool evening air deep into her lungs. She closed her eyes and continued to breathe, slowing her inhalations as her heart slowed its pounding.

"Better?"

Without thinking, Scotia grabbed her stick and whirled to face the voice, her body landing in the proper fighting stance without her consciously thinking about it. And then she realized it was Duncan's voice. It was Duncan who stood not far away, his expression an odd combination of concern and pride.

She relaxed, letting the stick once more fall to the ground. She lifted her chin. "Aye. Better."

Duncan tried to act calm. Scotia's passion always stirred him, but this—to watch as she controlled that passion, that emotion, funneling it into the movements of a warrior with a grace and lethal focus such as he'd never seen in her before— took his breath away.

"You were supposed to return to the caves with Rowan and Jeanette," he finally said quietly. He did not move any closer to her. If he did he would take her in his arms, he would kiss her again. He drummed his fingers on his thighs and wished he could take up the drill where she left off, for he did not trust the emotions and the desire that pulsed through him.

So he kept his distance.

Scotia closed her eyes for a moment, then looked at him, her face composed, her eyes clear. "I needed to work off some anger before I returned. You have told me I need to think before I act, and I was not thinking, not thinking well, anyway. I feared I would do something or say something and would embarrass myself . . . or you." She smiled at him then, but it was not the happy glowing smile she usually wore during and after her training sessions with him. This was dimmed by disappointment.

"I failed, Duncan, as I am sure you ken. Rowan and Jeanette must have already reported my failure to the entire clan."

"Nay, lass. They said nothing. In truth, I did not ken if I would find you elated or despondent, for they said nothing of what had transpired. Rowan just said I should find you."

Scotia turned away from him, her face raised to the sky and her hands on her hips. There was something new about the way she held herself. Her back was straight and strong with her midnight hair cascading down it. It wasn't the posture of Scotia angry. He was very familiar with that one—shoulders pulled up and forward, as if to defend her heart from attack. Nay, with her hands on her hips she stood strong, balanced, open . . . determined.

That's what he was seeing. Scotia determined.

"What are you thinking?" he asked.

She turned back to face him again, and he was pleased to see there were no tears, no glint of anger, just a calm he'd never seen upon her face before.

"Do not look so puzzled, Duncan," she said with a little shake of her head. "I am not that hard to fathom, am I?"

He approached her slowly, taking in all the little ways she held herself that were different, learning this new Scotia in case she decided to stay this way.

"Aye. In this moment you are a new person but I dinna ken why or how this came to be so suddenly. Failure, as you put it, for I do not see it that way, usually makes you unpredictable, angry . . . a brat," he added with a smile meant to take the sting out of the word.

"I am not a Guardian. That is a failure," she said. "That path is no longer in my future." She stepped closer to him, shrinking the space between them so much he could easily reach out and touch her, but she reached out and took his hand first. "If I am not to be a Guardian, then I am determined to help defend my family and my home the only other way available to me. We must redouble my training, Duncan."

She had his hand in both of hers, and her touch, her scent, carrying the slightly salty tang of her exertions as it wrapped around him, made it hard to think.

Scotia tugged on his hand. "Do you not agree?"

"Agree?" He had to think hard to remember what she was referring to. Her training . . . it came back to him . . . redoubling her training. "Aye. Agreed, and after what I have seen today"—now he took her hands in both of his—"you have handled yourself well all through this long, tiring day—I think you are ready for something a bit more difficult to master than the exercises and drills we have been working on."

Her impish smile returned. "What will that be?"

He could not help but smile back at her. "That is for tomorrow. Are you not hungry, lass? I am famished." He wrapped one of her hands in his, unwilling to release her just yet, and led her back to the trail. He was surprised to find himself very hungry . . . and not just for his dinner.

They did not speak as they made their way back to the caves, but he noticed she did not make any effort to let go of his hand. As they got close the sound of voices threaded through the trees, Scotia stopped, pulling him to a stop, too.

"Was I right?" she asked. "Allies?"

It was only then that Duncan remembered what . . . who . . . awaited them in the clearing.

"Aye, Scotia, you were right. 'Tis the MacGregor clan. Thirteen men arrived." He could not decide whether to warn her of Conall's arrival or to see how she reacted when she discovered him in the camp, but he did not want to test her new resolve so soon. "Conall MacGregor is among them."

She pressed her lips together and narrowed her eyes, but she did not take her hand from his . "I was wondering when he would turn up. Da did not skin him on the spot?"

"Nay." Duncan tried not to hold his breath as he waited to see if she was pleased or displeased that the lad had arrived. "Nicholas did not let him."

Scotia's brows shot up. "Did not let him? Nicholas, not Uilliam?"

"Nicholas, but he has gained a new oath from Conall. Will you make him break it? Will you help put the lad's life in danger again now that he is here?"

"Nay!" Indignation resonated in the single word as she stepped back from him quickly as if he'd slapped her.

"Why not?" he couldn't help but ask.

She huffed, but her shoulders did not rise. If anything, she stood taller, her shoulders down and back, like a warrior. "Because everything is different now. I am different now. Can you not see that? I have no time for trysting with a lad."

"Trysting?"

She stared at him, but did not answer the question that hung heavy in the air between them. Duncan found himself wanting to throttle Conall at just the idea that perhaps there was more than a few stolen kisses between him and Scotia. He should have kept a closer eye on Scotia, kept her away from Conall, away from that damned wall that could easily have killed both her and Rowan, and now it would seem Conall as well. He should have . . .

"Duncan," she said, her eyes narrowed, "you'll not hurt him."

"Why not?"

"We need every warrior we can get—"

"He is no—"

"Aye, he is. Not a good one yet, but he is a warrior. Do you think I would let just any lad kiss me?"

The minx taunted him, and he knew she saw that he was

concerned for more than her behavior with Conall in the past. He was certain she saw the slash of possessiveness that gripped him, a possessiveness that was heightened by the implication that she might let him kiss her again in spite of what she had said just a few hours ago.

"I have no intention of taking up with Conall again, Duncan." Her voice was softer now, low and soft, as if she wished to gentle his emotions, though her voice, her scent, and her hesitant touch on his arm did anything but calm him. "But I will not allow you or Da or Nicholas to harm him for what has happened in the past. The past is done and cannot be changed." She sighed and closed her eyes for a moment. When she opened them she said, "We must focus only on the future," as if she said the words as much to herself as to him.

Duncan's stomach chose that instant to growl, breaking the solemn moment. Scotia snorted, and quirked one finely arched eyebrow at him. "Perhaps we can think about the present, too." She hooked her arm through his and pulled him along. "At least until have we have supped!"

THE NEXT MORNING DUNCAN FOLLOWED SCOTIA JUST FAR enough to find where she had left the trail for her daily task of disguising her destination with a circuitous, hard even for Duncan to follow, route. He looked around to make sure no one would see as he slipped silently into the thick wood on the opposite side of the trail and waited, hidden by the bracken, just long enough to determine that no one followed either of them. Once he was sure, he headed through the wood, taking care that no one could easily follow him, either, and before long came to the training area in the bottom of the glen where either Malcolm or Uilliam drilled the lads each day.

Two of Malcolm's kin were there, sparring with such determination that the clash of sword on shield and the clang of sword on sword rang out through the clearing as if there were many more warriors battling. They did not seem to notice Duncan as he made his way over to a cone-shaped tent where the practice weapons were stored. He pulled a flap up, grabbed one of the wooden swords that was weighted with bits of lead wrapped in bands around the "blade" and pommel to better simulate the heft of a real sword. Scotia needed to strengthen her arm and her grip, and her sticks were not ever going to do that.

Her reaction to not becoming a Guardian yesterday had convinced him that she was ready to move forward in her training. She recognized the strength of her emotions and took action to manage them before she loosed her temper on anyone. 'Twas quite a milestone for the lass.

Of course he knew she would greet the practice weapon with a grin, or a smile, or a teasing comment, and he had to admit that was as much motivation for him rewarding her with the wooden weapon as were the needs of her training.

He left the training ground as if he had nowhere particular to be, then slipped back into the wood, took more time than he wanted to cover his trail, and finally arrived in the tiny open area in the forest where Scotia kept her weapons. He held the practice sword behind his back as he stepped from between two large oaks.

"There you are," she said without even turning to see him. She finished the drill he had her start each day with, a drill that was complicated enough to demand her complete attention and which allowed no room for wandering thoughts. "I thought perhaps you had returned to your sleeping blankets," she said as she held the final position for just long enough to check that her feet were where they should be, another thing he had her do at the end of every drill and exercise. He said nothing, letting her complete this warm-up. She turned, and a look of surprise lit her face, her dark brows arched like bird's wings over her sparkling eyes.

"What are you about?" she asked, closing the short distance between them. "What have you behind your back?"

He slowly pulled the wooden sword from behind him, then held it out to her, hilt first. She looked from it to him and back to the weapon.

"This is for me?" she asked.

"Nay, 'tis for wee Ian," he replied. "Do you think he will like it?" He tried to hold his smile in, but could not. "Take it, Scotia. You have earned it."

She tossed her stick into the wood, then wrapped her hand around the handle, lifting it from his hands. She immediately went into a fighting stance, moved through one drill, then another.

"Raise your arm," he said as she moved into a third. "You must increase your strength in order to keep the sword up where it will best serve you."

She did as he said, moving into a fourth and fifth drill before dropping her arm and letting the sword tip rest on the ground. She turned to face him, a huge grin on her face.

"'Tis very different than fighting with a stick."

"Aye."

"Heavier, so it moves differently. I move differently with it."

"Yet your body kens the movements, so you do not have to focus on your feet, or whether 'tis a parry or a thrust that comes next. Now you can strengthen your arm, your back, your . . ." He patted his stomach with his hand.

"And when I do that, I will get a real sword, aye? Then I will be ready to go into battle, to kill my first Sassenach." She lifted the practice sword and made as if to stab a man in the stomach, twisting her sword and lifting upward, to gut him. She spun and widened her eyes at him, clearly asking him what he thought of that.

The look of gleeful expectation saddened but did not surprise him.

"You will get a real sword when I deem you prepared, physically *and* mentally, for battle, Scotia. I do not think you understand the brutality of battle, the blood, the stench, the noise, and the harsh necessity to kill or be killed. Your life will be at risk every moment of a battle. Your skill and your kinsmen will be your only true defense against the skill of soldiers who are far taller, far heavier, and far more experienced than you. Do you really think you can stay focused on what you have to do to survive with all of that going on?"

To her credit she took a moment to consider what he said.

"I witnessed battle firsthand not long ago, at the Story Stone. I ken well what to expect, what it will be like."

"Really? What do you remember of that battle?"

"I remember relief when I found my clan had come for me. I remember fierce anger at the gap-toothed Sassenach who held a dagger at my throat. I remember the roar of the barrier Jeanette and Rowan created as it passed by me. I remember Gaptooth writhing on the ground, his life's blood pouring from the stump of his arm after you sliced off his hand."

"'Twas Malcolm who sliced off his hand. And you were shivering from the shock of it all, your eyes glassy, mute. I took you back to the burn where the Guardians and Nicholas awaited us, and we waited for the battle to end before we ventured forth from there. You saw little of the battle, and what you saw, I doubt you remember clearly."

"Nay, 'tis not true," she said, but he could hear the doubt in her voice and see it as she looked into the distance over his shoulder as if she sought to look into the past. "I was there. I remember."

"Do you? Are you certain you remember it just as it happened?"

She pressed her lips together and shook her head. "Nay." The word came out on a whisper. "'Tis a blur of images, sounds, the smell of blood, but then almost nothing until a day or two later when I realized that no one would speak to me. No one would even look at me." She swallowed. "Not even you."

"Once I learned how Myles had died, and why . . . nay, I could not look at you."

"What changed?" she asked, and he could almost feel her trembling again, as she had when he'd grabbed her hand and dragged her to the shelter of the wood and the protection of the Guardians that horrible day.

"I saw you training yourself. I saw a lass determined to do what was right in any way she could."

"And that is why I intend to go into battle, to kill as many Sassenach soldiers as I can, to avenge what they did to my mother, and what they did to Myles. To protect my home and my family."

He sighed at her continued adamance that she would kill English soldiers. In spite of what he had promised her, he did not think she would survive such a battle.

"Your intentions are good, but I still do not think you comprehend exactly what battle is like. There is no feeling of glory when you have brutally killed men with your own hands, even if you win the day. 'Tis brutal and terrible and should be avoided whenever possible. 'Tis why the battle at the Story Stone was particularly wrenching—it was not necessary until you became their hostage."

"But they killed Myles, too," she said. "We had to answer that heinous act decisively."

He looked at her, a decision coming to him fully formed. "He should never have been killed, aye, and he would not have died that day in that way if you had done as your chief commanded, if you had stayed in the camp."

"'Twas not my actions that killed him. 'Twas not my fault the English gutted him."

Duncan looked up at the heavy clouds that seemed to scud just above the treetops, weighing the dangers of what he meant to do against the lessons that needed learning.

"Bring your weapons," he said, turning to melt back into the wood.

CHAPTER TEN

SCOTIA TRAILED CLOSELY BEHIND DUNCAN, WISHING SHE WERE a wood sprite so she could lift a tree root to trip him as he stepped over it, or she could shift a stone and cause him to fall into one of the many burns they had crossed this morn. She looked up, wondering if it were indeed still morn, but the tree cover was so thick little light made it to the forest floor, and 'twas impossible to see how far the sun had traveled in the sky. She tripped, and only just avoided stumbling into Duncan's broad-shouldered back, thanks to her much improved balance from the training she had been doing.

"Do you need to rest?" he asked, but he did not slow.

"Nay," she said, "I do not."

"Good."

And he continued on, his ground-eating pace never wavering. She knew he was angry with her . . . or maybe just irritated. He hated it when she was right and he was wrong, but he'd never gone to such lengths to punish her for it. She wasn't wrong when she talked of killing English soldiers. She had seen men die before, recently even. A full dozen English soldiers had died at the Story Stone . . . At the thought of the stone she knew where they were headed, and it had nothing to do with the *knowing* of her gift. Duncan wanted to confront her with the battle, thinking it would change her mind about killing English bastards, but he was wrong.

She might not remember everything that had happened there, but she remembered enough and had the scar on her neck to remind her each and every day of what it meant to kill or be killed. Returning to the place would change nothing, but Duncan would not believe her, so she had no choice but to convince him by doing whatever he had planned for her.

However, as they drew nearer and nearer to the Story Stone meadow her stomach began to fill with the fluttering of dragonflies, and her heart started to pound in her ears. She let her heavy targe slip off her forearm, catching it by one of the sweat-damp leather straps that had chafed a raw spot on the inside of her arm.

Her targe banged into her anklebone and she must have made a sound, for Duncan looked back over his shoulder. He gave one slow shake of his head when he espied her shield, but said nothing.

The damn thing banged against her ankle again, and she quickly pulled it back onto her arm, wincing, but not letting a single sound free.

Bring your weapons. Hah. It was not as if she were going to use them on this venture, and this was the first day she'd had a real practice sword to work with. He'd said 'twould strengthen her arm. Ah, this trek with weapons was surely another of his ways of strengthening her as well as being a test of her resolve to do whatever he required for her training.

She felt like a fool for not understanding that immediately. Everything they did during their days together was part of her training . . . well, except for that kiss. She pushed away the softness the memory of that kiss always brought on. She had no time for softness. The English would be upon them again soon, and she had little time to prove her worth as a warrior.

She stood straighter, bent her elbow so she could hold her targe firmly up where it would protect her torso, and picked up the pace of her steps. She would prove that she was strong—strong enough to wield a real sword, not just a weighted wooden blade, strong enough to be a real warrior, not just a lass in training—and if it took a long trek with weapons and returning to the site of the Story Stone Battle to prove that strength, then she was up to the task.

DUNCAN STRUGGLED NOT TO DRUM HIS FINGERS ON HIS THIGH. Scotia was the one who had told him long ago that he did that when he was worried, and he did not want to give her any clue that he was having second thoughts about this lesson.

The bodies of the fallen had been buried, so the full loss of life would not be visible, but he knew there would be ghosts. The echoes of the battle would linger in the air just out of hearing. The fight would be all around them, like wraiths in the night. Anyone who had ever walked the ground where men died in battle would know what had happened here, would feel it in the prickles of their skin, would hear it in the unnatural silence that always blanketed such places. The Highlands were rife with battlefields, and even the animals tended to avoid them.

Scotia needed to understand that battle, that killing, should be her last choice, not her first. Killing was hard on the soul, even when it was justified, and certainly she was justified in her desire to protect and avenge her family and land. But Duncan could not bear to imagine how killing someone herself, looking into that person's eyes as the life drained out of them, would either destroy her or harden her heart, as it did warriors. Despite what anyone believed, he knew Scotia's heart was big and vulnerable, though she hid that with her rebellion and of late with her anger.

As they drew close, the muted light of the Story Stone meadow filtered through the dense wood. Duncan stopped, preparing himself for what came next.

"I ken well where we are, Duncan," Scotia said from behind him. He glanced back, surprised to find her changed from the bedraggled, tired lass she had been when last he'd looked back at her.

She stood tall, her targe held firmly where it should be, rather than dangling from her fingertips. Determination had replaced the glow of irritation in her eyes, and her chin was raised just enough to make her look strong and sure of herself.

"I ken why you brought me here," she said, but the words were not tinged with anger or disdain as he had expected, and there was something in the quiet of her voice that told him she was not as sure of herself as she tried to appear. The lesson had already begun.

"Do you?" he asked.

"Aye."

But he didn't think she really did.

"There is never good that comes of battle, Scotia. I ken you mean to fight the English, but do not fool yourself that any good will come of that. You will know the necessity of killing, but you will also know the torment of taking a life."

Her dark brows arrowed down over pale eyes, lending sharp angles to her face that offset the full, sensuous mouth that distracted every male who had ever been in her company. Or at least it distracted him.

"I will know no torment when I kill an English soldier, and neither should you." She took a deep breath. "They killed my mum. They killed Myles. I made a vow to avenge their deaths, and I will do that without torment or guilt."

"You will feel torment at the very least, Scotia," he said, forcing his wandering thoughts back to the moment. "It happens to everyone, especially in your first battle. I ken you are angry, hurt, and bent on vengeance—I want that every bit as much as you do."

"You do not act like it."

"I will choose my time to claim that vengeance, and I promise, if you are ready to fight, you will be right there by my side."

"I will be ready. If we had spent this day working with this"— she laid her hand on the pommel of the wooden sword—"I would be that much closer to ready."

"Nay, one day will not change things much, but you are growing more skilled each day, and today will strengthen you in ways you ken not. You are smart, strong, agile, and—" He almost said *passionate* but quickly thought better of that. "And a force to be reckoned with when you set your mind to something, as you have done with your training, but you are also impulsive, denying those strong traits in favor of letting your emotions sway your decisions. People died because of that—Myles in the forest, a dozen soldiers here. Can you say, truly, that does not haunt your dreams?"

She looked toward the meadow they could not yet see. "I can. The deaths do not haunt me. I was not responsible for the soldiers killing Myles. I was not responsible for the choice those same soldiers made to take me hostage and wait for the clan here. 'Tis unfortunate I did not set my mind to becoming a warrior sooner." She glared at him. "At least then I could have killed a few of them myself."

Duncan wanted to reach out, to touch her hand, or her shoulder, to see if she was as brittle as she sounded, but he did not. Now was not the time for softness on his part. Now was a time to see if she had any capacity for taking responsibility for these deaths herself, and to see if she could hold up under the weight of such a responsibility if she did. Only when she could master both would she be mentally, and emotionally ready to go into battle, to take a life.

"Follow me," he said, leading her past several graves where the earth had yet to settle from the recent burials of the English fallen. They quickly completed their journey to the edge of the meadow, to the edge of the battlefield.

"Look and see exactly what you wrought." He grabbed her wrist and pulled her out onto the spot where most of the melee had happened, where most of the English had died. 'Twas only providence that had kept their own warriors from the same fate.

"You and I were safely out of the worst of it, hiding in the wood with Rowan and Jeanette while the lads fought for their lives, for their homes, for their families," Duncan said as he scanned the scene of the battle, as he let the sorrow and pain of the place sink into his bones so he would never forget. "You are responsible for what happened here, Scotia. Your unwillingness to do as you were told by your father and your chief led to the death of Myles, the deaths of these English soldiers, and the injuries your own kinsmen sustained in a battle we were not prepared for. Can you not see that? Can you not feel that?"

He glanced over at her when she did not reply. Her fingers were tracing the still visible line at her throat where an English soldier had tried to slice her. Her eyes were big. Her breaths were so shallow and fast he could not see any rise and fall of her chest. She swallowed again and again. Regret made him sigh. He hated being so hard with her, but he knew he had to make this point. She could not go into battle thinking only of the killing, not of what the killing meant. For if she did not understand that, she would not understand that her own life was always at risk, too, and a warrior who did not understand that was a danger to every-one she fought beside.

"If you do not understand the consequences of taking a life, you will not value your own, and that makes you take unneces-sary risks. It makes you a danger to all you fight with and for, as Malcolm learned the hard way. Warriors will not trust you, no matter how well trained you are, until you prove that you hold their well-being at least equal to your own, until you prove that preserving their lives and your own is more important to you than taking one from your enemies."

"I understand all too well the consequences of a life taken, Duncan." She still ran her fingers over the scar on her neck. "I felt no remorse when you and Malcolm relieved that gap-toothed soldier of his life. I feel no remorse, no torment, no grief that all of those men had their lives taken here. They had no compunc-tion about taking a life. Why should I?"

"Do you really want to be like them?"

"Nay!" She turned on him, throwing her targe hard to the ground. "I am nothing like them. That you could ever think such a thing says you knew nothing of those bastard Sassenachs and know even less of me. I want vengeance. 'Tis a noble thing. They wanted only to rape, to kill all of us, to steal away the Targe stone and Rowan for their damned king. They fought because they were told to. I fight for vengeance. I am nothing like them."

And then she froze, tilting her head a little to the side as if she were listening to something he could not hear.

"Scotia? What is it?" He scanned the edges of the meadow, searching for anything that might catch her attention, but other than a few birds flitting in the trees there was nothing that he could discern.

"We need to go out to the Story Stone," she said, her attention still apparently on whatever she was listening to. "There is a sword there, the sword that belonged to the gap-toothed bastard. It is to be mine."

"How do you—'Tis a *knowing*?"

She nodded and turned her attention to him. "My first thought was to run directly out there without telling you what I was after, but that would be *reckless*, and might put you in danger, so I am not doing that. I am telling you I need to go out there. I *know* it. Will you help me do that safely?" And then she picked up her shield and settled it on her left arm and waited.

She presented him with as good a lesson as any since she didn't seem to get the one he had brought her here for. She would need a real sword eventually, and he had not thought how he would obtain that for her without revealing her secret, so they might as well collect one now. If he didn't trust her *knowing* he would never consider going out there, and he marveled that once again she was given knowledge of something that triggered a strong emotion in her—hatred, this time.

"How would you go about retrieving this sword while keeping us both as safe as possible?" he asked.

Scotia sprinted toward the Story Stone upon its hillock near the center of the wide-open meadow from the same place Duncan had emerged to rescue her the day of the battle—'twas the point where the forest was closest to the stone. Duncan was hard on her heels. She knew he was still uncomfortable exposing them like this, but they had found no sign of anyone, English or otherwise, who had been near the Story Stone meadow since the battle, so he had admitted he could find no reason to keep her from her prize.

She skidded to a stop as she reached the top of the small knoll. A hand, severed cleanly at the wrist and the flesh mostly gone now, lay palm up on the ground. The dagger that had come so close to ending her life, the blade smeared black with her old blood, was still clenched by bone fingers.

All at once the events of the battle came rushing back at her, as if the memories had been waiting here for her to return. It was almost as if it happened all over again, except this time she was watching from a short distance outside her body, as she was thrown to the ground, then bound to the stone so tightly she could barely draw breath or move her arms. She watched as the twelve English soldiers formed a ring around the stone, as she screamed at them, yelling whatever she could think of to discomfit them. She saw herself praying for the death of each and every one of the soldiers—a horrible, painful, lingering death. And she remembered the moment she had heard the clan's signal, a quiet call of a tawny owl, like a war cry in her mind. It was only then she had realized that she hadn't been sure they would come for her.

"Scotia?" Duncan rested his hand upon her shoulder, startling her out of her memories. She shrugged him off as she turned her attention away from the gap-toothed bastard's severed hand, to the stone where she had sat helpless for hours as the soldiers amused themselves by taking turns telling her the vile things they would do to her once they had dispatched her kin. The rope that had trapped her lay at the foot of the stone, sliced through by the gap-toothed man after she had kicked him in the ballocks.

As he had held her tight against him, his rancid breath rushing over her, and his dagger at her throat, he'd cursed her. "'Twould be safer to shelter with a nervous mother wolf than you," he'd hissed in her ear.

And that was when the wind hit, whipping up a maelstrom of dirt and grit. She hadn't known it was an unnatural wind at the time, driven by the twin gifts of Jeanette and Rowan, though she had felt the raw power of it. She still found it hard to believe there were two Guardians, with her, as always, the one left out.

She let her gaze drift up the ancient standing stone that was at least half again as tall as Duncan. She hadn't really seen it when they'd brought her here, and though she had heard of it she knew nothing more than its name, the Story Stone. She'd never actually been to it before that day, and even then she had not had much opportunity to look at it. She circled around it, taking in the weathered corners of the monolith, the dark silvery grey of the stone itself, decorated here and there by pale silvery-green lichens and bits of bright green furry moss. And carvings.

She stopped, staring at the side opposite the one she'd been tied to. The early afternoon sun hit the stone at a perfect angle to cast the shallow carvings in shadow while illuminating the face of the stone.

There at the top was the triple swirl within a circle symbol. She blinked, sure she was wrong, but there it was, the same symbol that was carved into the Targe stone Rowan always carried with her. It was also painted in the center of the ermine sack that held the Targe stone, and was incised on the large rock in the grotto where Jeanette had come into her Guardian gift.

And below it was another symbol: the broken arrow. It was just as she'd seen it painted inside the Targe sack just yesterday. It was the one symbol left without anyone to claim it.

"Duncan?" She looked about and found him scanning the forest at the edge of the meadow. "Did you see something?"

He glanced over his shoulder at her. "Nay, but that is no reason to let down our guard." He cocked an eyebrow at her, as if to admonish her for losing herself in her memories. "Do you remember that day any better from here?"

"I do." She shuddered a little and forced herself not to touch her neck.

"Good. Do you see that it was not glorious? Only painful and filled with death? Can you feel it all around you?"

She looked around, taking in the entire meadow, marveling that the battle itself had been mostly confined to a small area opposite where the Guardians had constructed their barrier, made only from the power of the Targe stone. The barrier had driven the English away from her at the stone, all except the gap-toothed bastard. But she could remember naught after Duncan had taken her hand and dragged her away from the stone. She nodded, unable to speak around the lump that lodged in her throat.

"There is no sword here," he said, disappointment pulling the corners of his mouth down. "We should go."

It was only then that Scotia remembered why she had insisted they come out here to the stone. She had *known* there was a sword here for her. Was she wrong? She looked about quickly, but the symbols on the stone once more captured her attention. As she looked closer she could see the faint lines of other symbols carved into the stone below the ones she knew from the Targe and its sack. She reached up and ran her fingers along another carving. This one, upon closer inspection, appeared to be a melding of the three symbols from the edge of the Targe sack, as if whoever had carved them here had carved them one on top of the other so that they were jumbled together, the broken arrow weaving through the other two.

"I have heard of this stone once or twice, but never has anyone mentioned these carvings," she said, mostly to herself.

"Carvings?" Duncan asked.

"Aye, come around and look at this side of it." He joined her, though his eyes were still clearly focused on the forest. She touched his arm to gain his attention, then she pointed up at the largest of the carvings at the top, the triple swirls within a circle. "Do you recognize that?"

Duncan glanced up at it, then shook his head.

"'Tis carved on the Targe stone, and painted inside the ermine sack."

That got his attention. He stepped a little closer to her, standing almost shoulder-to-shoulder as he gazed up at it.

"Do you see the symbol below it?" she asked.

"It looks like an arrow broken in two places." He glanced at Scotia. "Do you recognize it?"

"Aye. 'Tis the third symbol painted around the edge of the ermine sack. Jeanette and Rowan claim the other two are symbols of their gifts. That would make this one—"

"A symbol for another gift? Yours? I dinna ken how a *knowing* is symbolized by a broken arrow, though."

"Rowan and Jeanette said if I was a third Guardian I would understand what the symbol meant."

"And you do not?"

"I do not," she said, but her mind was busy working on a problem. When Jeanette had been taken by the power of the Targe stone she had found a large boulder with the swirl symbol incised on it, as well as the mirror that was the symbol of her gift of second sight. When she had found the two symbols together, in the grotto, her gift had overtaken her as the Targe claimed her. Would that happen here, to Scotia? If she was a third Guardian and the broken-arrow symbol was meant for her, perhaps indicating some gift beyond her *knowing*, would she be chosen by the Targe now?

She pressed her hand to the arrow and waited for something similar to what she had seen happen to Rowan, or to what Jeanette had told her about being claimed by the Targe, to happen to her.

She closed her eyes and searched within for anything unusual, anything different . . .

Nothing.

"Scotia? Is something wrong?" Duncan asked, startling her out of her concentration.

"Wrong?" She let out a shuddering breath. "Aye. Something is wrong. If I am meant to be a Guardian, finding these symbols here, together like this, should have been . . . should have made . . ." She shook her head hard, as if that would loosen the words that did not want to leave her mouth. "'Tis clearly not meant for me. I am not a Guardian."

"But your *knowing*, 'tis a gift."

"But not a Guardian gift. 'Twill serve me and the clan well in battle, aye? I do not need to be a Guardian to protect the clan. I will be a warrior." She glared up at the stone as if it had insulted her greatly. "I will be a warrior," she said as if convincing the stone.

She looked back over the meadow, the battle area notably empty of the early summer wildflowers that dotted the rest of the meadow with blooms of white and yellow and lavender. If she had harbored any hope of being a Guardian after yesterday's failure, she harbored it no more. Oddly, she felt relief at knowing for sure that she was not meant to be a Guardian. She need not wonder any longer. She need not feel hopeful, nor disappointed, and her decision to become a warrior was made all the stronger for the clarity gained this day.

"We should return to the cover of the wood," she said just as Duncan asked, "What are these other symbols?" He nodded at the jumbled symbols she had already forgotten about.

"I do not ken exactly. They seem to be a variation of the symbols associated with the Targe, but different, like they were carved one over the other." It was only then that she realized the circle with three swirls was carved below, but very close to, the superimposed Guardian symbols. It was much smaller, but clearly meant to be the same as the symbol at the top of the stone. "Perhaps that is the story the stone is named for?"

He stared at the symbols, his eyes squinting against the glare of the sun. "Have you ever heard what that story is?"

"Never."

"Neither have I. We must tell Jeanette of this. If they tell a story of the Guardians they might be important," Duncan said.

Scotia was about to agree with him when her heart started hammering. "Nay, we cannot say anything about this to anyone. If we tell her, or anyone, of these symbols they will want to know how we ken this and why we came here today. How can we explain why we were here without giving away our secret? I am not ready to reveal my plans to anyone else."

Duncan looked back at the stone. "We cannot keep this discovery from the Guardians, Scotia."

"We can. You promised."

"I did, but this—"

"We will tell them together, if and when there is reason to," she said, trying to think quickly. "For now, there is naught good for either of us that will come of telling anyone we were here."

He considered her words for a moment, and that alone made her feel he was remaining true to his word. "I would like to tell the Guardians and the chief that I brought you here today to teach you a lesson, to remind you of what can happen when you go off alone." He turned to face her, capturing her gaze with his. "'Tis the truth, and it will allow me to report that we have seen no English in the area as of yet, which is important news. I will not mention the search for a sword that brought us out to the stone, but I think we must tell Jeanette of these symbols. She might understand what they mean, or at least 'twill give her something else to search for in those Chronicles."

Scotia balked at the idea, but deep in her gut she knew he was right. If this new discovery was important, withholding it could bring more harm to the clan, and that she could not do.

"We will tell them only that this was a lesson for you," he said again, "to remind you of what happens—"

"The lesson is well taught," she snapped, then closed her eyes and shook her head at her own temper. "It is well taught," she said more calmly. "I agree that we must tell Nicholas and the Guardians what we have learned and seen." She looked up at him and found him staring down at her from his greater height. "'Tis also the truth. I did not realize how much I did not remember until I stood here."

"Will you remember all the symbols when we leave?" he asked.

She looked back at the stone, studying each symbol for a long moment until she was sure she could draw them in the dirt or on one of Jeanette's scrolls if she needed to.

"Aye, I will remember them," she said, though she did not relish revealing yet another failure on her part to become a Guardian, for both Rowan and Jeanette would recognize the similarities to the grotto stone. At least Duncan did not understand that part of what she had learned this day.

"We should head back to the glen," he said. As they left the hillock to make their way back to the nearest part of the wood, Duncan shook his head.

"What?" she demanded.

He sighed. "Did you *know* there was a sword out here? Or did you just hope 'twas so?"

She stopped and realized she had once more forgotten all about finding a sword. "I *knew*."

She closed her eyes and concentrated on the *knowing*. She turned a little to the left, opened her eyes, and walked away from her companion. Not ten paces from Duncan, she squatted down and brushed dirt and dead leaves away from something that had caught her eye, glinting in the afternoon sun that was beginning to break through the thinning clouds. There, lying in wait for her just where she *knew* it would be, was an English arming sword.

CHAPTER ELEVEN

Rowan watched as Duncan made his way to his place near the fire at the mouth of the main cave where he typically slept. Scotia had gone to bed as soon as she had devoured her meal and startled the Guardians with her news of the symbols on the Story Stone.

"There is something he is not telling us," Rowan said with a glance over her shoulder at Jeanette.

Jeanette nodded. "I agree, and yet he and Scotia have told us much this evening."

Rowan rubbed the spot between her brows with the heel of her hand and sighed. She turned back to her cousin. "They have. Do you think the Story Stone is another place the Targe draws power from, like the grotto stone?"

Jeanette cocked her head. Her eyes narrowed, and Rowan knew to give her time to consider the question and all the lore she knew.

"We were able to create a barrier there during the battle, though I thought the power simply came from the Targe stone at the time. 'Tis possible it is another place of power for the Targe, like the grotto. Perhaps that is what the symbols Scotia found will tell us. Can you fetch a light?" Jeanette asked as she moved to the council circle where Scotia had drawn the series of symbols she had seen on the Story Stone. Rowan grabbed a lantern that sat near the mouth of the main cave, a single stub of a candle burning in it, and followed Jeanette.

They both stopped, one on either side of the drawings scratched into the dirt. Rowan held the lantern close to the first symbol, the triple swirl that was so familiar, then slowly moved it down over the broken arrow, then over the muddle of shapes that Scotia said were the three symbols superimposed on each other, and finally to the smaller triple swirl.

"Do you think the broken arrow is for Scotia?" Rowan asked, deferring as always to Jeanette when it came to matters of Guardian lore.

Jeanette looked up at her and took a deep breath. "It seems likely, but the Targe has not claimed her." She pointed at the first two symbols. "'Tis not unlike what I found on the grotto stone when I was claimed as Guardian, yet she says nothing happened when she found this." She stood, took the lantern from Rowan, and walked around the drawings slowly, moving the light around to cast the shadows in different ways. "I still have found nothing to explain what the broken arrow means," she said, "or what gift it represents, but then I have not discovered such information for your symbol either." She reached for the lantern and held it over the jumbled-together symbols. "This looks as if each symbol was overwritten, perhaps with the passing of each Guardian?" She moved the lantern back and forth for long minutes, once more examining every line Scotia had scratched in the dirt. "'Tis hard to tell if the order they appear is simply from the way she drew them or if they appear in that same order on the stone. Tomorrow I must have her draw these on a parchment for me, and I can ask her more about them then. I will search the Chronicles of the Guardians to see if I can discover more about the Story Stone, though I do not remember seeing any reference to it before."

"It does seem there is something important we must understand here," Rowan said, trying not to let her frustration show in her voice. She did not want to put more pressure on Jeanette than her cousin already put upon herself to understand this new situation of two Guardians . . . or perhaps three.

"Aye, it does. It feels as if this is a key of some sort. I just wish I knew what lock it opened."

THE NEXT MORNING DUNCAN CHEWED UPON A FRESH BANNOCK while he waited for Scotia to join him to break her fast. Apparently he was not the only one awaiting her. Conall sat on the ground, his back to the outcropping of the ben that formed the mouth of the communal cave where Scotia and many of the other women slept. Conall tried not to draw attention to himself, but Duncan was not fooled.

Conall had not approached Scotia last night, with all her kin about her. Of course she and Duncan had been questioned first by Nicholas and Malcolm, and then Scotia had been taken to the council circle to tell the Guardians about the symbols she had discovered, so the lad had not had a moment to get her alone, if he was daft enough to try, given the promise he'd made to Nicholas. But this morning while most of the clan still slept, Conall was conveniently awake and situated such that he could claim to simply be enjoying the morning air, while being strategically positioned to see Scotia the moment she left the cave. Perhaps the lad wasn't as daft as Duncan thought he was.

Conall looked up and caught Duncan staring at him. He quickly looked away as if something near the council circle drew his attention. Duncan was not fooled, nor was he amused.

When the lass appeared a few minutes later, she strode out of the dark maw of the cave and made directly for the cook circle and Duncan without even noticing Conall. The young man leapt to his feet and followed her. Duncan did not move, nor say anything, only handing a bannock to Scotia as she joined him on the log near the cook circle.

"Good morn," Conall said. He slowed his pace as he neared them. Scotia looked up but only nodded. "Are there more bannocks?"

Duncan pointed to a pile of them on the far side of the fire, where Peigi had left them to warm. He tried to ease the tension in his muscles, tried to breathe slowly and deeply, tried to talk himself out of the grip of possessive anger that the young man ignited in his gut. Conall had no claim on Scotia. Hell, he'd be a right wee dafty if he even wanted a claim on the difficult, mercurial lass. And yet . . .

He closed his eyes and counseled himself to be patient, to see what Scotia would do.

A rustling sound had him slowly opening his eyes.

Conall had seated himself near Scotia, but Scotia was paying him no attention.

"How fare you?" Conall asked.

She nodded, but did not look at him. "Well enough."

As well as Duncan could usually read Scotia, he could not tell if she was feigning indifference toward the lad who, not long ago, had been the focus of her every thought for months, or if she really had left her infatuation behind.

"I am sorry I did not come here sooner," Conall said pitching his voice so low it was hard for Duncan to make out the words. Conall leaned forward and braced his arms on his knees. "My mum needed me, but as soon as I settled her with my uncle near Loch Awe, I joined Dermid and came to fight the English."

"I understand," Scotia replied, glancing up at him. "She is well?"

"Aye."

Duncan was swinging between satisfaction that this conversation was so stilted and mistrust, doubting that it would have been stilted at all if he had not been sitting next to her. But he said nothing.

After a long, uncomfortable silence. Scotia stood, brushed the bannock crumbs from her skirts, and gave him a look that spoke louder than words that she knew what he was up to. With a smirk, she headed off into the wood as she did every morning, stopping only when she got to the head of the path. She turned then, her face covered in feigned innocence.

"Are you not following me this day, Duncan? If you let me get too far ahead of you, you might not find me before I get myself in trouble." There was just an edge of mirth in her taunting words, and Duncan knew he was in for a long day of teasing.

Conall started to his feet but Duncan beat him to it, pinning him down with a scowl. "If you value your hide, you'll not follow her today or ever again."

To Conall's credit, he sat down with a quick nod and returned his attention to his meal.

Duncan followed Scotia and her trilling laughter down the ben while he cleared his mind of the myriad emotions the lass always managed to stir up in him, though if he was honest with himself, the emotions were easy to rouse. But today, all her mirth and attention had been focused on him. She'd all but purred like a kitchen cat as she gave Conall her indifference, as if she knew Duncan was waiting for her to reveal her true feelings for the lad.

Was it her *knowing* that gave her such insight? Curiosity and a hunch had him catching up to her quickly, as a plan for the day's training took hold of him.

"You ken there is more to being a warrior than sword fighting, aye?" he asked her as he matched his stride to hers.

"Of course. There is running, and climbing over things, strength, finesse, dirks, targes, strategy—"

"Aye, strategy. You have this *knowing*."

"But I cannot call upon it at will." She stopped suddenly as she spoke, and he had to backtrack.

"But still, you have it," he said, coming to a halt in front of her. "So let us figure out how it might be used. What do we know about it?"

"It is in the present, not future-looking as Jeanette's second sight is. I do not ken what triggers it, though."

Duncan considered the problem for a moment. "You knew the child Maisie was missing, and you knew where to find her."

"Aye."

"You knew where to find your sword, too."

"I did, though it was not exactly at the Story Stone, only close."

He nodded, but his gaze was inward, reviewing each instance of *knowing*. "And you knew the allies were in the glen, though they were just barely in the glen at the time. What else do you remember *knowing*?"

"I knew wee Ian was trapped in the kitchens during the fire, and now that I think about it, I knew Nicholas was coming to rescue us, too."

He looked at her but was careful not to meet her gaze. Whatever had spooked her the last time they had spoken of that day might be revealed if she did not think he was pressing her for it.

"I am sure there must be more events," she continued, "but I did not realize that I knew things other people didn't know, so they did not seem memorable to me."

Duncan's disappointment was fleeting. She did not trust him with whatever the other event was, not yet. He knew better than to press her to tell him, so he let it rest for now.

"And when Jeanette tested you?" he asked instead.

"She hid her healer's bag. I could not tell her where it was. I could imagine where she might have hidden it, but I did not *know*. It is clear I cannot call upon the *knowing* at will. More's the pity, for that would at least be useful."

Duncan let the bits and pieces of information flow through his head, as he looked for commonalities between them . . . two children in danger, a sword that had belonged to her enemy, allies arriving to help them defend her clan—but not a simple bag of herbs that belonged to her sister, a sister who was in no trouble, nor even any turmoil over the hidden bag.

All but the last were events rife with emotion . . . strong emotion. Even the sword, for she believed it belonged to the gap-toothed English soldier who had almost slit her throat. That must be the key, emotion, but he would not tell her that yet. First he would test his own theory.

CHAPTER TWELVE

SCOTIA HAD TRIED TO SIT ON A STONE NEAR THE SMALL lochan, but it was beyond her ability to sit still. Ever since Duncan had disappeared, leaving her wondering what this mysterious new part of her training would be, her mind had been swirling like a whirlpool, sucking in every possibility but lingering on none. Her feet were as active as her thoughts, and she'd spent the time since they had parted pacing, first up and down the trail, then across the ben to the lochan, and now along the edge of the small body of water, back and forth. She snagged another stick as she walked, peeling the bark off and shoving it into a cloth sack that hung at her waist. At least she'd have a good supply of tinder for the fire to show for her time waiting for Duncan.

But he was coming now.

The thought popped into her head, quieting all others. She closed her eyes and tried to see if she could *know* from which direction he was coming, the same way she had found her sword yesterday. She turned slightly, still with her eyes closed, until the *knowing* grew louder in her mind. She opened her eyes just as he became visible through the leaves.

Excitement shimmered over her skin until she realized he had no weapons with him. In fact, he had nothing with him out of the ordinary.

"What have you been doing?" she demanded as he stepped into the sunlight filtering through the trees.

Duncan stopped, as if he was surprised to find her waiting

for him even though that's what he'd told her to do. "Preparing for your training today."

There was a hitch in his voice that caught her attention but before she could ask him about it he stopped in front of her.

"Do you ken where your sword is, lass?" he asked her. His eyes were narrowed as if he did not expect her to know.

"Of course," she answered, crossing her arms but not stepping away. "It is . . ." She was about to say "in the clearing where we train" but suddenly she stopped as she *knew* it was not there. "It is not where we train anymore, is it? What have you done with my sword?"

Duncan held himself so still she could barely tell he breathed. "Where do you think it is?" His voice was flat.

Scotia closed her eyes and she *knew*. "You have moved it."

"Can you find it?" His voice was still flat.

Without a word she turned and made her way around the lochan and into the wood on the other side. She headed down the ben, cutting through dense underbrush, and around long, reaching canes of thorny brambles, until she arrived at a boulder with a large tree literally growing around it. Her first thought was to look around the base of the tree for her sword, but when she stopped and quieted her thoughts she *knew*.

She looked up and found it high in the branches of the ancient oak.

"You ken climbing is not easy in a gown, aye?" she said as Duncan slowly joined her. She waved her hand to stop any answer he might give. "I know, I know. I must be able to do anything a warrior can do while in my gown, for I will not know when I might need to fight." She kilted her skirts up into her belt and flashed him a grin. "Except perhaps now I will *know*."

She made short work of retrieving her sword and was quickly back on the ground next to Duncan. She expected that wonderful broad smile that he gave her when she'd accomplished one of her training tasks particularly well, but his face was still unreadable.

"There is more to this test?" she asked, but he said nothing. "Very well." Now that she knew what the training was today she was anxious to continue it. She let her mind drift, waiting for that moment when she *knew* something. And then it was there, in her mind. "You have hidden the dagger that killed my mum," she said. "If I find it, 'tis mine again."

Duncan nodded. "That seems fair, but first you must find it."

She closed her eyes and returned to the *knowing*, but this time she added a silent chant: *the dagger, the dagger, the dagger.* She did not say anything but headed up the ben, past the lochan, and on up the steep slope until she found a downed tree. Without hesitating, she reached inside a rotted-out portion of the trunk and pulled the dagger from under leaves that had gathered in it—or that Duncan had added to the hollow after he'd hidden the knife. She turned and showed it to him.

"'Tis mine once more," she said, sliding the sheathed blade into her belt.

"Do not lose it again," Duncan said.

"Never." She pinned him with a look. "Why is this working when it did not for Jeanette's healer's bag?" she asked. "These are but things—blades both," she said, putting one hand on the pommel of the sword and her other on the haft of the dagger, "but things nonetheless."

Duncan looked at her but his usually readable face was still a mask to her. "You did not ken Conall was among the allies when they arrived, did you?"

"Nay, though I would not have mentioned him if I had. I did not ken exactly which allies were arriving, only that some were."

"You kent I was joining you at the lochan, did you not?"

She nodded slowly. "How did you know that?"

"You were standing as if you knew exactly where I was coming from, though 'twas not a direction any of the trails or any of our usual locations lead from. And while you looked a bit irritated with me, you did not look surprised to see me coming that way."

"I *knew* you were coming, and then I closed my eyes and . . . I do not ken how to explain it exactly but 'twas as if I felt for where you were. I turned until the feeling was strongest, and that is where you came from."

She watched as her words sank into him.

"And you were irritated with me for keeping you waiting so long?"

"Of course."

He nodded and looked about him before he turned back to her. "Emotion is the key for you, Scotia," he said. "You must have a strong emotional connection with the thing . . . or person . . . in order for you to *know* where they are."

"But I dinna give a rat's ass about you," she said quickly, and to his unexpected satisfaction, not very convincingly.

"You do. You always have, but since we kissed 'tis stronger. Can you not admit that? Since then you have known where I was, have you not?"

Scotia wanted to deny it but what he said was true, though she had not realized it until this moment. "Aye, though not all the time. But if I think of you, or someone says your name, I ken exactly where you are. I do not remember being able to do that before . . . before you kissed me."

"An emotional connection," he said.

"But I do not feel—"

He stepped closer to her and touched her hand. Her heart thumped harder in her chest.

"You do. 'Tis why you ken where I am even when I am not here with you."

"But why?"

"Why?"

She pulled her hand away from him. "Why just you? I have kissed Conall, but I get nothing even when I say his name. Rowan, Jeanette, they are important to me. Why do I not know where they are?"

"Do you not?"

"Nay!"

"Then why have you always found it so easy to elude them when they were looking for you? Think about it, Scotia. Calm your thoughts and think back to a time you did not want to be found. How did you stay hidden?"

Her eyes grew wide. "But that is nothing new, nothing special. I thought everyone could do that."

"It may not be new, but it is special. Tell me, is it the same now as it was then, or has this *knowing* grown stronger of late?"

She had to really think about that. "It grows stronger. Clearer, really. I used to get this . . . itch . . . in my mind when Rowan or Jeanette drew near and I did not wish to be found. Now it is as if the thought 'Rowan is on the trail to the burn'—" She looked at him with her brow scrunched together and a startled look in her eyes. "Rowan *is* on the trail to the burn. She is. Right now."

Duncan smiled, that broad grin that she loved, that he seemed to save only for her. That thought stopped her. Surprised her.

"And Jeanette, do you ken where she is?"

Scotia closed her eyes and thought about her sister. "Aye. She is studying the Chronicles at the back of the main cave."

"Is there anyone else you can *know* about?"

"My da. Uilliam sometimes, but only if he is angry with me. I knew Nicholas came for me and Ian in the fire, but that is the only time I have known where he was."

"Emotion is the key, Scotia. There was no emotion involved when you were asked to find Jeanette's bag of herbs, but you have a soft heart for the weans, so you were able to find both Maisie and Ian when they were frightened and alone. Nicholas feared for your life in the fire. The sword almost took your life. And the dagger . . . I suspect you will always be able to find that dagger no matter how well it is hidden, or how far away you must travel to retrieve it."

"And you. I *know* you."

He nodded, holding her gaze with his own. "Aye."

She would not let herself look away from him, from his dark brown eyes gone soft as he waited for her to say something, to do something. But she would not let herself close the small distance between them. She knew herself, and she knew Duncan. They would drive each other daft if there was anything more between them than teacher and student, big brother and bratty wee sister. And yet she did not think of him as brotherly anymore. There was nothing brotherly at all in the way Duncan had invaded her thoughts, and her dreams. Nothing brotherly when he had kissed her. And there was nothing sisterly in the desire for him that swamped her at odd times.

Besides, they both knew she was a fickle creature. Her infatuation with Conall had only lasted until she had other things, more important things, to fixate upon. And there had been lads before him, fleeting flirtations, a few stolen kisses. Of course things had gone a bit further than kisses with Conall. She turned away from Duncan then, pretending she had heard something behind her. She was not proud of what had happened with Conall, though at the time it had been thrilling to know he wanted her so much, to know he would put his life in danger to lie with her. It had been a heady rush of power that she had never experienced before. It had been an escape from the impending death of her mother. And yet she had found no joy in learning of his arrival at the caves.

But she did find joy in her time with Duncan, and not just from the training. She found herself looking for his smile when she finished one of his tasks, and was disappointed if it did not appear. Spending time with him made her forget, sometimes, the things that had happened, and managed to suspend her fixation on the battle to come, allowing her to simply be with him, in the moment.

Daft. She was daft. She wanted no escape from the horrors that had befallen her and her clan since those days of naïveté. Now she wanted to hold the pain, the anger, the sorrow, and the grief close to her so she would never forget, so she would stay focused on what mattered, on vengeance, on driving the English devils from this land, on killing as many of them as possible so they could not return, yet again, to try to break Clan MacAlpin of Dunlairig. She had two deaths to avenge. If she gave in to whatever this was between her and Duncan she would lose her focus, her edge, her burning anger.

She realized she still stared into Duncan's eyes, but at least her resolve was once more in place.

"How can we use this ability of mine as a weapon against our enemies?" she asked, turning the tension between them back to what she really wanted.

Vengeance.

FOR THREE DAYS DUNCAN HAD DRIVEN THEM BOTH HARD WITH sword practice, testing her gift, obstacle courses in the wood, tracking practice for those things she could not find with her *knowing*, discussions of strategy . . . anything he could think of to tire the two of them out so much and so thoroughly that neither had the energy to dwell on the change in their relationship, for even though she had not admitted as much, the very fact that she could *know* where he was at all times spoke volumes about the emotions she refused to acknowledge.

That alone, hiding her emotions, was remarkable and told him in no uncertain terms that she did not want the feelings she held for him. Which was fine. He did not want these new feelings she was engendering in him, either.

But Scotia fought like a demon now that she had a real sword. No longer did she dance through the lessons he set her. The sword, and a better understanding of what her gift could and couldn't do for her, had honed her to a fine edge, making her move through the exercises with more force, more grace, and far greater purpose than ever before.

"Ouch!" he said as Scotia landed a blow with the flat of her sword on his upper arm.

"If you held your targe where you should, I could not hit you like that," Scotia said, her sword once more up, her targe in place, and a wicked smile upon her lips. "If 'twas a true battle, I would not have turned my blade, and you would be without that arm." She shifted her weight side to side, her sword at the ready, enjoying far too much his momentary distraction and her momentary victory.

Duncan attacked. Swords clashed, and for a moment his focus was absolute. Scotia put everything she had into her parries and counterattacks, forcing him to think fast to keep up with her.

She fluttered her eyelashes, the smile still in place, drawing his attention away from her fighting stance to her eyes. The moment his focus wavered, she spun, landed a vicious blow on his targe, then used that force to propel her into another spin. He stopped her next blow with his sword, the blades sliding down each other until the cross guards stopped them, jamming their weapons together and bringing Duncan within inches of Scotia. Her eyes locked with his as she fought for control of the battle.

Duncan could barely hold his ground, struggling to keep his mind on the battle now that she stood so close he could feel her rapid breath upon his face, but they were at a stalemate.

"Enough?" She licked her lips, and he was lost.

Somehow she hooked a heel behind his knee and pulled him off balance, toppling him to the ground. He managed to hold his weapons away, pulling hers free of her grip at the same time, but that meant he could not break his fall. He landed hard with an "Oof!"

In one motion, so fluid 'twas like a dance, Scotia drew her dagger and straddled him, her knife point coming to rest just under his ear. At least she was breathing hard from the exertion. He could barely breathe at all, and it had little to do with the knife at his throat, and everything to do with the woman who sat atop him in a position far better used for pleasure than for war.

Scotia was motionless, her gaze, still locked on his, showed surprise, and awareness.

His body stirred. She did not move. Her breath stuttered and grew unsteady.

And then she closed her eyes and caught her lower lip between her teeth and rolled her hips almost imperceptibly. Duncan groaned. He swiftly relieved her of the dagger, throwing it away from them as he rolled and pinned her beneath him so he lay in the cradle of her thighs. She reached up and pulled him down into a kiss that was every bit as fierce as their first, though there was no anger, no argument, this time.

Duncan's focus was absolute.

The slide of her lips against his, the touch of their tongues, fanned his desire. She let her hands roam over his back, pulling him tighter against her, then she slid her long fingers into his hair as he deepened the kiss, urging her mouth to open for him. It was all he could do not to push her skirts and his plaid out of the way and do what clearly they both wanted right then and there. One bit of sanity and a promise he'd made to himself kept him from that. But that promise didn't keep him from enjoying the moment.

He slid his hand slowly down her side, his palm skimming over the side of her breast, then down the curve of her waist.

The fervor of her kiss slowed, as if her attention had shifted from his mouth to . . .

"Ahhh," she whispered against his lips as he ran his fingers over the exposed soft skin of her thigh where her gown and kirtle had bunched up, until he found her damp and ready. Before his mind could catch up with him, he pressed a finger into her and felt her shudder. She let her head fall back, and closed her eyes. The look of utter concentration on her heart-shaped face almost undid him.

He pressed deeper into her, then out, and in again, and she began to move her hips against him, matching the rhythm of his fingers. He found her bud and ran his thumb over it as he delved his finger into her, all the while watching her as intense concentration gave way to intense pleasure. She tensed, arching her back, pressing her breasts against his chest and her sex hard against his hand.

She let out a long, low moan of pleasure, her flesh pulsing against him, and it was all he could do not to join her in her release.

He let his forehead rest against hers for a long moment, breathing in the scent of her, letting it wrap around him and settle into him, and he realized he had truly lost the battle, and not the one with swords and shields.

"Get off me, Duncan," she said but he could not tell her mood. He pushed back and sat down facing her, grateful when she settled her skirts back where they belonged. She said nothing as she got to her feet and found her dagger. She looked at it in her hand as if only seeing it for the first time.

"We cannot do that again," she said, sliding the dagger into its sheath at her belt.

"I ken that." He got to his feet and gathered his own weapons. "'Twas not my intention."

"Nor mine," she said. "I should have stopped you, but . . ."

"'Twas the heat of battle," he said, though he knew it was far more than that. "It riles the blood." 'Twas a poor excuse for letting his desires get the best of his intentions. "'Twill not happen again."

"I will not let it happen again," she said, but she wasn't looking at him and there was none of the heat he expected in her voice. "It cannot happen again. No kissing, no . . . touching." She cut her gaze to him and he could see the pink in her cheeks, but he did not ken if the color was because she was embarrassed by what had transpired here or because she was angry about it. She let her hand rest on the hilt of her dagger, the dagger that had killed her mum and Myles, the dagger that she had just used to remind herself of her goal. "I cannot be distracted from my vow, Duncan. I'll not let you nor any other lad distract me."

Duncan sat across the fire from Scotia that evening after the meal, hoping the crackling flames and quiet conversation would distract him from the tension that still rode his body and his mind. But it was useless. He could think of nothing else, and every time he let himself be drawn back to the events of the afternoon, followed by Scotia's silent return to the caves with him, he wanted to groan or grab her and pull her into the forest with him. Clearly he had not been thinking when he let himself, when he let them, get carried away like that, and now he was paying the price. Somehow she had turned the tables on him. He was the one distracted by desire, while she remained steadfastly focused on her goal.

"If you keep staring at her like that, lad," Nicholas said, "Kenneth is likely to pluck out your eyeballs."

Duncan closed his eyes and rubbed the spot between his brows. "Is it that obvious?"

"Aye." Nicholas sat next to him. "But from what Rowan has told me, and from what I have seen from the moment I met you, you have always had a soft spot for the stubborn, selfish—"

"She is not—"

Nicholas laughed quietly. "Not anymore, 'tis true. It seems she has grown up at last, and while circumstances of late pushed her there, you appear to have something to do with her transformation, too."

"Transformation?" Was their indiscretion that apparent?

"You are not blind—yet—and neither am I. You have been training her with weapons." Duncan gave silent thanks, then realized what Nicholas had said. "If I had not seen it myself," Nicholas continued, "I would know from the way she carries herself."

"Seen it?"

"You forget that my first calling was as a master spy. Did you not think I would keep an eye upon you and your charge when she has caused so much trouble?"

Duncan sighed. "'Tis a measure of how preoccupied I have been that I did not consider that."

Nicholas chuckled. "She is a distracting woman. But as I said, even if I had not seen her training myself, I would know. No longer does she wander about, swaying her hips, and looking for mischief as she did when first I saw her trysting with Conall." An unwanted flash of anger had Duncan scanning the gathering for the blond warrior. "She moves differently than she did even a tenday ago. Now she strides about like a warrior, her eyes scanning for trouble, her reactions swift and often ending in a fighting posture. And I daresay she is getting quite good with her weapons, given the number of bruises and cuts I have seen on you in the last few days."

Duncan looked down at his nicked hand, and rolled the shoulder she had whacked with her blade just that afternoon, knowing there would be a fine bruise in evidence by morning.

"She does not want it known until she is ready to join the warriors, and aye, she is getting very, very good with her sword and shield." He could not help the pride that he was sure Nicholas could hear his voice, nor could he keep from glancing across the fire at Scotia, catching her watching him. Flustered, they both looked away.

"Does she expect to fight with the warriors?" Nicholas's tone was flat, as if he did not want Duncan to know how he felt about that possibility.

"She does, and I have promised her she will when the time comes."

"That will not sit well with her sister and my wife," Nicholas said.

"I do not think Scotia cares about that."

"I am sure she does not. Have you any understanding of this *knowing* Rowan told me about?"

Duncan was grateful for the turn in the conversation. He explained the testing he continued to do with Scotia, and what they had discovered about why and when she might *know* something and why and when she did not.

"We must determine how best to use this gift of hers in our fight against the English," Nicholas said, tossing a pebble into the fire. "It might just give us the advantage we need. Do you ken if proximity has aught to do with how or when she receives a *knowing*?"

Duncan had to think back to all the tests he had given Scotia in the last few days. "She had the *knowing* about Sherwood, so that was from afar. She kent the allies were arriving in this glen before the guards at the pass blew the horn, but not long before. She kent where her sword was." He looked at Nicholas, knowing this next bit of news would not sit well with the chief. "We found it just near the Story Stone, though she did not ken it was there until we were already at the meadow. Other than that," he continued, "everything we have worked on has been within the confines of the glen."

"Do you think she is ready to venture further afield with her training?" Nicholas asked.

"I think she is chafing at the bit to venture further afield."

Nicholas laughed as he looked across the cook circle at Scotia, then back to Duncan. "Always, with that one, aye?"

"Always," Duncan agreed.

"I have just the task for the two of you, but Rowan will insist you take more warriors with you to keep Scotia safe."

"If this is a test for Scotia, then warriors will interfere. She does not want anyone to know what she is about until she is sure she will be a boon to our fight. I have promised her to keep this secret—though neither of us thought you still in the spy business." 'Twas another good reason not to let what had happened between him and Scotia happen again, he only then realized. "You have placed her in my care, and I have earned her trust." Unless he had lost it today, but he did not say that to Nicholas. "I will not jeopardize that by pushing her on this. Not yet."

Nicholas took a moment to consider Duncan's words, looking from Duncan to Scotia again, who seemed to purposely look anywhere but at the two men.

"Very well. You have done well with her so far. I will give the lass a little more time to hone her skills in privacy, but only a little, for if Jeanette's visions are true, Lord Sherwood and his detachment will be here very soon. In the meantime . . ."

CHAPTER THIRTEEN

EARLY THE NEXT MORN, DUNCAN MOVED SILENTLY THROUGH the wood, fully armed and only a little concerned for the safety of his companion. When he had roused Scotia well before dawn and told her the plan for the day, a combination scouting expedition and training day, she had glared at him at first, then leapt from her blankets without a word, and before he knew it she had led him up a deer trail he had never explored and out of the Glen of Caves, easily skirting the doubled guards around the passes.

As soon as they began to descend the ben, Scotia seemed to relax. She had stopped just as the sun's wan light turned the eastern sky shades of subtle pinks and purples, and bade him to lead the way as she did not ken where they were bound. Ever since, she had followed behind him quietly, but he kept feeling as if she stared at his back. Whenever he looked over his shoulder—to make sure she was still there, he told himself—she was simply trudging along, her eyes on her feet, or searching the forest around them.

Last night her eyes had been on him, as if she battled with her feelings for him, the feelings he knew she held but did not want. But this morning she was more settled, and it seemed her battle had been won. And yet he could swear she tried to stare a hole in his back, though he could not catch her at it.

He fought his own battle this day. When he had gone to wake her this morn, she had looked so peaceful, so sweet, it had taken all his resolve not to touch her, not to run his fingers over the smooth plane of her cheek, or to take her hand in his. It had taken all of his resolve to keep himself from simply watching her sleep. He had said her name quietly and her eyes had popped open immediately. He was glad he had controlled his desires and not made a fool of himself.

Even now, as they neared the outer watches set around the castle, he struggled to keep his mind off Scotia and what she might be thinking and feeling. He struggled to stay focused on what they were about. The English lord would probably send advance parties ahead of the main force to scout out the land, the whereabouts of the MacAlpins, food sources, likely ambush locations, and anything else they could learn that might be of use to the lord when he arrived. It would not do for Duncan and Scotia to stumble into one of those advance parties because he was preoccupied with the lass.

He held up his hand, his signal to halt, and looked about him. This would be as good a place as any to begin the day's work.

"Hide yourself," he said to Scotia. "You need to be close to where an enemy might pass—within striking distance, but not seen."

She cocked an eyebrow at him, shook her head a little, then set about gathering fallen branches, twigs, and a vine that grew up the side of an ancient tree. In a shorter time than he expected, she had disappeared under a mat that looked like the rest of the forest floor. To his surprise she had even thought to draw her sword and dagger before she had taken cover. She would be ready for any enemy who passed by her.

"Stay there," he said. "I will return shortly, and I expect you to hold your position until I do. Even if Lord Sherwood himself rides by you, do not engage. Do you understand?"

"You are quite clear, Duncan. Go now so that you might return sooner." The edge of irritation in her muffled voice was familiar.

He faded back into the wood far enough that she would think him gone, then climbed a tree to keep watch, to make sure she did exactly as he bade her. If he did not ken where she crouched in her leafy hide, he did not think he would ever notice she was there.

When he was reasonably certain she really was heeding his order to stay hidden, he climbed down from his perch and made his way toward the castle. When he was out of her earshot, he made the call of the tawny owl, and listened. In the distance the call was repeated so he made his way in that direction, using the owl call twice more to find Brodie MacAlpin sitting high up in a tree, keeping watch over the castle and the surrounding land and loch.

Duncan made a hand signal that meant "What news?" and watched as Brodie made another, indicating there had been no sightings of their enemy. Duncan nodded, waved good-bye, and decided to return to check on Scotia rather than move on to one of the other two men keeping watch today. He trusted her to keep to her task, but still, she was Scotia and it was only prudent to check on her.

When he drew near, he climbed the tree once more, and had to search to make out her hide, right where it had been when he'd left her. As far as he could tell nothing had changed. Relief swept through him, loosening the muscles in his back that he had not realized were tense.

"You can come out now," he said, as he neared her place.

"Of course," she said from behind him.

He spun and found her standing within striking distance of him, a second hide scattered around her feet and a grin of triumph upon her heart-shaped face.

Anger and pride fought within him. She had not followed his order as a good warrior should, but she had hidden herself so well, even he had not discovered her true hiding place.

"You were not to move," he finally said.

"But this was better, aye?"

Duncan fought the desire to return the grin that lit up her entire countenance. He fought the desire to sweep her up in his arms in celebration of her excellent ruse that would serve her well in battle, if not her fellow warriors.

He clenched his teeth and pressed his lips together until the urge to smile was under control. "Nay," he said. "Following orders is better." He watched as the delight sparkling in her eyes dimmed. "If you cannot do that simple thing, I can never recommend you to fight among the clan's warriors. In order to defend the clan together, you must be relied upon to follow the orders given you. Everyone's life will depend upon you doing what you have been told." He looked away to the west, hating that he could not tell her also how proud he was of her for thinking for herself, but as hard as this was, 'twas a necessary lesson.

"This was a test, Scotia, and you failed."

SCOTIA WATCHED AS DUNCAN STRODE AWAY FROM HER. HER mind was reeling at his harsh words. She had seen the surprise, and the instant of pleasure that had made Duncan's dark eyes shine, but then it had been replaced with an awkward anger, or maybe just disappointment.

Failed? She had not failed! She had surprised him, Duncan, the best tracker in the clan. She had hidden herself even better than he had asked her to, waiting patiently until she knew when he had climbed out of that tree and gone to find a watcher. She had already noted where more branches, vines, and bracken lay nearby before she'd even completed the first hide, so it took only moments for her to construct the second one and take her place beneath it. From that point on she had followed Duncan's orders, awaiting his return while staying alert for any passing English.

Anticipation of his appreciation for her ingenuity had made it easy to crouch, weapons in hand, her attention and senses fixed on the area around her for a long time. She had known the moment he had climbed that damned tree again, and it was only then that she found it hard to await his return.

Now she wished he had never returned. Damned man.

"Where are we going?" Scotia hissed from behind him, still picking leaves from her hair.

Duncan sliced a hand through the air, his sign for silence, and kept going, irritating her beyond her ability to keep silent.

"Duncan!" She knew better than to yell at him, which is what she would have done even a fortnight ago, but she was determined to explain why she did not follow his instructions exactly but that she *had* followed what he had intended by them.

When he kept moving without even that stupid hand signal for silence, she said his name again. "Duncan!" This time she let her voice be a little louder. "I did nothing wrong."

Still he ignored her, though his pace increased, making it harder for her to keep up with his long strides.

"What is wrong with you?!" she asked. "I did—"

"Haud yer wheesht!" he said over his shoulder, but he didn't look at her.

Stupid, idiotic, bothersome, irritating, silent man. Scotia let the litany of angry descriptions swirl in her head, over and over again, until she could barely contain her anger at his dismissal and withdrawal from her. She had done almost exactly as he had required, so she would not endanger his agreement to train her. That one small change had not put her in any more danger than she might already have been in, and it made her position even more secure. Duncan should be proud of her for making his order even better.

"Duncan," she tried again, "stop! You know as well as I that I did not fail to follow your orders."

The only sign that he even heard her was that stupid hand signal once more.

Irritation turned to ire. She was not wrong. He was, but he would never admit that to her. He would never admit that she might have done something strategically better than what he had told her to do.

Something snapped in Scotia's head, or maybe it was in her gut. Either way, she charged Duncan, racing up behind him and leaping on his back, her arms around his neck, her legs around his waist, her lips at his ear ready to demand he stop, but before she could form the first word the world flipped around on her. She flew over Duncan's back and landed hard on hers. Her left arm was wrenched at a painful angle in Duncan's powerful grip, his foot on her neck. Thankfully, the waterskin she carried had pillowed her spine, though the cool wet that she lay in told her it had not survived the impact.

And then Duncan released her as if he had been burned.

"What were you thinking, Scotia?" he demanded, though he kept his voice hushed. He stepped back from her. "I could have killed you." And then his face went from anger to shock, and he knelt beside her. The similarity of their positions to the much more intimate moments of yesterday seemed to hit them both at the same time, and the awkwardness she'd been trying to ignore burst to life between them.

"Och, lass, did I hurt you?" His words were soft with concern.

"Not as much as I shall hurt you," she said, pushing herself up to a sitting position, "once I get my breath back." She glared at him, intent on returning their relationship to what it had been before . . . before it had changed. "At least I got your attention," she snapped at him.

Duncan sat back. "You always have my attention."

"Only when I dinna want it." She tried not to wince as his eyes went hard, but she did not let his reaction stop her. "I did what you bade me. Are you angry because I made your order better?"

"Nay." But he did not look at her.

"Do not lie to me, Duncan. For a moment you did think well of what I did, but then you denied that, to yourself and to me.

Why? Why would you do that? Is it because I forbid you to"—she hated that her voice wobbled—"to touch me again?"

Still he did not look at her. She started to rise, and he reached out and grabbed her arm, holding her in place. "You are right, Scotia," he said looking at her now, but she could not read the emotion in his eyes. "What you did was smart. You used your knowledge of strategy creatively—"

Warmth began to wash through her with his words and the feel of his hand on her. She started to smile but he pressed his lips together and sighed.

"—an excellent trait in a leader, but you are not a leader. You might become one, one day, but that is a long way off."

"And you are a leader?" she asked, getting to her feet and picking up the useless waterskin.

"When you and I are training, aye, I am. In battle, nay, I am not. I have not the knowledge and experience of Malcolm, Nicholas, Kenneth, or any of the other seasoned warriors of this clan. In battle I must do exactly as I am told. To do anything else will put other lives in danger, and likely my own, for I will not be where I am needed, or prepared to do what is needed, if I change the plan on my own."

He looked up at her, then stood slowly, locking his gaze to hers.

"'Tis why Myles is dead," he said, his voice quiet but his words ringing like a blacksmith's hammer in her head. "You did not do as your chief bade you, to remain in camp where you put no one's life at risk, where you could not draw someone else—Myles— from where he was supposed to remain and into danger. If you had not taken it into your own head to change the order Nicholas gave you, Myles would very likely be alive today, and you would not be shunned by your own clan."

"'Twas not me who killed Myles," she said, though her heart pounded as his accusation circled in her mind. "I did not—"

"You did not strike him down yourself? 'Tis no excuse. He

would have been safely hidden in that tree if he had not had to climb down to follow you, to stop you from doing something even more dangerous than you had already undertaken by leaving the protection of the warriors' camp."

She started to deny it, but the words refused to leave her mouth. She blinked. She swallowed. She shook her head.

"I thought you were on my side. I thought you were different from the others of the clan." She shook her head harder. "You only meant to keep me under close watch after all. Yesterday was just another ploy to bend me to your will." She pivoted and strode through the wood, not caring how much noise she made as she remembered the feel of his kiss and his hands on her, as she remembered the way he had looked at her over the fire last night, the way her heart had softened until she struggled to remember that her purpose left no room for soft feelings for anyone. She turned back and Duncan almost crashed into her.

"And that look you gave me over the fire last night." She poked a finger hard against his chest. "You feigned the cow eyes of an infatuated lad when 'twas only another weapon to keep me close, and I almost fell for it. I almost fell for you. I am truly an idiot, a complete bampot. I knew not how skilled you were at mummery." He had played her as masterfully as a bard on a clarsach, a harp. He was a master of strategy in a completely different way than he had taught her.

"Scotia, none of that was—"

"Dinna lie to me!"

"I have never lied to you." Now his ire grew. He narrowed his eyes and stood his ground. "That kiss was real. What happened yesterday, though I never meant for it to happen, was real. I ken not what the look on my face was last night, but the feelings I had . . . I have . . . for you are changed every bit as much as you are changed . . . or at least as I thought you had changed."

"I have—"

A cry resounded through the wood. A man's voice in surprised pain. And then just as suddenly as it had started, it ended.

"Brodie," Duncan said, sprinting back in the direction they had come from. Scotia followed without a word, the rush of emotion that had fueled their argument now fueling her feet. After they had covered a good distance, Duncan slowed and gave her the hand signal for silence that had irritated her so much not long ago, and another to hold her ground.

Without a thought, she ducked behind a large tree, and worked hard to quiet her rasping breath as Duncan crept forward. She tried to quiet her mind, to *know* something of use, but all she *knew* was that Duncan was still nearby. The quiet call of a tawny owl had her peeking around the tree enough to see Duncan signaling her to join him. She moved silently, and when she was even with him, she crouched beside him. He pointed through the thick greenery.

There, at the foot of an ancient oak tree, her kinsman Brodie lay crumpled and broken upon the ground, a Welsh arrow through his heart.

Scotia and Duncan returned to the Glen of Caves well before sundown, just as the clan was gathering for the evening meal.

"Get something to eat, Scotia," he said, giving her a little push toward the cook circle where a kettle bubbled over the fire, sending a mouthwatering scent through the clearing. "I must report to Nicholas."

Scotia glanced at the council circle at the other end of the narrow clearing and found, as she'd expected, Nicholas, both Guardians, and Malcolm there.

"You'll not tell them of our bargain," she reminded him.

Duncan closed his eyes and sighed. "Nicholas already kens what we have been about."

Scotia's eyes grew big. She blinked. "He kens? You told him? You promised—"

"I did not tell him," he interrupted her, pulling her as far away from the people gathered for their meal in the clearing as was possible.

"Then how?" Scotia just glared at him, and he could not help himself, he smiled at her consternation and shrugged.

"I am not the one who carries herself so differently 'tis obvious to at least Nicholas that you are training with weapons. And he spied upon us."

"What? When?"

"I dinna ken, but I do not think 'twas yesterday."

"But—"

Out of habit, Duncan used the sign for silence that had set her off earlier. "I did not tell Nicholas, and I will not tell the rest, though 'twould surprise me if Nicholas had not already told Rowan, and if she had not told Jeanette, and of course then Jeanette would tell Malcolm."

Scotia glanced from him to the council circle and back. "'Twas Nicholas who sent us out today, aye? Not you. What were we to do?"

"As I said, a lesson in tracking. I must report to the chief," he said. "We cannot keep your secret from everyone for much longer." He inclined his head toward the cook circle, hoping she would get herself something to eat, then he headed for the council.

"What news?" Nicholas asked, taking a seat on the large boulder that commanded the circle by being a little higher than the others.

It was tricky to report on their scouting trip to Glen Lairig without revealing why he'd taken Scotia out of the Glen of Caves to the Guardians and Malcolm, in case Nicholas had kept the secret, but he managed it.

"After we found Brodie, we tracked the English—only two of them," he added before Malcolm asked. "It looked like they sought the other watchers but they did not find them. I relayed the news of Brodie so our men would know to be even more vigilant. We followed the tracks most of the way to the castle, but did not go any further."

"And Brodie?" Nicholas asked.

"We went back and buried him in a shallow place we found near where he fell. We covered him with stones, but more will be needed. We did not dare linger there too long."

"And why did you take Scotia along with you on this scouting trip?" Jeanette asked.

"'Twas my command," Nicholas said, drawing all eyes from Duncan to him. "I needed to be able to use the skills of our best tracker, but he is also the only one who has been able to keep Scotia in hand. He assured me that she would do as he said, that he would be able to see to her safety, so this was a way to accomplish two tasks in one."

"But—" Rowan started.

"But nothing, Guardian," Nicholas said, marking that part of their relationship. "I am chief, love, and Protector of the Guardians. I would make the same decision again."

"She did as you bade her all day?" Jeanette asked Duncan.

"Enough," he said before he thought through exactly how to respond. Nicholas's attention was fully on him with that response. Duncan was more tired than he'd realized to be so careless in choosing his words. "Aye, she did as I bade her," he added. "And she was much-needed help when it came time to lay Brodie to rest." He hoped the mention of their dead kinsmen would distract them from the tracking questions, though he knew 'twas not an honorable thing to use a fallen warrior in such a way.

"Scotia can be very helpful when it suits her purpose," Rowan said, "and she is a decent tracker herself. Has she gotten more canny about tracks and tracking in her daily attempts to evade you?"

Duncan wanted to tell Rowan just how much better Scotia had gotten at tracking and so many other things, but he could not betray his promise, especially now that it was clear Nicholas had kept the truth to himself.

"She has learned a few new tricks," he said with care, "but she cannot evade me without using her *knowing*."

There was a short silence as that piece of information sank into the small gathering.

"Did she *know* anything about these English?" Jeanette asked.

"Aye, once she saw Brodie 'twas as if a sunbeam lit the two English soldiers so she could almost see them, or so she said to me. 'Twas Scotia who did most of the tracking after that, like she did when wee Maisie went missing."

"Could she have directed you to exactly where they were, if you had wanted to engage them?" Malcolm asked, leaning forward, his elbows on his knees and his hands clasped tightly together.

Duncan had to think back to all the tests he had put her through these last days, and to what she had told him of her *knowing* this afternoon. "I dinna ken," he said slowly. "Perhaps if she knew them, had actually seen them, or if they carried something important to her, like the dagger used to kill Lady Elspet, she might. Today, I do not ken if 'twas as specific a *knowing* as would be needed."

Malcolm let that sink in before he continued.

"'Twould be a formidable weapon in our fight against the English"—he looked from Nicholas to Duncan—"especially if she were to be trained in the ways of warriors."

Duncan's heart stopped, then started again with a hard staccato thumping. Malcolm knew of Scotia's training. Duncan quickly glanced around the group but could not tell if the Guardians also knew or if their husbands and Protectors were also keeping Scotia's secret.

"My sister would never make a good warrior," Jeanette said. "She is too headstrong, too impetuous."

A movement in the deep shadows of a small cave near the council circle drew Duncan's eye, and he realized Scotia crouched there. He knew not how long she had been listening to their conversation.

He turned his attention away from the cave. "Aye, but she is also smart, agile, strong of heart and mind, and has a gift that, while it may not aid you Guardians in your task, can aid the clan's warriors in ours."

"Only if her gift can be used at will, though," said Malcolm. "Can it?"

"Not reliably, nay, but 'tis something we are working on together."

"Together?" Rowan asked. "So you are not just tracking her, are you?"

"I told you so," Jeanette said. "You are spending much time together, aye? 'Tis why she has been so different of late. What else are you doing together, Duncan? Tracking? Her gift? Are you training her to be a warrior?"

Duncan froze. He did not want to lie to a Guardian, or anyone, for that matter, but he also knew he dared not break his word to Scotia or all the work they had done together would be for naught, for she would not trust him enough to go into battle with him.

"He is," Scotia said, striding into the circle.

CHAPTER FOURTEEN

Now Scotia understood why it was not a good idea to keep secrets. Once they were revealed there was nothing but trouble, no matter how good the intention. Chaos had taken over the council, with Jeanette jumping to her feet demanding details, and Rowan fussing at Nicholas for hiding the truth from her. Which made Jeanette turn on Malcolm, who at least could honestly say he'd only guessed but had not known for sure.

Duncan tilted his head to beckon Scotia over to him, then made room for her next to him on the log that served as a bench.

"You did not have to do that," he said quietly while keeping his attention focused on the two Protectors and the two Guardians who were, for the moment at least, consumed by finding out who knew what when.

"I did not know I was going to until I heard Jeanette's question. 'Twas time to reveal the secret. Nicholas knows already. The English are upon us. Either I am prepared to go into battle with the warriors or I am not." In truth, she had not known what she was about until the words came out of her mouth, proving her sister's assertion that she was too impetuous, though in this case it was the right thing to do. She was sure of it. Whatever argument she and Duncan had had earlier in the day, for the full length of the afternoon they had worked perfectly as a team, and her gift had helped them track the two soldiers, proving she was ready to fight the English as a warrior.

Kenneth and Uilliam wandered into the campsite from the near end of the clearing and immediately joined the six in the council circle, but the Guardians were still demanding answers from the Protectors and did not notice. Kenneth and Uilliam exchanged a look of surprise, then joined Duncan and Scotia.

"What did Nicholas and Malcolm do?" Kenneth asked with a chuckle.

"Malcolm withheld a suspicion. Nicholas withheld knowledge. Neither Guardian is happy they were not included in the secret," Duncan said.

"Secret? What secret?" Uilliam said, pulling hard on his thick black beard.

"My secret," Scotia said. "Duncan has been training me with sword, shield, and dagger, as well as in tracking, strategy, and in learning how my gift works." Funny, now that the news was out, she did not ken why she had kept silent about it for so long, but then she realized her father was no longer laughing at the four people who were still "discussing" the secret. She looked over at him, happy that he sat on the far side of both Duncan and Uilliam.

"Why?" For some reason his question caught the attention of the others, and they went silent, turning to face the four on the log.

"Aye," Rowan said, putting her hands on her hips, "why?"

The accusatory tone lit Scotia's temper. "So I can go into battle with the warriors and avenge the deaths of Mum and Myles, and so many others, of course."

Duncan pressed his lips together. "'Tis more complicated than that, though that was the leverage I used. The day I was put in charge of her I found her training herself." He looked over at Malcolm. "She'd been watching you train the lads and could repeat the exercises herself near perfectly." He glanced at her, then gripped his knees and sighed. "I offered to train her in exchange for her staying in my company at all times when she was away from the caves. The bargain was struck that when the time came to fight, *if I deemed her ready*, I would make sure she was part of the battle."

"And do you deem her ready?" Kenneth asked, his voice unnervingly even.

Duncan hesitated, and all the tiny hairs on Scotia's neck rose.

"Tell them, Duncan," she said. "Tell them how I have trained hard. I am quick with my blades. I think well in the midst of a fight—"

"A fight?!" Kenneth was on his feet.

"Sparring, Da," Scotia said, holding her hand out as if that would stop his ire. "Today was the closest I have been to an actual confrontation with our enemies since my training began, but Duncan pulled us back to bury Brodie, even though I thought we should attack and keep the scouts from reporting back to Sherwood."

And still Duncan was silent, except now so was everyone else. If only she could know his thoughts. Now that would be a truly useful gift. But she did not. She could only ken where he was, naught else, and she did not need her gift to ascertain that right now.

"Duncan, tell them I am ready. Tell them how I proved myself this day." And still he sat mute. "Duncan?"

"She is not ready, then," Nicholas said. His rescue of Duncan had Scotia on her feet. If he would not proclaim her ready she would have to do it herself.

"I am ready." She held her hands loosely at her side, as Duncan had taught her so that she did not look threatening, but also so that she could grab her weapons quickly if the need arose. Of course her weapons were hidden in the forest, but she would not have drawn them on her family anyway. "If you wish to test my skills, I am willing, but Duncan can attest to my strength, my speed, my agility."

"I *can* attest to those. She is a quicker study and a more focused student than any I have seen before. She has worked hard to hone her skills and strengthen her body." That brought him a glare from both Kenneth and Uilliam, but Duncan did not let it stop him. "She is also good at strategy, showing a creative mind for it."

"So she is ready?" Nicholas asked.

Duncan looked at Scotia. "I am sorry." Then he looked Nicholas in the eye. "She is not."

Scotia pivoted to face her new foe. "How can you say that? You promised me! How can you lie to everyone? I am ready. I proved it this very day. Why do you lie?!"

Duncan ran his palm over his face and slowly rose to face Scotia. He reached for her hands, but she ripped them out of his grasp and crossed her arms over her chest.

"I do not lie, Scotia, and you well ken it. Yes, this very day you did well in the afternoon, but in the morning you did not, and that impulsiveness, that lack of being willing to follow orders exactly as they are given, not as you wish them to be, or at all, *that* will get someone killed. Perhaps you, perhaps someone else. Most likely both. I cannot support you going into battle when I do not fully trust you to do as you are told. No one should die because I was not willing to tell the truth, no matter how much it might hurt you, though that is not my intention." He looked at each person in the circle, Uilliam rising to join everyone else as he met Duncan's glance, until finally his gaze landed on Nicholas.

"I wish I could report otherwise, but I cannot. Scotia is not ready to join the warriors in battle."

DUNCAN COULD FEEL A MUSCLE IN HIS CLENCHED JAW TWITCH as he watched Scotia storm toward the main cave. When she disappeared into the darkness, he dropped to his seat on the log, his back to the angry lass. He was angry, too. Events had conspired against him teaching her this last and perhaps most important lesson, forcing him into a corner where he either lied to Nicholas and Scotia, telling her what she wanted to hear, or he told the truth to both of them.

He could not lie, not to Nicholas, not to Scotia, and now Scotia would likely never speak to him again. He knew that in her eyes, he had betrayed his promise to her. But she was not ready for battle. If they had been able to finish their argument she might have understood why she was not ready, and she might not have pressed him into a corner where he had to deny her what she so badly desired.

She was smart. She learned quickly when the motivation was strong. He had no doubt she would understand what she needed to do, and would master it. And when she did, he would go to Nicholas and change his recommendation.

But he could do none of that if she refused to listen to him.

So he would have to make her listen—if he had time.

"When do we leave the Glen of Caves?" he asked Nicholas.

"Most of the warriors who have remained here will leave at dawn. We'll want more watches now that the English are nearly here. We'll have to set the lads to watching the passes." He looked at his wife. "Rowan, I think 'tis best if the Guardians remain here for now."

"Aye," she replied. "We will use the time to continue our studies and prepare what defenses we can, but we will have to move closer to the battle eventually, love. We will not be able to assist from here."

Nicholas nodded. "That means Malcolm and I remain here as Protectors. Kenneth, Uilliam, you take command of the warriors in Glen Lairig. You ken the land far better than I do, and you ken the men and their particular strengths well. You can continue the preparations until we travel to meet you."

"So I am to go with them?" Duncan asked, hoping that would give him enough time to make Scotia understand what she had yet to master.

Nicholas narrowed his eyes and was quiet, then finally nodded as if he'd made a decision. "Nay. I think 'tis best if you remain here and continue to keep watch over Scotia. 'Twould not do to have her take it into her head to join us on the battlefield despite our conversation here. You are the only one who has been able to keep her . . . contained. I am sorry. You would be a great asset in the coming battle, but we cannot let her create chaos when control is what we are after."

Duncan fought to breathe. Not part of the battle? "But . . ."

"Nay, Duncan. No 'but.' We need you to keep Scotia safely away from the fray. The lass never means to bring harm to others, but it has happened, and we cannot risk the distraction she would be."

Duncan knew he would make the same decision if he were in Nicholas's place, but that did not mean he liked it any better. He took a deep breath and reminded himself of the lesson Scotia needed to learn.

Take an order, and execute it as directed.

LORD SHERWOOD PULLED UP HIS COURSER AS THE TWO SCOUTS he had sent out days ago pounded toward him on their palfreys down the pitiful excuse for a road he and his detachment traveled toward Glen Lairig. He shouted at the column of men not to stop as he pulled his horse out of the flow to await the scouts.

Information had been all but impossible to gain as they made their way across the rolling landscape and into the first of the mountains. Even those few Scots they had managed to capture alive during the nightly skirmishes had given not even a hint of how many MacAlpins there were, what their defenses were, or if they were indeed in Glen Lairig as King Edward thought. The first two scouts he'd sent to spy on the secretive clan had never returned, and he could only assume they were dead, either by the hand of one of the clans that harried the detachment each night or by the MacAlpins themselves. At least these two had survived.

"What news?" he demanded as the two bedraggled men stopped beside him.

"We found the castle, m'lord," the older of the two said, "but it has been abandoned."

Sherwood blinked. "Abandoned?"

"Aye, and with good reason."

The two scouts looked at each other, and the younger one swallowed, then took up the report.

"Abandoned. One whole side of the curtain wall, the north wall, has collapsed, though from its position at the top of a steep embankment that leads down to the lake we do not think it was caused by a siege engine, or even by battering rams. The embankment gives no room for such an attack."

"So it just fell?" Lord Sherwood asked. This man needed to get to the point.

"That is the only explanation we could arrive at."

"And the rest of the wall?"

"It stands and for all appearances seems sound. There is a small tower that stands unscathed, and outbuildings that will provide shelter for your soldiers."

"But?"

"But the only other building—the great hall by the size of it—is nothing but a burned-out shell. There are no useful supplies left."

"So these rats of the Highlands abandoned their ruined castle and took everything of use with them." Lord Sherwood could feel a twitch in his left cheek just where his jaws met. "Where. Did. They. Go?" He let each word drop like stones between him and the scouts.

The two men looked at each other again, and the story once more passed to the older one.

"We could not find them, m'lord. There was at least one watcher, perched up in a tree not far from the castle, and there must have been more, for the moment he spied us he started to cry warning, so Bryn shot him to keep him quiet. We looked for others but found none."

"So they have not gone far if they still post watchers on the castle," Lord Sherwood said, thinking out loud.

"'Tis likely, but we found no trace of them in any numbers."

Before Lord Sherwood could frame another question the younger one cleared his throat. Sherwood glared at him but nodded for him to speak.

"M'lord, we did find out what happened to the last soldiers sent against the MacAlpins."

When the man stopped, Sherwood just glared at him.

"There is a large meadow with one of those standing stones, marked with carvings, in the center of it. 'Tis clear there was a recent battle there, and we found graves in the wood nearby. It did not take much effort to determine the bodies were English." His face turned a pale green and he swallowed several times before he could continue. The older scout kept his gaze focused somewhere between his horse's ears, but looked almost as disturbed as the other. "Twelve in all," he finally added. "Is that not the number that was sent?"

Lord Sherwood nodded. "Any Scots in those graves?"

"Nay," the younger one replied, his color once more returned to its more normal pale appearance. "It seems unlikely they would have buried their dead next to English, though."

He agreed. "Could you tell aught of their numbers, or their battle style?" He was getting rather desperate for information that would help him. Everything except the dead watcher seemed to weigh in the MacAlpins' favor.

Once more the narrative shifted to the older scout. "It was hard to tell exactly, but it looked like they were probably evenly matched, or nearly so. The English appeared to have taken the high ground around the stone. There are ropes still looped about the bottom of the stone as if they held someone prisoner. The Scots came from the wood near where we found the graves, but the odd thing was that the English didn't hold their ground."

"What?"

Both scouts nodded, and the older one continued. "They abandoned their position, or were driven from it, though we could not tell of anything or anyone that might have done that. They engaged the Scots near the Scots' position."

Sherwood tried to calculate how much time had passed since those soldiers had been sent in to do the job he had now been given—a fortnight at least. Long enough for the MacAlpins to regroup, to plan, to lay traps as he and his men had encountered many times along this godforsaken road.

"Is there any way we can salvage the castle?" he asked, his mind working furiously with what they had told him, looking for anything that might help him plan what looked to be more than a quickly fought battle.

The older looked once more at the younger.

"Aye, m'lord. Someone had started erecting a palisade of small trees to close the gap where the fallen section of wall is. If we put everyone but those required to keep watch to felling trees and setting them, I do not think it would take more than three days to finish that and secure the castle for our use."

He realized the two were a good match for the job he had set them. The elder scout seemed well versed in battles and the younger in the finer points of castle defenses.

"What are your names?" he asked.

"Adam of Hoveringham," the elder said.

"Bryn of Beaumaris."

"Did you gain your knowledge of curtain walls at Beaumaris, Bryn?"

"I did, m'lord. My father was a mason there, but I was a good shot, so I was trained as an archer."

"Very well," Lord Sherwood said. "This is not the information I desired, but we will use it to our advantage."

"M'lord?" Adam said.

"Aye?"

"There is more. The road is blocked in several places starting just another mile or two further along. We were able to make it back to you in one night, even though we kept off the road whenever possible, but the road is hemmed in on both sides by dense forest or steep slopes most of the way into Glen Lairig, and the risk of ambush is high. It will require clearing as we go and will still be hard going with the supply carts."

The tic in Sherwood's cheek returned, making him clench his jaw even tighter. The Highlanders were in for a surprise if they thought such tactics would slow him down. He shouted for his captains as he pivoted his horse and raced for the front of the column of soldiers.

CHAPTER FIFTEEN

Scotia stood in the darkest reaches of the main cave. Her lungs strove to pull in air, but still she could not breathe. She swallowed again and again, but her throat would not open. Her hands fisted so hard her nails cut into her flesh. She wanted to run, to leave, to put this betrayal behind her forever, to leave behind the disgrace that Duncan had served up to her.

If she never saw him again, that alone would make her happy.

She found herself at the mouth of the cave, not even aware of how she came to be there, so she turned and hurried back to the dank dark where no one could see her, where no one could deepen her humiliation.

She had trusted Duncan, she had begun to have soft feelings for the man, and she had fully expected him to keep his word to her, but when the time came for her to step up and join the warriors, he denied her.

He denied her even when he admitted she had skill, learned quickly, and had a gift that would help the MacAlpins fight the English. But he still denied that she was prepared to fight beside the clan's warriors.

How. Dare. He.

Once more she found herself at the mouth of the cave and discovered that the sun had set behind the western bens. Night would soon be upon her. Night, where she would be trapped here in this cave with women, weans, and bairns who fussed through the dark hours; where she would be surrounded by people who already shunned her, but who now would also think her so much less than she was. Neither a warrior, nor a Guardian. Just a bothersome, stubborn, troublemaking lass.

'Twas beyond bearing, and 'twas all Duncan's doing.

She was a warrior with a gift of *knowing*, and while it might not be a Guardian gift it was still of value in this fight, yet she was not allowed to go to battle.

She was not allowed . . .

Scotia was a MacAlpin, born of a long line of powerful, independent women with gifts beyond measure and understanding. She was the one who owed vengeance to the English for the deaths of her mum and Myles. Justice must be had, and 'twas clear now she would never receive Duncan's help, nor Nicholas's permission to join the battle.

She retreated to the back of the cave one more time, but this time she grabbed a plaid and arranged it under her blankets so it looked like she was sleeping, donned the trews and tunic she'd kept hidden for just this sort of need, then grabbed another plaid and wrapped it about her, pulling an edge of it over her head like a hood. She returned to the mouth of the cave and peered out to see where everyone might be, especially Duncan. She could not let him see her leave the cave site, though he would determine she had done that sooner or later and follow her. Why had she let herself believe he had started to feel something for her besides his duty to keep her out of trouble?

She was a fool. Her humiliation doubled, writhing about her gut and strangling her heart. She pulled those feelings close and held on to them tightly. She would never fall for such a ruse again. She would never fall for Duncan.

She caught sight of him, a Duncan-shaped shadow in the gathering gloom. He still sat on the log in the council circle though it would appear that everyone else had retired to the evening meal at the cook circle. Good. He would not see her, and 'twas easy enough to fool the others. She had always been able to slip past them.

She stepped out of the cave, keeping to the darker shadows, moving at a pace with everyone else so she would not look out of place. With luck anyone who saw her bundled in her plaid would think her just one of the many women in this camp, and by the time her absence was discovered even Duncan would not be able to find her, no matter how good a tracker he was. This time she would use her gift against him. She would *know* where he was at all times.

And soon everyone would know exactly how good a warrior she was, how much of an asset she would be in their fight. Soon she would be vindicated. She would avenge the deaths of her mum, Myles, and now Brodie, all by herself if necessary.

Her decision made, she calmed her thoughts and the pounding of her heart, and waited for her opportunity, the perfect moment to melt into the wood and once more take her fate into her own hands, armed with knowledge and *knowing*.

DUNCAN HAD MOVED JUST INSIDE THE MAIN CAVE SOMETIME IN the middle of the short summer night when rain had begun to fall. He sat there still, waiting for the first hint of dawn, sleeping little. He scrubbed his face with his hands, then drew his plaid about him more tightly, as if it could shield him from the coldness in his heart and his mind.

He had been right about Scotia, though he took no joy in that. Her reaction to the truth was not unexpected, but he had hoped she would choose to respond to it with more thought. If he had only had the opportunity to finish the lesson he was trying to teach her this morn.

But he had not, and her reaction only proved what he had suspected—that for all the lessons she had learned, she had failed to grasp the most important one: thinking before acting. He had seen it in the way she did not understand his anger that she had not followed his instructions to stay hidden exactly as he had stated them. He shook his head. He knew she was a self-centered lass, spoiled and used to the attentions of all around her. She was used to being indulged, to getting what she wanted with a smile, or a fluttering of her inky eyelashes, or, when that failed, with temper and willfulness.

But she wanted to be a warrior, and he knew this was a lesson all warriors must learn, though most learned it easier than Scotia did. Too bad she was not as adept at this as she was with all her other lessons.

As the night sky began to give way to the first hints of dawn he rose, settled his sword at his hip, his dagger already in place. He prepared himself for more anger from her, perhaps even tears if she thought manipulating his feelings for her 'twould help her cause. 'Twas an uncharitable thought, but a true one. At least it had been true until the last few weeks. He rubbed the heel of his hand against the center of his chest, trying to ease the ache that pulsed there. He had surely killed whatever feelings had been growing between them, but he could not dwell on that. No matter how much he rued the loss of her smiles and soft touches, no matter how much he yearned to take her into his arms and lose himself in her kisses or watch her lose herself to passion, no matter what she did or how she reacted, he owed it to her to complete her training. Only then could he keep his promise to send her into battle.

Duncan waited no longer, making his way deeper into the cave to rouse Scotia.

It did not take him long to discover her ruse. He berated himself silently, doing his best not to wake the bairns and weans sleeping with their mothers as he strode back to the cave mouth. He should have known Scotia would not meekly take to her bed in her anger and disappointment. He should have known she would see his denial of her readiness to go into battle as a betrayal of their agreement. But her changed behavior this last fortnight had lulled him into thinking she really had transformed herself, that she would stay in the caves, honoring her promise not to leave them without him in spite of her ire.

He had let his hope that she really had learned to think like a warrior instead of a spoiled, hard-headed wean, his pride in her skills, and his growing attraction to the woman he thought she had become cloud his clear-eyed understanding of her.

He stopped for a moment, wishing he had Scotia's gift of *knowing* so he could find her as easily as she found him, but he did not. He had to depend upon his tracking skills and an understanding of his quarry. There had been no moon last night, no light to travel by unless she'd taken a lantern with her. Of course if she'd taken a lantern the light would have drawn someone's attention, unless she waited until she was well away from the cave site and then lit it. 'Twas what he would have done, but when she was riled, she did not think clearly, as evidenced by her disappearance, and if she had not thought of taking light, she would not have gotten far in the night.

Light or none, the one thing he was certain of was that she would not have gone anywhere without her weapons.

AS SOON AS THERE WAS LIGHT ENOUGH TO SHOW THE DIFFERENCE between the dark shadows of the trees and underbrush, and the clear spaces between them, Scotia crept out from the thick bushes she had sheltered under all night, brushing pine needles and bracken from her trews before settling her targe on her arm. Quickly she resumed the task she had set herself the night before: getting out of the glen and joining the battle without Duncan stopping her.

Despite what he thought, she had learned his lessons well, so she spent a lot of time moving slowly through the wood, first down the ben, then slogging back up in the frigid water of a burn, then across a rocky ledge, back down a ways, then finally, when she was sure even Duncan could not follow her, she stopped to catch her breath and drink from the burn she'd been following for a while. When her thirst was slaked, she looked up, peering through the leafy canopy where she could just make out a shallow dip between peaks, though it was almost completely blanketed in rain-heavy clouds. She had found this poor excuse for a pass soon after she arrived in this glen, an almost impassable way out of the valley and back into the world beyond. Almost. She told herself she was well pleased with her decision to keep this pass to herself, her own secret bolt-hole should she need it, but a tiny, niggling whisper of a thought dimmed the pleasure with the hope that Duncan would find her, stop her, before she did something that she would rue.

Nay, she would rue nothing. She had kept her part of their bargain, training hard, reining in her emotions, doing everything Duncan required of her, and it had gained her nothing.

Never again would she fall for his lies.

She grabbed the round shield from where she had laid it by the burn and set out again, trudging up the ever steeper benside as fast as her tired legs could take her, justifying her every step with his betrayal, his damning silence when the time had come for him to step up and keep his word. She would show him. She'd show them all that though she might not be a Guardian, she was a warrior, and she would have her part in the battle to protect her home.

The sudden sound of something, or someone, moving quickly toward her through the dense underbrush had her whipping around, her sword in hand and her shield in place.

"Do not take one more step if you wish to keep your head." Each word sliced through the quiet of the benside like a claymore parting flesh, the strength of her roiling emotions lending each one the weight of certain death.

"You do not want another death upon your conscience, Scotia."

Duncan. Damn the man.

"I have no deaths upon my conscience!" She knew her voice was louder than necessary but she could not control it.

"May I approach you?" His voice was calm, lacking any emotion to tell her what he was thinking, or what he might be planning. "May I?" he asked again.

Everything in her head, in her heart, in her gut screamed *nay*, yet she found herself nodding, though she knew not if he could see her, unwilling to expose her raw feelings by speaking again.

But he must have been close enough to see her, or he simply knew she would not harm him, at least not with her sword. Her words, if she let them fly, could hurt him as much as his silence had hurt her, and she would not show him mercy while she eviscerated him with them.

"You cannot leave like this," he said as he drew to a stop a few steps out of her sword range. No one could call Duncan uncautious.

"I will leave how and when I wish. You broke your promise to me, so you have forfeited your right to any say in what I do." She waved her sword in his direction for good measure.

"I have not broken my promise—"

"Am I to join the battle as a warrior then?" she asked, knowing full well she was not.

"Nay, but—"

"Yet you espoused my skills, that I had learned your lessons well, that my gift of knowing . . ." It was only then that she realized she had not *known* he was the one following her. Why had she not *known*? Had her gift fled her, too?

"What is it?" Duncan asked. "Is there trouble?"

"Nay, not for me. There will be for you if you try to stop me."

He threw up his hands, as if surrendering to her. "I am not here to stop you."

"You lie." She narrowed her eyes, glaring at him, and tried to see if she could *know* if he lied, but there was nothing, as if she had never had a gift at all. She took a shuddering breath at the thought that she had lost the one thing that really set her apart and made her an asset to the clan who probably wished she'd never been born.

"I would never lie to you. I am not here to stop you, only to explain why I did not . . . do not believe you are ready to go into battle with the warriors."

"I need no explanation for betrayal. It does not matter why you betrayed my trust, only that you did."

"It matters greatly if you will but listen—"

"If you are not here to stop me from leaving, then turn around and go back to the caves."

"I cannot. If you leave, I will go with you, though you ken as well as I that this is not the way to get what you want."

"You are wrong. This is the only way to get what I want. It is not battle that I thirst for, Duncan. Surely you ken that."

"Vengeance. You want vengeance above everything else."

"Aye." With that made clear she sheathed her sword and spun away from him. "Go back, Duncan. You have no taste for vengeance."

She had not taken two steps when she was grabbed at the shoulder and found herself facing an angry Duncan, who gripped her hard by both shoulders.

"No one should have a taste for vengeance, Scotia." He shook her hard, accentuating his words, as if the shaking would rattle the vengeance out of her head. She wrenched herself free of his grip and stepped back.

"Have you learned nothing from me this last fortnight?" he continued, matching her glare with his own. "Vengeance is all about emotions running amok, and that is not the right mind to face battle. A mind fixed on vengeance is not capable of thinking through the ramifications of rash action. A mind fixed on vengeance is not capable of any soft feelings. Do you not have a single soft feeling within you, Scotia? Do you not have the ability to see how this choice you are making will cause trouble for all you claim to love?"

"Then it should cause no trouble for you, Duncan of Dunlairig." She notched her chin up and cut him in the only way she knew would truly hurt him. "I have no love for you." He winced, as if she'd slapped him hard across the face, and she knew the lie in her words, for her heart twisted at his pain.

"'Tis unfortunate," he said, his voice low and thick with an emotion she did not want to think about. "For though it shames me to admit it, I have loved you for a long time."

Shock took her breath. Loved her? He could not. He was Duncan . . . he had kissed her, touched her, but both had been in the heat of the moment. And yet, if she thought about the time they had spent together, his patience, his rare smiles and the compliments he had paid her skills even as he betrayed her. And her gift, at least until today when she was so angry she could not think straight, it had let her find him, always.

He drummed his fingers on his thighs, then shoved his hair out of his face. He paced back and forth along the path, then stopped in front of her, close enough that she could feel his breath upon her face, but he did not touch her.

"How I could ever love anyone so childish, so self-centered is beyond me. How could I ever have believed that you would grow out of your spoiled behavior? And now," he scoffed, "now your need for personal vengeance even at the risk of your entire clan . . . I must be daft. Or stupid.

"I thought you were changing, that you were embracing the things I was teaching you. I thought you would be able to take those lessons and use them in service to your clan, but you still fixate on vengeance. Vengeance is not worthy. Vengeance is born of hatred, and as long as hatred is your motivation, rather than the well being and prosperity of those you claim to love, your need for vengeance will only continue hurting everyone around you."

She stood there, desperately denying everything he said, though doubt hovered over her like the rain clouds overhead. And yet, she could find no words to defend herself.

"The thing is, Scotia, I think the one you hate is not the English. You blame them, but the one you really hate? That is yourself. I do not understand it, but it is the only thing that makes sense to me."

Silence stretched between them.

"Will you stop me?" she asked.

"Have I ever successfully stopped you from doing anything you really wanted to do?"

She thought of all the times he had come to her defense, even as he'd berated her for whatever folly she had fallen into at that moment. She thought of the times she had disappeared into the wood after a row with her sister, or a reprimand from her father, and how Duncan had followed her, watching over her, but never forcing her to return to the castle until she was ready. She remembered how he had stood ready to do whatever she needed in the days after her mother had been killed. And she thought of how he had helped her learn the skills needed if she ever went into battle.

"Nay, you have always looked out for me, even when I did not see it. Even when I did not want it." She looked away from him, as she struggled with what she wanted, and what he expected of her. "If I go, will you look out for me now?"

"Still you do not see that you cannot go into battle. Not now. Not this way. No warrior will trust you if you go against the wishes of your chief. No warrior will stand beside you in a fight when he cannot know if you will risk your own life for his."

"Not even you?" She saw a chasm opening up between her and Duncan, and was surprised at how lost she felt, knowing he stood on the far side. "You said you loved me. Would you not go into battle with me?"

He shook his head and stepped away. "I wash my hands of you, Scotia, as the rest of the clan was smart enough to do after Myles's death." He put more distance between them. "I have been blinded by my feelings for you." He took a long breath. "If you do this, no one will ever trust you again. If you do this, you will be beyond redemption."

CHAPTER SIXTEEN

SCOTIA STOOD WHERE DUNCAN HAD LEFT HER FOR A LONG time, her mind both full and blank, unable to form a coherent thought. She stood there long enough that the sun broke over the ben, burning away the clouds and casting warmth upon her back as if beckoning her to turn and walk into the sunshine, and out of the Glen of Caves. She stood there waiting for Duncan to come back to her.

Duncan always came back.

But as much as she wished it were true, in her heart she knew this time was different.

Anger surged, and she fought the need to stomp her feet and shriek at the unfairness. He had trained her. She had done everything he demanded of her. He was the one who had betrayed her trust, and yet he threw that in her face. *No warrior will trust you if you go against the wishes of your chief*, he had said.

"The wishes of my chief would be different if Duncan had but kept his part of the bargain," she muttered to herself as she turned and climbed the short distance to the shallow pass. "The wishes of my chief would be different if Duncan had but told him that I am well prepared in every way to take my rightful place in the coming battle." She clambered over the broken stones that littered the pass, and began her descent over the slippery scree that covered this side of the ben, her concentration consumed for the moment by the need for care. She'd never join the warriors if she broke her neck.

When she reached the more sure footing of the wood, partway down the ben, she dusted her hands off on her trews, and set off toward the castle. She knew not where the warriors were positioned, but she knew there would be guards near the castle who could direct her to . . .

It was only then that she remembered that her da and Uilliam were in charge of the warriors in the glen until Nicholas and his champion, Malcolm, could bring the Guardians closer to where the battle would be joined. If they beat her to the warriors, she knew her da would deny her the right to kill their foes, just as he had the day he took the life of the English spy who had killed her mum before she could ask for the honor for herself.

But it did not matter. She would simply hide close enough to watch the warriors, and when the battle began, she would take her place on the battlefield.

With luck her skills would be apparent before anyone realized who she was and tried to force her from the battlefield. Her conscience flinched at sneaking into the fight when she wanted their trust, but it was the only way. Once she had proved herself in battle, regardless of how she came to fight with them, they would have no choice but to let her continue.

She was a warrior. She had a gift of *knowing*—

"And what do we have 'ere?"

Scotia skidded to a stop.

"A woman in pants? I knew the Scots were barbaric, but that is more than I expected."

Scotia stared into the eyes of a large English soldier not twenty feet away, dressed in a dirty padded gambeson, a helm with enough dents in it to speak to much time in battle, and a sword like her own, drawn and pointing right at her. A slighter man stood a little behind him. This one was dressed in a particolored tunic, half a dirty white, half a faded blue. He held a bow already nocked with an arrow.

All the angry, hurt thoughts and feelings that had been wheeling through her head and gut ceased instantly as she slipped into the warrior-mind that Duncan had trained into her, saying nothing until she must and quickly assessing her opponents.

The older one was clearly in charge, both from his demeanor and his position in front of the other man. She judged she could not take him in a sword fight, for he was both taller than her and outweighed her, but she could outrun him with ease. Then she looked at the younger man. She had seen firsthand what an archer could do to a man perched high in a tree. He carried the longbow of the Welsh, and she doubted he would miss hitting her at such close range even if she were running away from him.

She held her hands up, away from the sword she so wanted to draw. She did not drop her shield, but with her hands up, they could see that she carried no hidden weapon behind it.

"Have you nothing to say for yourself?" the older one demanded.

"What are you saying?" she asked in the Gaelic, buying herself time to figure out what to do.

"Who are you?" The younger one spoke for the first time, and her suspicions were confirmed. He spoke a variation of the Gaelic, but the accent was not any she had heard before. Welsh, fighting for the English.

"Speak English, both of you!"

She looked at the younger one, with her eyebrows raised and what she hoped looked like confusion in her eyes.

"I do not think she speaks English, Adam," the younger man said. "Do you?" he asked her in the Gaelic.

"Do I what?" she responded as if she had not understood what he had said in English, not falling for his trick. The two men looked at each other, and she took a quick step backward. 'Twas little extra room, but it was better than standing still.

"How are you called?" the Welshman asked.

"Mairi," she replied, "Mairi of Kilfillon." They would not ken that she made up such a name or such a place. "I am lost. Can you tell me where I might find shelter and a meal?"

"I think you are MacAlpin," the Welshman said to her. He translated what he had asked and how she had replied for his companion. She took a quick glance around her while their attention was off her, looking for something that would help her escape, for she would die before she would allow herself to be taken prisoner by English soldiers again. She had skills this time, knowledge, and some experience at fighting, though not as much as she wished. If only Myles were standing at her back *now*, they would have a chance . . .

She stopped herself from thinking of that, of his death and her part in it, and focused only on getting away.

"What should we do with her?" the younger one asked Adam.

Adam looked over at Scotia, who did her best to look like a woman who knew nothing.

"She carries no food, no travel sack, and she did not approach us as if she were lost," he said, clearly thinking out loud, which was useful for Scotia, though it made it difficult to continue to feign ignorance of English. He motioned for the archer to circle around her, and the man slowly moved to her left, as if moving slowly would not scare her into running. "She carries weapons like a Scots warrior," Adam continued. "I did not know they armed their women."

Scotia moved closer to a tree, the only cover she could find with a quick glance about her. It would stop an arrow, though it would only be a moment before the archer was in position, so the tree was no hindrance to him, and the swordsman could easily slash around the trunk if he had to.

She expected the man to keep talking, to tell his partner that they could not take her prisoner because it would only slow them down, though they could torture her to find out what they needed about the MacAlpins. The one thing she was sure of was that they had no intention of letting her go.

Adam lunged for her with his blade, and she barely had time to lower her shield to stop the blow. Without thinking, she spun around and sprinted off into the wood. An arrow flew so close she could hear the faint whistle as it cut through the air. It struck a tree just in front of her with a solid thunk.

She darted off her course, cutting into a denser growth of trees. The arrows followed her. With each one, she changed directions, like a rabbit evading a wolf. If she could get far enough ahead of him the trees would protect her completely, but the man was quick both of foot and with his bow. She could not stop to make sure, but she thought she heard the other man crashing through the forest behind her and the archer.

Her mind raced through all the possibilities she could imagine. She needed to draw these two as far away as possible from where they met her in the hope they would not be able to find that place again. If they did find it, 'twould not be difficult to follow her trail right back into the Glen of Caves, for in her anger and hurt she had not remembered to hide her tracks.

Duncan was right about her . . . The words ran through her mind, but she refused to think about them. Not now.

She slowed, just enough for the archer to glimpse her through the trees. She watched as he loosed another arrow, judging where it would land but forcing her legs to move faster than ever, before it could hit exactly where she had been standing. She sprinted through the forest, her lungs burning, her mind focused on finding the best path, sometimes running down felled trees, as Duncan had her do so often, leaping over small burns without hesitation. She raced down a ravine, only to trip on a tree root, and tumble the rest of the way to the bottom. She lay there, looking up at the sky as she tried to get her breath back, but a shout from nearby had her scrambling to her feet and up the other side.

Once she made the top, she crossed a burn that rushed into the ravine not far below where she had fallen, then ran hard to put more distance between her and her pursuers. As she ran, she searched for the perfect place to turn up the benside, a place where her tracks would simply disappear. She found such a place in a recent tumble of rocks that reminded her of the curtain wall at Dunlairig Castle after it had fallen, a pile of rubble and nothing more. She hopped quickly from stone to stone, taking time only to check with care that she had left no print, no broken leaf, no overturned pebbles to mark her passing, until she reached the far side of it, where she purposely left the faintest mark for them to find, a single partial footprint where she let her heel touch down as she stood on a small stone.

With even greater care, she managed to return to the rubble field without leaving any sign that she had doubled back, and crossed the stones once more, heading up the ben this time. As she reached the edge of the stone-strewn area, she found enough rocks to make her way up the ben a short distance without leaving any sign of her passing. From there she stretched to get up on a fallen tree and picked her way further up the ben on it. When she reached the end of it she climbed off and crouched down in the lee of its roots that had been pulled out of the ground when it fell, and listened for the men who followed her.

After long moments she heard nothing but the usual sounds of the forest, birds twittering overhead, rustlings in the undergrowth, but none of the sounds of people, especially of men who had tried to keep up with her as she ran.

So where were they, and how could she find out without putting herself in jeopardy?

"I am a warrior," she whispered, reminding herself of all the things she had learned and needed right now. "I am skilled at tracking and at hiding my trail. I am a creative strategist. I have a gift of . . ."

Of course. Her gift! 'Twas her greatest weapon though not reliable when she needed it—it certainly hadn't told her Duncan had followed her to the pass, and it had not warned her of the English soldiers, either, but she had been so wrapped up in her anger, in Duncan's betrayal, that she might not have noticed if she had *known* either.

She took a long, slow, calming breath, quieting her mind and her body. She prayed that she could call upon her gift now, when she needed it so badly, but as she listened for the soldiers both with her ears and with her mind, nothing came to her. Nothing. Had her gift truly deserted her as much as Duncan had?

As she thought of him she *knew* that he waited for her below the pass inside the Glen of Caves. If he had followed her she would not be alone now. Anger threatened her focus, so she took another slow breath and turned her thoughts to the soldiers and to her gift, remembering only then that her gift was drawn to things and people she had an emotional connection to—like Duncan.

But the only emotional connection she had to the English swordsman and the Welsh archer was that she wanted to escape them. It would have to be enough.

She closed her eyes and brought to her mind exactly what the two scouts looked like, but then focused on the archer and his skill with the bow, even in the thick forest, and she realized 'twas likely he was the one who had killed Brodie as he sat high in a tree. 'Twas likely he was the one she had vowed to kill, and with that thought and the burst of determination that came with it, she *knew*.

Scotia made good time getting back to the main pass into the Glen of Caves while still being careful to make herself hard to follow. As she drew close, she gave the tawny owl call and slid behind a tree where she would not be seen from outside the glen, even though she *knew* the two soldiers were backtracking her original careless trail as she had feared, and would quickly end up at her private, unguarded pass. She shifted from foot to foot, trying to keep her impatience at bay so that her gift would not be hampered by it, waiting for whoever was guarding the pass to approach her.

"Why are you here, lassie?" Denis asked as he stepped onto the path that led into the glen. He looked about, as if only then taking note of the direction from which she had come. "How did you come to be outside the glen on your own?"

"I left by another pass, over the bens that way." She pointed south. "Two English soldiers are on their way there now. We must send guards to stop them. They will find the pass, but they must not be allowed to live to tell of it."

Denis moved closer to her in his odd side-to-side steps that spoke loudly that his knees were ailing him. She tended to forget that 'twas not just the women and weans who were kept here. Living in the wood could not be any easier on him and his old bones than was living in the caves for Peigi. Both needed to get back to the comforts of a real shelter, a real home.

"And how do you come by this information?" he asked. "Have you snuck out of the glen without your keeper and brought more trouble to us, Scotia? We've no time for more trouble than we already have." He stopped in front of her, a scowl that looked to be part pain, part irritation, pinching his face.

She started to deny what he clearly understood, then stopped. Denial would serve no one, not even herself, as she *knew* the soldiers would find their way to the other pass very soon.

"Aye, that is exactly what I have done, though 'twas not what I meant to do. You must send men to guard the tiny steep pass where the twin peaks of the next ben meet. If they do not go now, 'twill be too late."

Denis stared at her.

"Denis, if you do not believe me, 'twill mean the death of all you seek to keep safe."

"Why should I believe you, Scotia? What scheme are you about?"

"None, I swear it. What is the worst that will happen if you send men and I am wrong? They will have trekked there for naught but the discovery of a pass unguarded? But if I am right, then you will serve the clan as you always have, watching the gates and keeping them secure. I ken you have at least five men guarding this pass—I got past two of them without being seen, and with your knees—"

He winced, but she thought it was more irritation that she had noticed his pain than pain itself.

"—with your knees you must have at least two men who can fight for you if the need arises."

"Duncan has taught you too well."

"Aye, he has, and not well enough, or we would not be having this problem right now."

Denis stared at her, then shook his head. "Conall! Angus!" he shouted, then he whistled, three sharp notes. Conall and Angus arrived from either side of the pass, while she heard a third warrior coming up behind her. She refused to turn around, though, even when he said, "You did not pass unseen."

She looked over at him and found he was one of Malcolm's kin who had come here to help them fight the English, though she could not remember the young warrior's name.

"Tell them what you want them to do, lassie," Denis said, crossing his arms over his chest and leaning a little away from her.

Scotia looked at each one, only then realizing that she did not *know* if she was sending them to defend the clan or to die, perhaps both. Her breath caught in her throat, and she found it suddenly hard to breathe. But as she was getting so good at, she pushed that thought, that possibility, to the side and quickly told them how to find the pass and everything she could remember about the two soldiers, then Denis sent Conall and Angus on the way. As soon as they took their leave Denis turned to the MacKenzie man.

"Hector, take her to the chief," Denis said, "and make sure he kens exactly what has happened here." He gave Scotia that pinched scowl again. "And why."

CHAPTER SEVENTEEN

DUNCAN RAPIDLY PACED THE SAME STRETCH OF A DEER TRAIL he'd been pacing for hours, as he watched for Scotia to return from her secret pass, as he waited for her to do the right thing. But she did not come. Each time he paced north he decided he needed to return to the pass, find her, and drag her back to the caves before her rash actions caused more harm, but then, as he turned back southward, he reminded himself that he had washed his hands of her.

He had an actual ache in his chest at that thought. He'd abandoned her, and even though she deserved it with her return to her impulsive, selfish decisions that might put someone else in danger of dying, it was not something he did easily. She had been his to watch over for as long as he could remember.

A heaviness settled over him. He had failed in so many ways. He thought he had guided her to a real change, given her a purpose that focused her vibrant energy and challenged her sharp mind. He had believed her feelings had changed—for her purpose, and for him—but he had been wrong. It was as if everything they had done together these last weeks was a lie. She claimed he had only wanted to keep her close, but he knew now that she had only wanted him to blindly support her quest for vengeance.

He could not fathom what had possessed him to tell her of his feelings. He could not fathom why he had such deep feelings for her, or why it had been such a shock when she had denied them so vehemently.

He heard the horn blast once, and his first thought was that Scotia had returned, but if she came from the main pass that meant she had left the glen after all. In truth, he had known she would, if for no other reason than that he'd told her not to. Nothing good could come from such an expedition.

And then three long blasts of the horn made him forget everything except his duty to the clan.

Three blasts meant trouble.

SCOTIA LED THE WAY DOWN THE TRAIL INTO THE GLEN OF Caves with Hector right behind her, her sword, dagger, and shield now in his possession.

"Ye are a right wee eedjit," he muttered.

He was right.

"If Conall and Angus find their deaths this day because you brought the English right to this glen, 'twill be a mark against yer soul the likes of which you cannot redeem yourself from," he said.

"I ken that," Scotia replied. Never had she knowingly caused someone to be put in such a place of danger before. Conall was sweet, if not too smart. He did not deserve to die before he found a lass to love him better than she ever had, to give him bairns, and keep him warm on a cold winter's night. And Angus's bairns and his wife needed him. What would she do if either man died because of her folly this day?

"If yer chief has any ballocks he shall lock you in chains and keep you somewhere where you can never cause trouble again," Hector grumbled. "'Tis what I would do with you, were it my decision."

Scotia stumbled at the thought of being so helpless, but caught her footing before she fell. After being held captive by the English at the Story Stone she had sworn to herself she would never be held in such a way again, that she would never allow herself to be put in such a helpless position.

If Nicholas commanded this, would she be able to do as her chief ordered? Duncan would say it was her duty to do as Nicholas said, even if it meant a certain death.

She swallowed hard, pressing back the panic that just the thought of being tied up again raised within her. She should run, flee, before they had a chance to do such a thing to her, but—Duncan's voice whispered in her mind—if she allowed it, or any other punishment without a fight or an argument, it might show her contrition and her understanding of what she had done.

"I might add in a flogging, just to make sure you remembered the lesson," Hector said. A note of satisfaction in his voice made it sound like he'd just said they would have honey cakes for dinner.

The trouble was, she knew he was right. 'Twas what she deserved. She could not deny that she had failed in every one of her lessons.

She had failed to keep her temper in check. She had failed to think of others before herself, or how her actions might cause harm. She had failed to cover her tracks. She had failed to kill the soldiers herself, running instead. She had failed in every way possible, letting down everyone she loved.

She had failed Duncan most of all.

He had been right. She was not ready to be a warrior or she never would have left the glen when her mind was so full of anger and betrayal. If she were truly ready to be a warrior, she would have afforded him the respect to listen to him, to heed his warning. But she didn't.

She could see all too clearly now that he was not the one to break faith with her. She was the one who had broken faith with him. He had always been clear that when he deemed her ready, he would champion her right to join the warriors in battle, and she had agreed. She had broken the pact between them, all because her pride was hurt and her drive for vengeance was stymied. No wonder he was so angry with her. No warrior would go back on his, or her, word. For all her accomplishments with sword and shield, she had failed to learn this most basic lesson.

And now, not only was she not ready to be a warrior, she had thrown away the man who believed she could become one. She had betrayed the trust of the one person who was her constant champion, the one person who truly loved her.

The one person she loved above all others. The thought almost stopped her heart. She loved him. And now she realized that she had been lying to herself for a long time. She loved Duncan. He was always in her mind, by her side, encouraging, teaching . . . hoping she would grow up enough to one day return his love, despite what everyone thought of her, despite her own behavior. And it was only now that she had lost his love that she realized she had loved him all her life.

She was a selfish chit.

If she had listened to him, to allow him to explain the lesson she had just learned the hard way, none of this would have happened. If she'd only trusted him she might be folded in his arms now, telling him of her feelings for him, instead of facing her family and revealing yet another failure on her part.

They should bind her to a tree.

They should banish her to a lonely life where she could bring no more harm to anyone she loved.

It was what she deserved.

It was *exactly* what she deserved.

DUNCAN SKIDDED TO A HALT AS HE ARRIVED IN THE CAVE clearing just as the Guardians emerged from the path that led to their bower by the burn. Nicholas and Malcolm, along with all the lads they had been training, stood at the far end of the clearing, weapons at the ready, while the women and the weans scattered into the forest, all except Peigi, who sat in her accustomed place near the cookfire.

He looked at her with raised brows, asking without the need for words why she remained.

"I am too auld to caper off into the forest, lad," she said, waving a wooden ladle in his direction. "If 'tis the English they will find a fight on their hands from more than you warriors and Guardians!"

Duncan laughed quietly, grateful to the old woman for reminding him that sometimes a person just had to stand one's ground, no matter the consequences.

"If it comes to that, Peigi, I will gladly fight at your back."

"Of course you will." She leaned a little to the side to look behind him. "Where is your charge?"

He sighed. "I dinna ken. I fear she has gone off and caused whatever trouble is coming into the glen, and 'tis my fault for leaving her alone."

Peigi rose to her feet and stood before him. "She is no child, Duncan." She accentuated each word with a poke of her finger in the middle of his chest. "For all her foolish tempers, she is a woman grown, and it is she who is responsible for her actions, not you."

He nodded and rubbed at the place on his chest, where he was certain a bruise would form. "I ken that, but still I feel responsible. I thought she had changed. I was certain of it, but she has not, and in my anger and disappointment, I left her."

Peigi clucked her tongue against her teeth. "You canna see the lass clearly, Duncan. She has changed these last weeks, but perhaps not enough. Not yet. Do not give up on her altogether. She just might surprise you."

"She surprised me today when I discovered she has thrown aside all I have tried to teach her and retreated back into her selfish ways."

Peigi twitched a gnarled hand toward the far end of the clearing. "It seems she has returned."

The clenched fist in Duncan's gut loosened. She was alive and appeared unharmed, but Malcolm's cousin, Hector, accompanied her.

"Go, laddie!" Peigi gave him a push. "Find out what trouble our Scotia brings with her."

Scotia stood silently next to Hector, facing Nicholas and Malcolm, as Hector relayed what had happened. She dared not look at Duncan as he pushed through the line of lads who still held their weapons—swords, dirks, and rocks—at the ready behind the chief and his champion. If she saw the disappointment still there in Duncan's eyes, or worse, hatred, she would ken that she had truly lost him. She pressed her lips together and fought to keep her composure.

He stopped just behind Malcolm.

"Denis sent Conall and Angus to watch the pass this one"— Hector glared over at her—"did not tell us of, but they will need help. The archer will make it impossible for our lads to attack them in the open of the pass, and they cannot guard the pass and hunt down the soldiers all alone."

"I ken where the other pass is," Duncan said, his voice harsh as if he, too, fought to contain his emotions. She glanced up, unable to keep herself from looking at him, but he did not look at her. "I can follow Scotia's trail out of it and find the soldiers faster than anyone else can."

Malcolm and Nicholas both looked back at him. "You ken where this pass is, and that she had left by it, and you said nothing?" Nicholas almost snarled at him.

"He only learned of it today." Scotia took a step forward to defend Duncan, then stopped when he took a step back, the reality of the loss of him, of his support, of his love, only then really sinking in. She stepped back, squared her shoulders, and looked only at Nicholas. "'Tis my fault alone that this has happened. He tried to stop me"—she took a deep breath but did not let her gaze falter—"but I refused to listen to his good counsel."

Scotia heard Peigi's wheezy laugh and saw her behind the line of lads, nodding her head, her gaze locked with Scotia's, and Scotia almost felt a push from the auld woman to keep going.

"Time is of the essence, Nicholas," Scotia said. "The soldiers may have already found their way to the pass. I will go with Duncan. This is a mess of my making, and 'tis only right I should help clean it up."

"Nay—" Duncan said, but Malcolm cut him off.

"Clean it up?" Malcolm asked. "Do you think this is a spilled kettle?"

"Nay, I do not," Scotia said. Her temper flared like a flame igniting in her gut, but she kept it in check, calling on all the training Duncan had given her to keep a cool head, to think clearly even in battle, for in truth, this was a battle for her place in the clan. Her life, her future, and the future of her clan depended on how she managed herself in this moment.

"I do not think 'tis a spilled kettle," she said calmly. "I understand *exactly* what this is. I understand that I have let my selfish needs drive my actions for too long. I have shamed myself. I broke my promise to Duncan, and I take full responsibility for whatever happens. I understand exactly what I have done and how it has put the entire clan in danger, just as I put Myles in danger and it cost him his life."

That statement caught her by surprise, but she knew she spoke from her heart, that what she said was true. She *was* responsible for Myles's death, just as everyone had been telling her. Remarkably, she found it was a relief to understand what she'd done, to admit to it. No longer would she have to defend herself, for she understood there was no defense of her actions. None of them.

"I was responsible for Myles's death, though I did not intend it to happen. I am responsible for leading these soldiers to this glen. I did not intend it to happen. 'Tis a recurring theme in my life, but do you truly think I want to see the same thing happen to my entire clan, to see them wiped out by the damned English? Do you think I want the Highlands overrun with the vermin because I have prevented the Guardians from having the time to learn how to create the true Highland Targe? Everything I have done was in pursuit of vengeance, beginning with my mum's murder and my failure to prevent it."

"You could not have prevented that," Jeanette said, surprising Scotia. She had not noticed the Guardians standing in the shadow of the trees to her right. "I was there and I was not able to prevent it."

Scotia closed her eyes for a moment and heard Duncan's voice in her head. *The thing is, Scotia, I think the one you hate is not the English. You blame them, but the one you really hate? That is yourself. I do not understand it, but it is the only thing that makes sense to me.*

If she had any hope of keeping her place in the clan, she knew she could keep secrets no longer, no matter what they thought of her afterward. A warrior must be trustworthy. And though she knew she would never be allowed to join the warriors, if she ever wanted anyone to trust her again she must begin with the full truth.

"I *knew* the spy was in the tower," she said to Jeanette. "I *knew* his intention. My fear over losing Mum was already so strong I denied what I *knew*, and instead acted on another *knowing*, that wee Ian was trapped in the burning kitchen. If I had been stronger, braver, she might yet live."

A silence unlike any she had experienced before wrapped around her as she waited for the hatred she knew she deserved. She had allowed her mother to be murdered because she was too much a coward to face her fear.

"Nay, she would not." Duncan's voice slid through the silence. "She was already dying. She was in pain. You told me that yourself." He stepped up to stand on Malcolm's left where he could look at her. "Just that morn, Jeanette told me Lady Elspet would not likely live another day. Ian is but a child with his full life ahead of him. Given the choice, your mum would have made the same decision. 'Tis what she would have wanted you to do."

"Duncan is right," Jeanette said as she moved toward Scotia and took Scotia's cold hands in her own. "Sister, nothing could have prevented what happened. Mum drew his attention trying to protect me. Then I told him Rowan had the Targe in an attempt to get him to leave Mum alone. It was then he killed her and knocked me out when I tried to stop him. She did what she could, even in her state, to keep us all safe. Do you not think rescuing wee Ian would have been her choice for you, rather than putting yourself in the path of that monster?"

Scotia tried to understand what her sister said to her, shocked by the softness and concern Jeanette was showing her. A heaviness she had not known she carried started to slide off her shoulders.

"Truly?"

"Aye. Truly. She would not want you to blame yourself for what happened. She would want you to learn from it, aye, but not seek vengeance for something she chose to do."

"Even if what you say is true—"

"It is," Jeanette said. "I was the one there, and you ken well that Mum was a gentle soul. She would never want you to cause harm to anyone for her sake, especially not to yourself."

Scotia swallowed and looked about, waiting for someone to . . . she knew not what she expected, but it was not understanding. "But I *am* responsible for Myles's death, and I have led the English to this glen. I know that now, and I need to do something to atone for that." Something tickled the back of her mind, but she could not grasp it.

Nicholas cleared his throat. "Are you sure there are only two soldiers?" he asked Scotia. "Are you certain?"

"I am. An English swordsman named Adam and a Welsh archer. I dinna ken his name, but I think he must be the one who killed Brodie."

"And why did he not kill you?"

"Duncan taught me well."

Nicholas sighed. "Duncan, take Hector and two more of your choosing and hurry to the pass. Capture these English soldiers if you can and bring them back here, blindfolded and in such a way they will not know how to return here if they were to get away. If you cannot capture them, do not let them live to tell this tale." He looked at Scotia, but he was still talking to Duncan. "Return here as soon as you can. It seems we have a decision to make, and you must be a part of it."

Duncan nodded, but his eyes were on Scotia before he pointed at two more of Malcolm's kinsmen, and led them quickly out of the clearing. Nicholas sent the lads scurrying into the forest to join the women and do what they could to keep them safe if it came to that.

Nicholas looked over at his wife, then at Jeanette and Malcolm, the only ones left in the clearing except for Peigi.

"Rowan, can you keep the three of you safe in your bower?"

"Aye. The barrier we erected there is very strong."

"We will take Scotia there"—he looked back at her—"but I want her secured, bound hand and foot if no other way."

Jeanette started to interrupt him, which warmed Scotia's heart more than it should have, but Nicholas stopped her.

"I ken she is your sister, but she is a danger to this clan. Every time she roams free, trouble happens, and we have enough trouble already. I am the chief. I say she will be bound until Duncan returns and we can decide what to do with her."

Jeanette started to speak once more, but this time Scotia stopped her. "Sister, he is right"—her voice wobbled just a little, but she was determined to take without complaint whatever punishment he deemed necessary—"and though I have no intention of bringing further trouble here, I cannot promise it won't happen, for I have never meant to bring trouble to our clan."

Nicholas nodded at her, but his eyes were unreadable.

CHAPTER EIGHTEEN

NIGHT WAS FALLING. A CRACKLING FIRE CAST A SMALL CIRCLE OF flickering light around the Guardians where they worked near the burn, leaving Scotia alone in the dark. Her back was beginning to hurt. Her hands were numb, and so were her feet. Malcolm had trussed her up like a deer ready for roasting, then tied a rope around her waist and the tree, just as she'd been tied to the Story Stone. It had taken every bit of courage she could muster to let him do that to her without complaint. She hadn't said a single word.

She did not think she had another word in her after her confessions of this afternoon anyway. She had told the truth about almost everything, not knowing if it was too late to make a difference. She still didn't know, wouldn't until Duncan returned and she could tell him that she had lied when she said she held no love for him.

She closed her eyes and concentrated on Duncan, saying his name over and over in her head until she *knew* he was still alive. He felt closer now, as if he were heading back to the glen. Would he even give her a chance to tell him of her heart?

He must, even if he could no longer love her. It was her last secret, held so tightly she had hidden it even from herself.

Something passed over her, a sensation that made every hair on her skin stand up.

"How often do you have to renew the barrier?" she asked, recognizing the sensation as the same one she felt when she entered and left the bower, passing through the barrier.

"I thought you had gone to sleep," Jeanette said, but did not look at her sister. She was moving her hands through the air in one of the blessings their mum had taught both of them many years ago. She had discovered that it strengthened a barrier once it was created.

"I could never sleep like this," Scotia said, holding her bound hands up to make her point.

Rowan looked over at her. "That is the first time you have even made reference to your situation. 'Tis most unlike you, cousin."

"Do you think I cannot change?"

"I think that remains to be seen." Rowan held the Targe stone up in front of her, face high, and a light breeze whipped up, swirling around the bower.

"What are you doing?" Scotia asked, desperately needing something to take her mind off the pins and needles in her hands, and the chill of the ground that was creeping into her backside.

"Practicing. Just as you have practiced your sword skills with Duncan, we must practice using our gifts through the stone."

The breeze grew stronger as Rowan closed her eyes and concentrated. A branch cracked overhead, then flew across the bower to land, broken end buried in the ground. Rowan opened her eyes and grinned.

"'Tis a handy thing to be able to do, aye?" she asked no one in particular.

"Wheesht," Jeanette said. She was staring into an overfilled cup of water sitting on the ground in front of her, one hand held out to Rowan, who moved the stone close enough for Jeanette to touch it.

"Can you see where the English are?" Scotia asked.

Rowan and Jeanette both shushed her.

Scotia watched as her cousin and her sister did things she would never be able to do. They prepared for battle in their own ways, not warriors with sword and shield, but warriors all the same. Scotia knew she would never be a warrior of any sort.

She was still trying to understand what Duncan and Jeanette had said to her, that she had not been responsible for letting the spy get to her mum. Even if she had not caused her mum's death, the belief that she had and the guilt that came with that belief had changed her, moving her in a direction she never would have imagined, filling her with pain, and hatred, and a need to see vengeance done.

That need for vengeance had driven her to seek out the English on her own, which had put Myles directly in danger and had cost him his life. He had died right next to her, and she had not even been allowed to give him comfort as he did. That lay heavy on her conscience too, turning her in yet another direction—preparing herself for battle so she would never put another warrior in a position to protect her when she should do that herself.

Two deaths. Two times her world was broken and put back together in a new way . . .

She looked at the ermine sack that lay on the ground between the Guardians.

Twice broken . . . like the arrow on the sack and on the Story Stone. Was it possible? But if she was meant to be the third Guardian, if the twice-broken arrow really was her symbol, then why had the Targe not claimed her the day at the Story Stone, as Jeanette had been claimed when she found her mirror symbol on the grotto stone?

And then Scotia realized she knew the answer. She was not worthy to become a Guardian. Not then, but now? Now that she understood the things she had done wrong, the things the fear and hatred in her heart had led her to do, the things that she had admitted to and taken responsibility for, now would she be worthy?

If she was, it would mean they had yet another Guardian to help protect the clan and the Highlands. If she was, would her gift of *knowing* become stronger? Would she be able to use it at will? 'Twould make her gift an even more formidable weapon against their enemy.

And if she was not worthy? That would be yet another thing she would have to take responsibility for, for if she was not worthy, 'twas no one's fault but her own, and the clan would be the one to suffer for her failures. She could not bear to let anyone else suffer because of her.

She needed to talk to Duncan.

Scotia waited for Jeanette to sit back on her heels. Her head hung down as if she were tired, or sad.

"Well?" Rowan asked.

"I cannot tell where the English are any better than I could this morn. If only I had traveled toward Oban once or twice I might be able to identify the land I can see around them."

"Well, at least we know they are not in Glen Lairig yet," Scotia said. "That means they must still be at least a day's march from the castle, aye?"

Jeanette lifted her head and shifted off her knees to sit so she could see both Rowan on her right and Scotia on her left.

"I suppose it does, and that alone is useful," she said.

"I might have something else of use," Scotia said, trying to scoot more upright, but only succeeding in scratching her back on the tree's rough bark. "I think the third symbol really is mine."

DUNCAN ARRIVED BACK AT THE CAVES WITH THE THREE MacKenzies and the blindfolded archer, who was injured but not badly enough to keep him from answering questions.

Nicholas came out of the surrounding trees without a sound. "The other one?" he asked.

"Dead," Duncan replied.

Nicholas nodded at the three MacKenzies and pointed down the path to the Guardians' bower. They took their leave, clearly meant to take up posts guarding the Guardians.

"What's your name?" Nicholas asked the prisoner.

"Bryn of Beaumaris," he answered without hesitation as Malcolm joined them from the same path the others had taken.

"An archer, aye? From Wales?" Nicholas asked.

"I am."

"Why did you let yourself be caught?" Duncan asked. It had been exceedingly odd that as soon as the older soldier had fallen, Bryn had thrown down his bow and given himself up.

"I have no love for the English. I was taken from my home and my family and impressed into service in Edward's army when I was ten and five. I was good with a bow. All of us who had any skill with the bow were taken by the king's army."

"Why did you not escape and return home if you have no love for the English?" Malcolm asked.

Bryn's head jerked as he looked in Malcolm's direction, though Duncan was certain the man could see nothing. "I have no home to go to. My father was a mason. We followed the castles and lived in the work camps. It has been at least ten years since I became an archer. I know not where my family might be now."

The three men looked at each other. Duncan shrugged, not sure whether to believe the man or not. It would be useful if one of the Guardians could tell if someone spoke the truth.

That dragged his thoughts away from Bryn to Scotia. What had Nicholas done with her? He knew better than to speak of clan business in front of their prisoner, but he was worried about her, regardless of how angry he still was with her latest debacle. He was not pleased with himself for worrying. He should be done with her, but he could not stop his concern. The look in her eyes when she was exposing all her fears and mistakes, when she took responsibility for Myles's death, and her mum's, had been so sincere, so without guile or pretense. He had forced himself to keep away from her, though he had not been able to stand there and watch her blame herself for her mum's murder.

It all made sense now, though, the changes in her, the choices she'd made.

"How far away are Lord Sherwood and his forces?" Malcolm asked.

Bryn sighed. "They are at least two days away unless he leaves the supplies and everyone but the soldiers to make their way separately. If he brings only the soldiers and they are all on foot, a day, perhaps a day and a half."

Duncan looked to Malcolm, who was nodding his head slightly.

"How many men does he have?" Malcolm asked.

"He started with two score, but they have been harried almost every night since we arrived by other Scots. Perhaps a score and ten now? I am not sure as I've been scouting this area for several days."

"Take him to the training area, Duncan," Nicholas said. "Secure him there. Gag him. I will send someone to take over his watch. We have another situation to see to."

"You do not mean to kill me now I've cooperated?" Bryn asked. "According to Lord Sherwood all Highlanders are murderous brigands, but then that's what he says about the Welsh, too."

"Do not count on your future just yet, archer," Nicholas said and signaled Duncan to take the man away.

The wood was dark and the moon had not risen yet, so it was slow going taking the man down into the glen. Duncan had barely secured Bryn in the training area when one of the older and more able lads arrived. He motioned for Duncan to head to the Guardians' bower without so much as a sound. Clearly he had been instructed not to speak in front of the prisoner. Duncan pulled hard on the bindings.

"If you continue as you have begun," he said to the archer, "and we do not find that you have lied to us, there is hope for you. Cross us, and you will be dead before you see it coming. You"—he looked at the lad—"stay standing. 'Tis too easy to let your mind wander or your eyes close if you sit."

The lad nodded vigorously, and Duncan headed back up the ben, fatigue and an empty belly finally catching up with him.

When he reached the bower he found the Guardians and their husbands huddled together near a small fire. Scotia was tied to a tree, and he could tell she was focused entirely on the whispered conversation, though he doubted she could hear much of it. She looked tired, but something about her had changed once again. Where she had lost her unique spark earlier, when she confessed her sins, she now almost glowed with it.

"You have missed much, laddie." Peigi surprised him. He must truly be tired not to have noticed her sitting on a large stone just next to where he stood. She held out a hand to him, and he helped her to her feet. "I set aside a few bannocks for you, though I was not able to bring the evening's stew with me when they forced me out of the cave site." She opened a pouch hanging from her belt and handed him three bannocks.

They were dry, but he was hungry enough he cared not.

"Duncan is here," Peigi announced then, startling the group by the fire as if they, too, had not known she was there.

He heard Scotia say his name, but he did not look at her. He was afraid he would forgive her for what she had done this day, and he was not ready to do that.

"What has happened?" he asked.

"It would seem the Guardians have a plan for Scotia, and they will not condone any sort of punishment for her until they are done with her," Nicholas said, clearly irritated with the wife he adored.

"I believe—" Scotia started to speak, and he almost looked at her.

"She makes a compelling case that she is the third Guardian, Duncan," Rowan said. "We must find out if she is right before we do anything else."

"But nothing happened when she found the broken-arrow symbol upon the Story Stone," he said. "When Jeanette found—"

He stopped. He looked at Scotia, and suddenly he understood. "What makes you think you are worthy now?"

THE FORCE OF DUNCAN'S QUESTION PUSHED SCOTIA BACK against the tree. His eyes were narrowed, and his hands were fisted by his side. The pain and distrust she saw in him opened up a hollow place in her chest that she feared only he could fill. She tried to rub it away with the heel of her hand, only to be harshly reminded that she was still trussed up like a prisoner.

She dropped her hands back into her lap, took a deep breath, and tried to steady her nerves. This was too important not to tread carefully, but absolutely truthfully, with Duncan.

"I dinna ken if I am worthy," she began, choosing her words with care, "but I understand the symbol now, and Jeanette said only the one meant for that symbol would understand it." She explained what she had figured out to him, just as she had twice already, once to the Guardians and once to their Protectors. She watched him as she spoke, trying to determine if he believed her, but she could see no change in his expression or posture.

When she stopped speaking everyone waited for him to say something, but he just stared at her.

"We must take her back to the Story Stone, Duncan," Jeanette said, her voice pitched low, as if she spoke to a wild animal easily spooked. "We must find out if she is truly meant to be a Guardian. She may be the piece that we are missing. She may be the key to creating a true Highland Targe. Rowan and I have tried and tried to create one without success. Small barriers, aye, we can do that, but we cannot make one that could protect this route into the Highlands. If she is a third Guardian . . ."

"It is too dangerous to take anyone to the Story Stone meadow," Duncan said. "The English could be as little as a day away. Lord

Sherwood may have sent other scouting parties ahead. There is no cover there, no way to keep two Guardians safe."

"We can keep ourselves safe, Duncan," Rowan said, an edge to her voice that Scotia well recognized from when she did or said something her cousin did not like. "We, the Guardians and the Protectors, have decided this must be done. Malcolm has a plan for how to make it as safe as possible for everyone. We leave before dawn."

"So she has convinced you to put all of us at risk for her scheme?"

"Duncan!" There was scorn in his words, but Scotia knew they were meant for her, not Rowan, and that he would hate himself come dawn for speaking to the Guardian in such a disrespectful manner, and that, too, would be her fault. "Duncan, please, listen to me."

She desperately wanted to stand. Sitting looking up at him as she said what must be said left her feeling helpless and all too vulnerable, but there was naught she could do about that right now. "I ken I have hurt you and destroyed whatever trust I had earned from you, but this is not for me. This is for the clan. This is a way that I can be of service to everyone I have wronged. It may not change the way I am thought of, but that is not at issue. The safety of the clan, the protection of the Highlands, and the chance to do what needs doing for the right reasons, that is what is important. That is what you have taught me, though I was late to understanding the lessons. If I fail to be chosen as a Guardian, so be it. But if I can make it possible to create a true Targe, then we have to try. Aye?"

"Listen to the lassie," Peigi said softly. "Listen with your heart and you will hear that she speaks from hers."

Scotia pressed her lips together and blinked away the moisture that tried to gather in her eyes. Peigi believed her.

"There is one more thing I must say to you, Duncan," Scotia said before he said anything that might dash the hope that still flickered in her. "There is one last lie that I must own up to, and for it I ask your forgiveness, for I told it to hurt you when you did not deserve any more hurt than I had already caused."

He looked away from her, and she thought he closed his eyes.

"Please, Duncan, look at me. Please?"

He turned his gaze back to her, but his face was devoid of any emotion as if his heart had frozen against her, and she knew it was too late. She could not mend what she had broken so completely, but she still must tell him the truth. She had promised herself no more lies.

"Duncan, I told you I held no love for you in my heart. 'Twas a lie. 'Twas an evil, hateful lie. I dinna ken when it started, but I ken now that I have loved you for as long as I can remember. At first I idolized you like a big brother, but you are *not* my brother, and as I have grown, so my feelings have changed and grown, too. You have lavished your care and attention on me my whole life. You have watched over me, kept me safe, even from myself at times. You have been my teacher, my guide, my rock, and lately you have been my friend, and I threw it all away with my . . . when I should have . . ."

She steadied herself, determined not to shed a single tear though her heart was truly breaking, and she knew beyond doubt that she had done this to herself.

"I am sorry, Duncan, more than you can know, that I did not have the room in my heart to allow these feelings out. I love you, Duncan, and I hope someday you can find a way to forgive me for the terrible things I have done. I hope, someday, we might be"— she took a deep breath—"friends again."

Duncan stared at her for a long, long moment, then without a word to anyone, he left.

CHAPTER NINETEEN

SCOTIA HAD NOT SLEPT AT ALL, EVEN THOUGH JEANETTE HAD decided, against both Nicholas's and Malcolm's wishes, to cut her loose from the tree. Sometime in the night she had heard Peigi join one of the groups of people passing near the bower on their way back to the caves and was grateful that they had not needed to abandon the glen altogether, and that Peigi could return to her heather mattress in the great cave. If the clan had not been able to return to the caves, that would have also been her fault, but as usual Duncan, with the help of the MacKenzies, had saved the clan from that necessity.

As Scotia lay on the cold ground, wrapped in a plaid, she stared across the small space at her sister, wrapped in the arms of Malcolm, and her cousin, asleep with her head in Nicholas's lap as he kept watch. A loneliness so deep it stopped her breath pulled at her, as if it might tear her apart, bit by bit, and the distance between herself and the others in the bower seemed to stretch and grow, leaving her more alone than ever.

She missed her mum. She missed the light that used to shine in her da's eyes when she was a wean and got into mischief. She missed the way Duncan would take her hand and draw her away from trouble with the promise of a story or a sweet when she was little, and how of late he had driven her in her training to be faster, stronger, better.

She missed the smell of him, and the sure touch of his hands upon her when he stood close behind her and helped her adjust the angle of her sword, or the position of her shield.

She missed the kisses they had shared, the passion he had roused in her, and wished with all her heart that she had taken it upon herself to kiss him just one more time before she had thrown everything away.

Duncan had loved her, though she doubted he ever would again. All she could do to prove that she had changed was to live the lessons he'd taught her, both the warrior lessons and the smaller lessons he had tried to teach her for years about how to be a better person, how to think of others first, and how to mind her emotions so they did not continue to put her and those around her in danger. He might never love her again, and for that she could not blame him, but perhaps, in time, they might find a way to be friends, true friends this time, for she would think of his needs before her own, as he always did for her. It was not all that she wanted, not nearly, but it would be something. It would have to be enough.

She rolled over, putting her back to the Guardians and their husbands, and pulled her plaid tightly to her as she tried to put everything out of her mind. But there, deep within, she *knew* that Duncan kept a restless watch not far away. Tears gathered but, as always, she refused to let them fall. She would always *know* where Duncan was.

As soon as the sky began to lighten with the coming day Jeanette had scried with her cup and could see no trouble for them at the Story Stone, though as always, she said she could not promise she had seen this specific day. Truly they did not have a choice, even if there was trouble waiting for them there. Once the English moved into Glen Lairig 'twould be too dangerous to go to the stone, and the Guardians were sure, as was Scotia, that if she were chosen as another Guardian, it would happen at the Story Stone.

When the two Guardians, their Protectors, Duncan, and Scotia left the Guardians' bower and the Glen of Caves for the Story Stone meadow, the sky was changing from pale grey to the bright blue of a summer's morn, embellished with lacy clouds in shades of pinks and purples. Birds twittered and sang all around them, a dawn chorus that usually pleased Scotia, but this morning she found the noise not melodic and beautiful but loud, and each bird at odds with the others until the sound battered at her senses, making her grumpy and out of sorts, though she did her best to keep her feelings to herself.

They did not take a direct route to the stone, but rather searched out Kenneth, Uilliam, and the contingent of warriors they had been working with to set up traps and ambushes for the English. That project would have to wait until this test was complete. For now, every warrior they could find must accompany them to the meadow, leaving only enough to keep watch for the English. The safety of the Guardians came before all else.

Each time they gathered more of the MacAlpin warriors, Duncan would move to the back of the growing group. He told Nicholas he would watch the rear, but Scotia knew, without her gift, that he really sought to put more distance, and more people, between the two of them. He had not looked at her all morning, nor answered her quiet "good morn."

She wanted to demand his attention, and she would have once gotten into some mischief to get it, but this time she knew better. She knew she could not force him to talk to her, or even to look at her, and she knew any "mischief" she got into now would put lives in danger, so she kept her place near the front of the group, just behind Jeanette and Rowan, and tried to forget that Duncan was not next to her.

The two Protectors, along with her da and Uilliam, led the group, and a contingent of six warriors surrounded the front and sides where the Guardians walked. Just behind Scotia came the rest of their fighting force, leaving Scotia as the only individual in the group with no particular role to play should they find trouble, though Nicholas had surprised her when they woke before dawn by telling her to bring her weapons. She had gladly strapped her sword and her dagger at her waist, and taken up her round wooden shield. Part of her wished they would find trouble so she could prove her warrior skills, but she knew that would be a terrible thing. Besides, if her wishes really could come true, Scotia would shortly find herself a Guardian, and she, Rowan, and Jeanette would, on the spot if they could, erect a true Highland Targe, stopping the English before they ever set foot in Glen Lairig. But wishing had never accomplished anything for Scotia.

Despite the cool of the deep wood, she wiped her sweaty hands on her trews and pushed the stray tendrils of her hair that always escaped her braid off her sticky face.

As they drew close to the Story Stone, Malcolm gave orders, spreading most of the warriors just inside the perimeter of the meadow to keep watch for anyone who approached, and to stop anyone who did, at all cost. Her da and Uilliam would join that contingent, as would Duncan. The remaining eight warriors were to come to the stone with the Guardians, the Protectors, and Scotia.

Duncan's eyes narrowed. "Last night you agreed I would be in the inner perimeter."

"Aye, but I had a chance to sleep on it and decided different this morn," Malcolm said. "Nicholas agrees."

"But he should come with us," Scotia said, then immediately regretted it when both Malcolm and Duncan turned black looks her way. She threw up her hands. "I am not a Guardian, so what I want has nothing to do with this." She turned away and bit her bottom lip, determined to keep silent until the she and the Guardians were at the stone, though she wanted him by her side as she faced her future.

He was the one who understood her gift best, better even than she did, so if things did not go as she and the Guardians hoped they would, his counsel might be of great help. But maybe that was why they sent him away. Maybe they did not want him helping her. She turned back to find him staring at her, but he quickly averted his gaze.

"Keep them safe," he said to Malcolm and Nicholas. The champion and the chief just nodded, and they all prepared to take up their positions. Duncan disappeared silently in the direction that Kenneth and Uilliam had taken. The women and the remaining warriors waited for the signal that all was clear in the perimeter, then headed carefully out to the standing stone.

As soon as they reached the hillock where the English had held Scotia, she led the Guardians around to the far side of the stone and showed them the symbols she had found the last time she and Duncan were here.

Jeanette stood, staring at the carvings, while Rowan knelt upon the ground, opened the ermine sack, and spread it so the Highland Targe stone sat in the middle, on top of the three swirls in a circle symbol. The unclaimed broken-arrow symbol was closest to the Story Stone. The warrior in Scotia was happy that she would have something to protect her back while, at least in the direction she was facing, she would be able to see any trouble approaching in time to prepare for battle.

"You may need to touch the Story Stone, Scotia," Rowan said, "as Jeanette was in contact with the stone in the grotto that holds the mirror symbol when she was chosen as a Guardian."

"How will I know if I need to?" she asked.

Rowan shrugged. Jeanette settled in her spot to Scotia's right, and shook her head.

"Trust your instincts," Jeanette said, as she pulled her small wooden scrying cup from a fold of her arisaid and held it up for Malcolm to fill it to overflowing with water from a skin. Jeanette set the water in front of her, near the edge of the ermine sack. "If you feel you should touch the stone, do."

"That is not much guidance, sister."

"It is not. Perhaps someday we will understand enough to teach the next Guardian better, but for now, this is the best we can do."

"Jeanette? The blessing?" Rowan said, her auburn brows raised.

"Aye." Jeanette said the words none of them understood while gracefully flowing her hands through the air in the series of symbols Elspet had taught her. "We should set up a barrier, too, as we have done in the bower."

Rowan nodded. Without a word she lifted the Targe stone in her hands and held it heart high. Jeanette touched the water lightly with the fingers of her right hand and the stone with her left. Almost immediately Scotia felt a prickle on her skin as a barrier that could not be seen, but could be felt, spread out from the stone until it surrounded the three women, the standing stone, and the two Protectors. The other five warriors created a perimeter just outside the edge of the barrier. Scotia was surprised.

"No wind?" She looked at Rowan. Usually Rowan's gift was accompanied by at least a breeze.

"Only when I use my specific gift," Rowan said, settling the Targe back on its sack. "Let us begin." Then both Guardians looked at Scotia.

"Am I to do something?" Scotia asked

"Do whatever makes sense to you," Jeanette said.

Scotia considered this lack of direction, then decided to look at it as Duncan had taught her to assess a foe she knew nothing about. She started with the little she did know, putting together the common pieces of both Rowan's and Jeanette's experiences. Rowan was touching Elspet when the Targe chose her, a direct transfer from the old Guardian to the new. Jeanette was touching the stone in the grotto with the symbol for her gift inscribed upon it when she was chosen and her gift burst through her.

Scotia looked over her shoulder and up at the stone that loomed over her head, then stood and faced it. She reached up and pressed her hands to its weathered face, as close as she could get to the broken-arrow symbol, though it was still just out of reach.

An almost painful rush of goose bumps raced over her skin, raising the hairs at the nape of her neck, but that was all. Nothing happened. She tried to quiet her mind as Jeanette did, but that never worked.

"It is useless!" she said, spinning to face the Guardians, but they were both looking at her wide-eyed.

CHAPTER TWENTY

ONCE DUNCAN CAUGHT UP WITH KENNETH AND UILLIAM, Kenneth instructed him to head west to look for the English, but Duncan knew 'twas Kenneth's way of sending him even farther away from Scotia, the Story Stone meadow, and the test that would prove what he knew deep in his bones: Scotia would be chosen as a Guardian *if* she had changed enough to be worthy of that position and that responsibility. As he strode away through the wood, he forced himself to keep going without looking back, without questioning the decision Malcolm had made to send him away, or Kenneth's to send him even farther. 'Twas what he wanted, after all, to be as far away from her as possible. 'Twas much easier to remember her failures, her lies, when he could not look upon her, when he could not see the change in the way she carried herself.

Her bearing this morning had been—He could not put a name to it, but she *felt* like a different person. She had looked at him calmly, but had done nothing except say "good morn" as she passed him and took her place behind the Guardians. He realized the look in her eye in that moment had been solemn, thoughtful, and yet he could tell she was nervous about the coming day.

As much as he knew 'twas best for himself that he was not present at the stone, still he wanted to be there to celebrate her success when she was chosen. If she was chosen. He could not decide if he was certain she would be, or if he was certain she was not worthy of the honor. In truth the events of the last day, the rapid changes in Scotia's behavior, her admission of guilt in the death of Myles, and the revelation that she blamed herself for her mum's death made him think . . . hope . . . that she was finally worthy. His breath caught in his throat as he realized that was the thing she would not tell him—of her belief that she was responsible for her mum's death, and that if she could not bring herself to admit that, then she could not admit to her part in Myles's death.

But she had.

Twice broken. Twice mended. Sometimes when something broke and was mended, it ended up stronger than before.

He stopped for a moment, debating with himself. Duncan knew he could not be present when Scotia presented herself to the stone, when she was chosen as a Guardian, though there was little in this world he hoped for more, for that would be a sign that she really had changed, that she really was worthy. He knew Rowan and Jeanette would be happy for Scotia, and that they would immediately start to determine how the three of them could work together to protect the clan. He knew Nicholas and Malcolm, as Protectors of the Guardians, would keep her safe from any danger that might present itself while they were so very exposed at the Story Stone. He knew the warriors spread out around the Guardians and their Protectors in two circles would hold the English soldiers at bay if they happened to come upon the place while the Guardians worked together.

But he also knew, no matter how angry or disappointed he was with her, if anything happened to Scotia he would not forgive himself for leaving her safety to the Protectors and the clan. He also knew that there was nothing he could do at this point but to keep walking, to keep putting distance between the two of them as Malcolm and Kenneth had instructed. He had no choice but to trust that she would prove her worth, or she wouldn't, all on her own.

Duncan stopped for a moment and settled his distracted mind by carefully cataloging the world around him, just as he often counseled Scotia of late. The sharp aroma of pine swirled around him on the breeze, the scent so strong he could taste it in the back of his mouth. Small birds chirped, flitting from one treetop to another, and somewhere in the distance he heard the melancholy *cruck cruck* of a raven. He noted the location of the sun through the canopy of trees, and though it was just barely past midday he could tell that he had veered off from his westerly course to a more southwesterly direction.

Much to his chagrin, he also noticed that he was being followed. He should listen to his own advice and pay attention to what was happening in the moment, not what happened yesterday or might happen tomorrow.

Without a sound, he slipped behind the boll of an ancient oak tree, setting his back tight to the trunk, and prepared to listen for his shadow.

"You did not feel the power?" Rowan asked Scotia.

"Power?"

"Like a sizzling under your skin, almost painful. I felt you call it."

"Nay, not that. I felt goose bumps, but that is not uncommon."

Rowan and Jeanette were looking at each other, the same small smile playing over their lips. The Protectors were standing nearby but facing out, watching for trouble.

"Is it so amusing that I have once more failed?"

"Nay, sister, you have not failed. Come, sit with us. Rowan and I will try to join with you through the Targe, for I am quite sure that you are meant to be a Guardian."

"But the Highland Targe has not chosen me. How am I to join with the two of you if I am not chosen?" Scotia struggled to keep her voice steady and even, determined not to show any weakness, even though she wanted to break something, or battle someone.

198

"I think you are trying too hard, sister. Sit." Jeanette motioned her back down to sit around the Targe stone with them once more. "Keep one hand upon the Story Stone and place the other on the Targe as I do. Do not try to do anything, but rather let us lead you, gently, easily, into the power of the Targe, and I am certain, this time, that you will be proved a Guardian."

Scotia wanted to believe her with all her heart, but her heart had been bruised by too much loss, and she was loath to feel any more pain. Nonetheless she was not one to run away from a challenge, and in truth she had nothing more to lose. She sat so she could easily touch the Story Stone and the Targe stone, then looked at Rowan and Jeanette.

It was not long before Duncan's suspicion was proved. Uilliam walked past Duncan's hiding spot, then stopped and looked around, turning in a full circle as he pulled on his beard and muttered under his breath. Duncan grinned and waited for the black-haired bear of a man to scratch his head, pull his beard again, and scowl.

"Damned man," Uilliam whispered as he turned back in the direction Duncan had been traveling and slowly walked that way, scanning all around him for a sign of Duncan's passing. "Damned, damned man," Uilliam said, a little louder this time. "Duncan, if you are about, make yourself known. Nicholas will have my hide for losing you if you do not."

Duncan chuckled and stepped from behind the tree. "We cannot have that, now can we, Uilliam?"

"Nay. It would seem you have learned all I taught you and then some, especially of late," the older man said.

Duncan realized his observation was true. "I have. Training Scotia has required me to stretch my own skills and invent new ways of training her. She is a fiercely smart warrior, that one, and catches on very quickly." Duncan couldn't stop himself from looking over his shoulder back toward the meadow. "You are here to keep me from returning to the meadow, aye? 'Tis not necessary."

Uilliam let his head bob in answer.

"I do not like feeling useless when the future of the clan hangs in the balance," Duncan said. "There is far more I can do scouting for English than I can do standing by as things do or do not happen there."

Uilliam bobbed his head again. "I ken exactly what you mean." He looked about, and Duncan knew from long experience that he was taking stock of their surroundings. "Following you has reminded me of how useless a task that is, though you were surprisingly easy to track for a while," he said. His eyes narrowed for a moment, then he strode off in a westerly direction.

Duncan almost had to run to catch up with Uilliam's long strides. "I was distracted."

"By Scotia."

"Always by Scotia."

"But more so of late."

"Much more so of late." Duncan sighed. "She used to irritate me. Now . . . When I was training her it seemed she had changed, that she had turned into the woman she was always meant to be: strong, focused, gifted not just with her *knowing* but as a warrior. Then yesterday, when she thought I had betrayed her trust, she was the same as she'd always been—impetuous, angry, thinking only of herself, not of the clan, not of what I taught her."

"You ken you did not betray her, aye?"

"I do. She was not ready to go into battle. She showed us that clearly enough."

"And now?" Uilliam stopped and scanned the forest again.

"I swore to myself I would have no more to do with her. Clearly I have not taught her what she needs to ken."

"Are you sure about that, laddie?" He took off, adjusting his direction back to the west. "It seemed last night that she had learned what she needed to, the hard way."

"Which had nothing to do with the lessons I tried to teach her," Duncan said, keeping up with Uilliam better this time.

"Did it not? In the past she would not have thought about her actions. She certainly would not have taken responsibility for the trouble she brought to our dooryard. Never would she have apologized for her deeds. In all the days I have known that lassie, she has never apologized for anything."

Duncan thought about the admissions Scotia had publicly made, and how even then he had come to her aid, how even after what she had done that day, the new trouble she had caused when she had left the glen, even then he could not stand by and watch her take responsibility for her mum's death. She had much to be held accountable for, but that was not part of it, and the harm she was causing herself with it had pulled on every instinct he still had to keep her safe and happy.

"I cannot get her out of my thoughts for even a moment," he said, with a heavy sigh.

Uilliam stopped, and when Duncan stopped next to him, clapped him on the back. "You have been smitten with the lassie for as long as I can remember."

"'Tis different now." Duncan caught himself drumming his fingers against his thighs and forced himself to stop.

"Aye. I have noticed that, too. Our Scotia has finally grown up."

"Do you think so? I was sure she was nearly there until yesterday."

"We are lucky you and the lads silenced the soldiers without injury to yourselves. 'Twas a stupid thing of her to do."

Duncan took off this time. "And yet you sound like you have forgiven her already," he said over his shoulder.

Uilliam was silent for a long time as they made their way

toward the entrance into Glen Lairig at the far western end of the loch.

"I think Scotia wants to change, lad," Uilliam said, startling Duncan as much by speaking in the silence as the words themselves did. "She panicked yesterday when she thought you, the one person she has always depended upon to protect and champion her, broke his promise, and in that panic she reverted to her old behavior, but then she realized what she'd done and did her best to warn us, to limit the damage her actions might bring to the clan. She took control of the situation by admitting her mistake in front of everyone. She even allowed herself to be bound like a common thief without word, tear, or any attempt to avoid her punishment. 'Twas most unlike her. In fact, she acted like an honorable warrior, though she had to know her revelations would only push everyone away from her even more." He cocked his head and listened intently, then he stuck a finger in Duncan's chest just where Peigi had. "Especially you."

"I do not ken what to do about her. One minute I want to . . . kiss her." What he wanted to do with her was far more intimate than kissing, but he would not say something like that to Uilliam, who was like an uncle to her. "The next I want to throttle her, though until yesterday throttling had not entered my thoughts for quite a while. What should I do about her?"

"First, that is between you and the lass," Uilliam said with a quiet laugh. "Second, I certainly have no right to give advice on women, *but* if her changed behavior is evidence at long last of your good influence, then I think for the entire clan's sake, ye'd best ask the lass to wed with you."

Duncan knew the idea of marrying Scotia should have sent him running into the wood like a deer with a wolf pack on its heels, but it didn't, and that alone was an interesting thing to know about himself. Could he marry the lass when he did not ken if he could even trust her? That was supposing she would consent to be his wife, which he had strong doubts about.

For the first time since Uilliam had shown up, Duncan wondered what was happening at the Story Stone. Was Scotia a Guardian? And if she was chosen, did that mean she really had changed? Did it mean she had finally learned the one lesson he had tried to teach her for years? Could she be a Guardian and not think of others before herself?

The questions galloped around his brain unanswered as he followed Uilliam to the edge of the forest.

ROWAN RAISED THE TARGE STONE HEART HIGH AS SHE AND Jeanette prepared to lead Scotia into the Targe's power. Jeanette placed the fingertips of one hand on the Targe stone while settling the fingertips of her other hand on the lip of the cup of water settled on the ground in front of her.

"Touch the Targe stone and the Story Stone," Jeanette instructed. "It might help if you close your eyes. Do not try to do anything, rather let Rowan pull the power of the Targe through you."

Scotia did as instructed, but her mind would not quiet, so instead she imagined herself drawing the broken-arrow symbol in the air in front of her with each curled line that embellished the zigzag shape as a way of both focusing her mind and keeping herself from trying too hard again. She fervently hoped that Jeanette had the right of it.

All of a sudden the goose bumps were back, racing over her skin, lifting every hair on her body this time. Her breath caught in her throat, and then it happened.

CHAPTER TWENTY-ONE

It was not long before Duncan and Uilliam found evidence of the English, and not just a party of outriders. The entire detachment, at least the soldiers, for there was no sign of carts, and only a few horses had passed by this point sometime since sunup. The two men looked at each other, then back at the clear evidence that the English had made it into Glen Lairig already, well ahead of when they were expected.

"The bastard must have left his supplies behind," Uilliam said, scanning the beaten path.

"Aye. 'Tis what I would have done, and what Bryn suggested he might do, but I did not think the English would leave behind their comforts to be taken by Highlanders in order to make better time." Duncan also scanned the clear evidence of the English force's march through here. "Even so, they travel the trail along the lochside, as if they head to the castle."

"How many, would you say?"

"Not the two score Jeanette saw, but not many less. It seems our allies were not able to carve away enough to give us an even fight."

"The Sassenachs will be tired from their march from the sea." Uilliam was still scanning the tracks.

"They will be. We must engage them soon, then. We cannot give them time to recover."

"We must get back and warn everyone," Uilliam said. "The Guardians must get to a safe place, and the warriors must return to their posts and prepare to attack."

Duncan was thoughtful for long moments. "You warn them," he said to his companion. "I will track the Sassenachs to make sure they are going where we expect them to. It would seem this Lord Sherwood may be better at tactics than Nicholas gives him credit for. I would not care for us to be taken unawares by underestimating him. Get the Guardians and Scotia to safety, and I will return to our rendezvous camp as soon as I am able."

"'Tis a wise plan, Duncan. Take care, and do not engage them on your own."

"The same to you, my friend."

Uilliam quickly turned to retrace their steps while Duncan took off at a ground-eating lope, following the English into Glen Lairig.

As if a dam broke within Scotia, a deluge of *knowings* pressed against her, vying for her attention. They came so fast and so furiously that she could not pull one from another to make a coherent thought. She *knew* so much that she knew nothing.

"Try to think of Da." Jeanette's voice filtered through the torrent, and Scotia grabbed onto it like a lifeline in a storm.

"Da?" She wasn't sure her voice worked, but she felt a hand give her knee a squeeze in answer—Rowan.

Scotia tried to calm her clattering heartbeat, to slow her breath, to call the face of her father into her mind, but instead she suddenly *knew*. "He is seated on a dead log. One of Malcolm's kinsmen, Jock, has a sword to Da's neck, but there is neither fear nor anger. Da never was any good at feigning that which was not true."

Neither Guardian said anything, so they must have known about this—a test of her gift, no doubt. And then she let her mind roam, searching for something they could not have prepared for her, something no one could have foreseen. She searched for the unexpected something that would prove that her gift could be accentuated by the power of the Targe, a *knowing* that would prove she was a Guardian, though none could doubt it now that she was joined with her sister and cousin in its power.

Duncan would be so proud of her . . .

DUNCAN RAN AS FAST AS HE COULD WHILE STILL SLOW ENOUGH to read the signs of the English detachment's passing. He had not gone far when he spied a side trail that was so well hidden he almost missed it. He followed it a short distance and determined that it was made by a small group of five soldiers peeling off the main force, heading south. He calculated how far he had come, and the general direction of the trail, and determined that if this group went due south they might skirt the meadow without ever realizing it was there.

But they might also cross paths with Uilliam, and, Duncan realized, if he had not wandered about quite so much before Uilliam caught up with him, he might have crossed paths with the soldiers long before now. He had been so consumed by thoughts of Scotia he had not bothered to take more than the basic care in hiding his tracks or paying attention to what was around him.

He weighed the need to warn Uilliam against the need to learn if more of these small groups had detached themselves from the main force. Uilliam was a seasoned warrior and knew the enemy was amongst them. He would be vigilant, and there were plenty of MacAlpins and their allies at the Story Stone meadow to keep the Guardians and Scotia safe.

Duncan loped down the trail left by the main English detachment, leaving Uilliam to fend for himself.

Twice more Duncan found side paths with small groups of English veering off—one to north, and another to the south, but this time he followed the southbound group. It did not take long for him to be certain that this group would come upon the Story Stone meadow with ease, and he could not let that happen. Not only would it put the Guardians in peril but, if the soldiers understood what they saw and lived to report back, the MacAlpins' advantage—that they had not one but possibly three powerful Guardians—would be lost, and they could not afford that.

Duncan raced down the trail of the soldiers without care that he would give himself away in his haste. He must draw their attention before they arrived at the meadow. He must distract them, hold them, loudly and long enough for his kinsmen to hear and find them. He could not let them reach the meadow, but he needed to let them get close to the outer ring of warriors to ensure they would hear him. He ran full out, his lungs working like the bellows in a blacksmith's forge, until he caught the flash of a helm through the foliage.

"Halt!" he yelled, as loudly as he could. "Do not take another step. You are surrounded, and we will not hesitate to kill each and every one of you!" he yelled again. He settled his targe on his left arm and pulled his sword free of its scabbard as he put everything out of his mind but stopping these soldiers from finding the meadow and the Guardians. He dared not think of what might happen if they saw the Guardians at work.

AT THE THOUGHT OF DUNCAN IT WAS AS IF SCOTIA'S GIFT WAS yanked away from her, dragging her attention so hard and so fast she felt as nauseous as she had once when she had been out on the loch in a small boat during a summer storm, tossed and pitched about on the waves until she could do naught but lean over the side into the tempest and empty her stomach.

Just as she felt sure she would do that same thing, the sensation stopped, and she knew Duncan was in peril.

She knew the English soldiers were upon him, but she might as well be blind and helpless, for though she knew exactly where he was, she could not see exactly what his peril was. If only she had Jeanette's second sight . . .

And suddenly she could see him, Duncan, fighting for his life with five English men-at-arms. She could see his mouth opening, as if he called out to someone, but she could not hear him. She could feel Jeanette's surprise and her dismay at what they were seeing, as if they were one.

And then there were MacAlpins converging on the scene, three, four, five. She could feel Duncan's relief and *knew*, though she could not hear, that he directed the fight, even as he battled for his own life.

Then suddenly the soldier he fought missed a block to Duncan's thrust and crumpled to the ground. She could see Duncan yell something to his kinsmen, then he took off at a run. Suddenly there was a long shafted arrow that shot past his head, so close it seemed impossible that it had not hit him. He spun around, raising his shield to protect himself at the same time, but he was not quick enough. A second arrow hit the edge of his shield and sank itself into his shoulder. He stumbled backward, fell, and did not move again.

Scotia screamed, Jeanette's voice entwined with hers, though she knew not if it was out loud or only in her head. Duncan was down. He was hurt. The archer was running toward him, another arrow already nocked, and still Duncan did not move. She had to do something. She had to do something now! At the same moment, Scotia felt a new power surge through her, an almost painful sizzle under her skin, and she knew Rowan was also there, lending her gift to Scotia. Scotia lashed out with a burst of

Rowan's ability to move things, and knocked away the archer who was almost upon Duncan, sending him flying until he landed hard on his back and lay still. Quickly she/they threw up a small protective barrier over Duncan in case there were more English soldiers close at hand.

Scotia yelled for Nicholas and Malcolm, though she never broke her connection to the Targe and its Guardians, but she did not ken if she spoke the words or only thought she did. She yelled again and heard Jeanette's voice nearby.

"What are you saying, Scotia? We cannot understand you!"

Scotia never took her "eye" off Duncan. If she were to help him, she must calm herself enough to tell the chief where he was and that there were still English soldiers battling with MacAlpins. She drew on all that Duncan had taught her to calm her mind, slow her heart, to think clearly, but the need to get him immediate help thwarted her efforts. Nonetheless, she tried again to tell the chief where Duncan was and what was happening, but before she could tell if he understood her this time, another *knowing* slammed into her.

Uilliam was also fighting for his life with another small knot of English soldiers. Without a moment's hesitation she forced Jeanette's vision to her will once more, grabbed Rowan's gift defensively, and one by one, with great precision and guided by the tactics she had learned from Duncan—the pain in her chest at the thought that he was lying hurt, perhaps dead, made her stomach roil again, but she forced her mind back to Uilliam—she protected Uilliam while flinging away the soldiers, one by one, until he was the only man standing. The look on his face was one of both consternation and wonder, and she was just glad he was alive.

She abruptly pulled herself free of the Targe and found Rowan and Jeanette sitting limply by her. Rowan looked stunned. Jeanette's pale eyes were just as astonished.

Scotia looked up at Nicholas and told him everything she had seen and everything they had done, as quickly as she could.

"We must get to Duncan, Nicholas," she commanded. "I do not ken if he is alive or"—her voice was so thick in her throat she almost couldn't get the last word out—"dead." She tried to rise but found her legs less than dependable. "We cannot let him die!" She knew her voice was rising, growing more strident as Nicholas and Malcolm pulled Rowan and Jeanette to their feet, just as Scotia's legs finally responded to her command. She reached for her sword, drawing it from her scabbard. Rowan bent to retrieve the Targe and sack, tying it securely to her belt, while Jeanette dumped the water from her cup and put it in a sack she had made for it.

"Hurry," Malcolm said, pushing the three women back to the wood, but in the opposite direction from where Duncan lay.

Scotia was confused for a moment, then realized they were not going after Duncan. "Nicholas!" she screamed, "We must help Duncan!"

Jeanette grabbed her sister by her shoulders. "You are a Guardian, Scotia. First the Guardians must be taken to safety. You ken this. 'Tis the way it has always been. Duncan will live or die, but he kens it, too, and would be the first to get you to safety before he found his own."

Scotia looked over her shoulder, back to where she knew he lay. She knew Jeanette was right, though she did not like it. She knew Duncan would tell her that the sooner she did as she was told, and found safety, the sooner the warriors could retrieve him, find Uilliam, and chase down the English.

She nodded, both to Duncan's voice in her head and Jeanette's words.

"Let us hurry," she said. "But," she said to Nicholas, letting the knowledge that she was a Guardian, just as Duncan had said she would be, lend weight and expediency to her voice, "I expect you to send someone for him as soon as we are safely away. He is alive," she managed to say, "but has not moved since the arrow found him and he fell to the ground. Find him, please, Nicholas, bring him back safely," she said. "I could not bear it if he lost his life because of me."

Nicholas nodded and Malcolm gave a grunt of agreement, then pushed the women to a run as they fled the Story Stone meadow.

CHAPTER TWENTY-TWO

As soon as the Guardians were clear of the Story Stone meadow the small group slowed and made their way with great care away from the open area. Scotia wanted to take the rear of the group, watching for anyone who might follow them but also minding any tracks the others left that were too easy to find, but Malcolm had insisted she walk ahead of him.

"You are a Guardian, Scotia," he said. "'Tis my place as Protector of the Guardians to keep you safe."

"More like you mean to keep me from returning to find Duncan. I give you all my word I will not do that." Though that was exactly what she wanted most to do. "I understand the Guardians must be protected, but you ken I can protect myself, aye?" she said.

"That remains to be seen, but it is seeming more and more likely," Malcolm answered.

She sighed. She might be a Guardian now, but that did not mean she would be trusted. If she was lucky, she might win the trust of her clan in time.

"'Tis my right as a Guardian to be concerned with protecting all of us, aye? We are too easy to track traveling this way. We need to split up," she whispered.

"We are not splitting up," Nicholas said quietly over his shoulder, and she was impressed once again with the man's talents. Hearing like that would serve a spy well. "We will be at the rendezvous camp soon. For now, we need to be quiet, and step as lightly as we can. The Guardians—all three of you—must be kept safe so you can create the Highland Targe, if you can. That is what is most important right now."

Scotia did not respond, but she agreed with him. She only hoped that between the three of them they could figure out how to raise a shield that would protect this route into the Highlands from England's greedy king.

It was not long before they came to a place where Nicholas gave the owl call, and it was answered. They moved silently onward into a dense part of the forest where the trees grew close together, their crowns blocking out all evidence that the sky still existed over them. The air was damp, cool, and carried the sharp scents of pine and balsam. Green, furry moss grew on the north side of most of the larger trees, and the ground beneath was spongy with a thick carpet of last year's leaves and pine needles.

As they moved deeper into the narrow fold of the mountain, it grew darker and colder beneath the trees until at last they reached the far end, where the rudiments of a camp had been left for just this moment.

"No fires," Nicholas said as they gathered around the cache. "We will wait here for the others, but we cannot linger here even so long as the night. Love," he said to Rowan, "can the three of you raise the Targe?"

Rowan looked at Jeanette, then Scotia, but neither of them knew the answer any better than she did.

"I dinna ken, but—"

The same tawny owl call interrupted her. Nicholas signaled for the women to take cover as he and Malcolm drew their swords and stood behind two large trees. Scotia drew her sword as well, and only then realized she had left her shield at the standing stone. She motioned for her sister and cousin to move further up the side of the tiny glen where there was a little undergrowth to hide in, but she remained behind a tree, close enough to Malcolm and Nicholas to fight with them if necessary.

The first people she saw were Uilliam and Jock. Uilliam had Duncan over his shoulder, and it took Scotia every ounce of her stubborn will to stay where she was until her chief and his champion, her Protectors, called for the Guardians.

"What are you waiting for?" Jeanette strode past Scotia, heading for Uilliam and Duncan. Scotia lost no time following her.

"More of the lads are behind us," Uilliam said with a grunt as Jock helped him lay Duncan on the ground. Scotia dropped to her knees and took Duncan's cold hand in her own. Blood stained his left shoulder, wet and red, even in the dim light of the forest. Dread made her shiver.

"Does he yet live?" she asked Jeanette as her sister ripped Duncan's sleeve away, revealing the wound.

"Aye," Jeanette said. She glanced up at Uilliam. "What happened to the arrow?"

"I took it out of his shoulder so I could carry him without causing further damage," he said to Jeanette, "but I had not time, nor anything to bind it with. How did you ken 'twas an arrow?"

"I saw it," she said without emotion as she rifled through her healer's sack and laid out a needle, thread, a smaller bag of moss, and a rolled-up strip of linen on a stone near her knee.

Scotia smoothed Duncan's hair away from his face, noting how soft it was, softer than her own, but he did not stir. "Why does he not wake?"

"He must have hit his head as he fell," Jeanette said. "He has a gash just here." She turned his head to reveal a small cut and a large lump not far behind his left ear. "Come sit here, sister." She indicated for Scotia to sit where she could cradle his head in her lap, then handed her a pad of moss. "Hold this to the cut to help it stop bleeding."

Scotia did just as she was told without a moment's thought or hesitation, letting the weight of Duncan's head rest in her lap as she pressed the moss to his injury with one hand, and continued to smooth his hair away in long slow strokes with the other.

"Will he die?" Her voice trembled just a little. Jeanette reached out and cupped her sister's cheek with one hand.

"The wounds do not look terrible, but there is always a risk of fever and festering." As if that reminded her of something, Jeanette pulled her healer bag back to her and rummaged through it again, finally pulling out a small glass jar with a piece of waxed leather covering the mouth and tied in place with a piece of deer sinew. "When this is all over I must travel to visit Morven. She never taught me how to make this salve, and it does seem to prevent festering." She slathered the pungent ointment into and around Duncan's shoulder wound, then had Scotia lift his head enough for her to slather some on that wound as well.

"Aye," Rowan said, scratching at what Scotia knew was a scar on her ribs from when Jeanette had used this same salve on her after the curtain wall fell. "But it smells terrible and stained my kirtles."

"But you had not the slightest hint of fever or fester," Jeanette said, a little smile lifting the corners of her mouth as she recovered the jar. "You should be grateful for the stinky stuff."

Rowan's teasing complaints and Jeanette's hint of a smile lifted Scotia's fears, at least a little. They would never tease if they thought Duncan was dying.

Jeanette then turned her attention back to threading the needle and using a little more moss to blot away the blood that had slowed but not stopped.

"Malcolm," Uilliam said, "when I got to Duncan, Jock here and the rest of your kin were fighting back the English who were still trying to get to Duncan. Our lads joined in, so Jock and I could get him away." Scotia looked up from Duncan's face and saw that Uilliam's eyes were focused on Jeanette as she took the first stitch. "You set up a barrier around him, did you not, lassie? The English were gathered around him when we arrived, but could not get near enough to touch him. I had no trouble."

"Well, I guess that proves your belief that those of ill intent will not be able to pass through a Guardian barrier," Scotia said.

"Aye, but"—Jeanette shook her head and glanced up at Uilliam—"'twas not me who set up that barrier, well, not me exactly."

"Rowan?" Uilliam asked.

"'Twas all three of us," Scotia answered him.

"Then you are . . ."

"I am a Guardian, aye."

"I knew you would be." Duncan's hoarse voice surprised them all.

Scotia looked down at him. "You are alive." She felt her lip tremble. "Thank God, you are alive." The joy that filled her was unlike anything she had ever felt before, as if the bright light of the sun burst within her, sending light into every dark crevice, every dark thought, every dark emotion, filling her with the love she had for this man. She would have hugged him, but she was not sure he would allow that. She satisfied her need by brushing his hair away from his face again, then ran the back of her fingers down his cheek before he could stop her. "How do you feel?"

"Thirsty." It was not what she was hoping to hear, but she took it as a good sign.

Rowan handed her a waterskin, and she helped Duncan drink a little, though 'twas hard to do while prone.

It wasn't until she set aside the skin that she remembered the others standing around them. Jeanette tied off her last stitch, snipped the end of the thread, and started to bind some moss over the wound.

"Are you finished?" Scotia asked, knowing that as soon as he could, Duncan would likely move away from her, as he'd done so dramatically last night, and this morning as they traveled to the meadow.

"I am," Jeanette said.

"I think I will lie here a little longer," Duncan said. "Can I speak to Scotia alone?"

No one replied, they just moved away from the couple. Scotia held her breath, not sure what was coming next, but all he did was to lean his head a little into her stroking fingers. Relief flowed through her at the small gesture that he did not mean to push her away, and she could not stop the water that gathered in her eyes.

She leaned down so he could see her face and judge the truth of what she said. "I thought I had lost you," she whispered. "I thought I had lost you before I could ever atone for the way I threw your care, your friendship, and your love away. I did not ken if you were dead or alive, so I did what I could to keep you safe, then I carried on, as you taught me."

He reached up and wiped her tear from his cheek, then smiled. "And I thought I had lost you when that arrow hit me. It makes me hopeful that you are so glad I am alive."

"More than you know," she said, and shyly leaned down further to press a chaste kiss to his lips, only to be surprised when his hand came up and cupped her neck, holding her in place as he kissed her back.

When he released her, he smiled. "I was wrong about you."

"You have *never* been wrong about me, Duncan."

"This time I was. I was angry with you, more angry than I have ever been. As much as you felt I had betrayed your trust, I felt you had betrayed mine."

"I did." She was not proud of that, but it was the truth, and she was determined to speak only the truth with Duncan.

"Aye, but Uilliam made me see that you quickly saw your mistake and took full responsibility for it, doing your best to protect the clan from the worst of it and telling the truth about many other things, too. When I left you last night I did not believe you worthy of becoming a Guardian, but today, with Uilliam's help, I understand why you are worthy, that you really have changed."

"Uilliam only had part of it right." Truth. She owed him the complete truth. "But you were right about me. As much as I took responsibility for the harm I had caused, I did not understand how I came to cause it until you abandoned me in the bower, bound and helpless. It was not until then that I had to face that I had brought everything upon myself. It was not enough to admit to my mistakes, I had to see how they came to be, and I knew, if I continued that way, I would never be worthy of becoming a Guardian, and I would never have a chance to win you back. If I had not seen that when I was with you I was a better person than I thought myself capable of being—a stronger person, who did not need to manipulate, or ignore what other people needed, in order to be happy—I never would have understood what I needed to do to be worthy. With you, I liked myself better. With you, I found a purpose and a focus that had always been missing from my life. With you, I found . . ." She blinked and determined to get it all said. "With you, I found my heart. You are my heart."

Scotia held her breath.

"And you are mine," Duncan said. "You have always been mine," He whispered as he pulled her down for another kiss.

Scotia thought she'd burst from the joy that filled her, but the moment was quickly interrupted by a sharp "ahem," from someone, drawing their attention to the arrival of Kenneth and several others.

"Does he ken you are a Guardian?" Duncan asked quietly.

"Nay, but there is that to tell." A sudden *knowing* came over her that she realized had come to her when the Targe took her but that made itself clear to her only now. "There is more, Duncan." She smiled down at him. "So much more! Da! Everyone, I have a story to tell you."

CHAPTER TWENTY-THREE

DUNCAN TRIED TO SIT UP AS THE COUNCIL AND OTHER WARRIORS gathered around, while Scotia tried to hold him down. In truth he would like nothing more than to stay just where they were, but he could feel the excitement vibrating through her.

"Do not move. You will open your stitches," she said.

"I would like to sit up," he insisted. "Can you help me?"

Before she could, Nicholas and Malcolm assisted him to rise enough to sit. Rowan had two men move a stone for him to lean back on, and when he was settled, Jeanette moved in to bandage his head, which explained the headache that started to pound as soon as he sat up.

Scotia stood beside him, waiting for him to be settled. He reached up and squeezed her hand. "Tell us."

"Are you a Guardian?" Kenneth asked.

"I am well and truly a Guardian, that much was made clear. My gift is *knowing*—"

"'Twas more than simple *knowing*," Rowan said.

"Aye, but even that—" She realized confusion raced through the gathering, and knew she had to back up even more. "When I was chosen by the Targe stone my *knowing* became stronger, and I was filled with a barrage of *knowings* so great that it was hard to focus on any one of them, but I *knew* Duncan was in trouble so I followed that *knowing* to him, but I could not see what was happening so I shared Jeanette's gift—"

"There was no sharing," Jeanette said. "You took it. It was as if I could only follow where you went with it, though I could see and *know* all you did."

"I did not mean to take it. I did not even know I could share it. We will have to experiment with that, sister."

"We will," Rowan said, making a point that there was another Guardian to include.

"As I said," Scotia continued, "I used Jeanette's gift to see Duncan just as he was shot. The archer who shot you"—she looked down at him—"was upon you, and in my fear for you I grabbed Rowan's gift and directed it to throw the archer—"

"'Twas not a throw," Rowan said, "she picked him up and hurled him away from you. Even I have not been able to do that."

"Anyway, that was when the *knowing* came to me that Uilliam was in trouble, too, so we created a barrier over you to keep you from further harm."

"And then you hurled the soldiers away from me," Uilliam said, a note of awe in his deep voice. "'Twas you who did that, aye?" he asked Scotia.

She nodded.

"You have taught her very well, Duncan," Uilliam said.

Pride warmed Duncan.

Uilliam continued, "'Twas as if an invisible warrior fought beside me, anticipating the moves of each soldier as they came for me, and incapacitating each in turn. You three lassies make one very formidable weapon."

There was quiet as Duncan watched that thought sink into each one there. Three Guardians, and one trained as a warrior who could combine all their gifts into a single weapon. Would Scotia be strong enough to control all that power without letting it overtake her? Clearly her training was not at an end, as he had thought. He would have to watch over her, teach her to claim her strength without letting it go to her head, or her heart.

Her heart was his, and he was not about to let it go.

"Did you leave them there?" Nicholas asked at last.

"Aye. 'Twas only me so I got out of there before any could rouse. When I made it to the meadow I heard the fighting and went to help. That's when I found Duncan."

"So the soldiers who lived will be able to report on what happened to Lord Sherwood." Malcolm said what everyone was thinking.

Uilliam sighed and pulled on his beard. "Aye, they will. Our lads are pulling back to guard this camp. We did not have enough to chase down the soldiers who lived and keep enough numbers to attack the main force."

Scotia cleared her throat, drawing Duncan's and everyone else's attention back to her.

"As I said, when the Targe claimed me as a Guardian I was filled with *knowings*, so many I could not tell you what most were. But one of them made itself clear to me just a moment ago as I was talking to Duncan."

She stepped forward into the center of the gathering and performed what he thought was the blessing that he had heard Elspet make many, many times over the years, but the guttural words were slightly different, and fit flowing hand symbols as they never had before.

"That is the blessing, is it not? And it is in the language you spoke when you tried to tell Nicholas and Malcolm about Duncan!" Rowan said. "I did not recognize it, for you pronounce it differently than Auntie Elspet did, and what you said was not any of the blessings I have learned"—she glanced over at Jeanette and twisted her mouth into a wry smile—"or tried to learn."

"Did I?" Scotia asked. "I do not remember that."

"Aye, you did. Can you speak the language now?" Jeanette, the ever-curious, asked.

"I do not ken if I can speak it on my own, but I understand it. I know what the blessings mean, as well as the symbols on the Targe and the other stones."

Everyone was silent.

"The words of the blessing are . . ." Scotia closed her eyes and seemed to be concentrating very hard.

"*Mother of all things, hear my prayer.*

Mother of the earth, the fire, the water, and the wind, protect us.

Mother of the Guardians of the Shield, protect us and

Fill your vessels with your abundant gifts so that we may protect you.

Oh, Mother of all things, hear my prayer."

"Guardians," Jeanette said. "Guardians of the Shield. More than one." Her curiosity was fully engaged. "It could mean Guardians through time, or it could indicate that having multiple, simultaneous Guardians is not as unusual as we thought. What else can you interpret now?" she asked Scotia.

"The words on the Targe sack," Scotia said.

"The words?" Jeanette asked as Rowan immediately opened the sack and spread it on the ground in the center of the circle, right at Scotia's feet where all could see. She set the Targe stone in the center, then stepped back to her place between Jeanette and Nicholas.

"What do they mean?" Duncan asked. Scotia looked down at him with a small smile that settled over her lips even though he could see lines of tension at the corners of her eyes.

Scotia knelt on the opposite side of the sack from Duncan so she was not blocking his view of it and pointed to the mirror. "The mirror is clear seeing, visions of the future, but also clear seeing of distant things, like you"—she nodded at Duncan—"in the present. The other, Rowan's symbol"—she pointed at the inverted V with three wavy lines beneath it—"it means what Rowan can do, moving things like mountains, the things of the earth, with the energy she draws from the ground"—she touched the three wavy lines—"the same source as the Targe's energy."

When Scotia did not continue, Jeanette said, "And the other one? The broken arrow? Is it the twice-broken arrow as you thought?"

Scotia looked up at Jeanette then. "Truly you do not understand the words?"

"Truly, I do not."

Scotia looked at Rowan but her cousin shook her head.

"It means . . ." She closed her eyes again. "It is so clear in my mind, but so difficult to put into words. It means the strength of the twice-broken . . ." Her eyes popped open, and she caught Duncan's gaze in her own. "Warrior."

A thrill went through Duncan as he realized how well that described her. "That is your symbol," Duncan said. "You are the twice-broken warrior. But how does that indicate your *knowing* gift?"

Scotia stared at him for a long moment while everyone else seemed to hold their breath, waiting for her answer.

"It indicates the wisdom that comes from surviving the breaks and seeing them mended, like a bone broken and reknit. For me, that wisdom comes through strong feelings, I suspect I am too stubborn to *know* things otherwise. Duncan has helped me understand that I must have strong feelings connected to the things and people I know things about—a form of wisdom." She looked over at her sister. "'Tis likely why the first time you tested me I could not find your healer's bag. I had no love nor worry for it, nor was I yet worthy of becoming a Guardian."

"I do not understand," Kenneth said. "What have I missed? Twice broken?"

Duncan realized that Kenneth had not been there when she had first admitted her mistakes and revealed why she believed the broken arrow was her symbol, that she was meant to be a Guardian.

Quickly, with neither tears nor any defensiveness, Scotia explained what she had learned to her father. She sat tall and she spoke with a quiet surety that held the confidence of the old Scotia and the wisdom of the new.

"I can only say that I will do everything within my power to honor both deaths," Scotia said, "to be mindful of them when I face a hard decision and unruly emotions, and to keep the good of the clan and my duty as a Guardian foremost in my mind at all times. I am the strength of the twice-broken warrior, gaining wisdom from my unforgivable mistakes and the training that Duncan has given me, to combine the gifts of the Guardians into one."

Kenneth moved to her, pulling her to her feet, then wrapping her in his arms, holding her tight. When he let her go, Duncan saw her quickly wipe away the water that gathered in her eyes again.

"The story is not done," she said as she picked up a stick, and brushed away the fallen leaves on the forest floor until she reached dirt.

She drew Rowan's symbol first, then drew Jeanette's mirror as if Rowan's symbol was reflected in it, and then finally her own symbol, the broken arrow, slicing through the other two.

"This is the story the stone tells: that the power to move things, the ability to see things, and the strength and wisdom of the twice-broken warrior must combine, as we learned this day."

"It does indeed," Rowan said quietly. "'Twas there for us all this time, but we did not understand—we did not *know*—what it meant. Is this the way we construct a true Highland Targe, the shield big enough to protect this route into the Highlands?"

"Almost. There is one more piece of this story, Rowan. Which brings me to the word incised on the Targe stone, the stone in the grotto where Jeanette became a Guardian, and on the Story Stone where I became one, too." She lifted the Targe off the sack and cupped it in her hands, taking it over to the other two Guardians.

"You do not understand this word, either, do you?" she asked Rowan, and then Jeanette, who looked at the stone but not at her sister.

Both shook their heads.

"The word"—she pointed at the three swirls in a circle that was incised on the stone—"means"—and a sound came out of her mouth that even she seemed surprised by.

"But what does it mean?" Jeanette asked, looking up at Scotia.

"It means . . ." she said. "It means . . ." she began again, but she had to stop, and that same look of intense concentration came over her face, just as it did when he set her a new lesson in her warrior training. "Again," she said quietly, "the word is as clear in my mind as the waters that run in the mountain burns, but there is no single word to translate it. It means the place of power . . . nay, it means the wellspring of power . . . the source of power. Yes, 'the source of power lies deep beneath the hearth.'"

There was quiet as what she said sank in.

"The hearth?" Jeanette asked.

"The hearth . . . the home . . ." Scotia shook her head. "I cannot say what it means in exact words, but I know for certain it means that the source of the Targe's power lies beneath our home, Dunlairig Castle. 'Tis where Mum performed most of the blessings. 'Tis where she built the protection over the castle after the wall fell. She may not have understood the word, but by training or some other understanding, she kent the center of our home, the bailey . . . where the water breaks the surface through the well . . . was a very powerful place for a Guardian and the Targe."

"That is where you first experienced your gift, love," Nicholas said to Rowan, taking her hand in his. "I felt the power that night as well, though not nearly as strongly as you."

Jeannette's head was slowly moving up and down. She took a deep breath and looked back at the Targe where it lay in Scotia's hands.

"Do you ken how to construct the true Highland Targe?" Scotia asked her. "Rowan can pull the power we will need, I can direct it with your vision and my *knowing*, but do you ken how to create such a thing?"

"Do you not, with your *knowing*?"

"Nay, my beloved sister, I do not. Is there a blessing that Mum taught you that there is no known use for? Perhaps something she taught you when I was not attending to her lessons?"

Jeanette got that look on her face that they all knew meant she was lost in the Guardian lore that filled her agile mind, and then Jeanette's eyes went wide as she stared first at her sister, then at her cousin.

"There is one. Mum taught it to me not long ago. She drilled me for days until I had it right, as if she knew I would need it, though she knew not what it was for." And then she recited the words and the motions, and a grinning Scotia translated them for the Guardians.

"Nicholas." Rowan smiled at her husband. "We need to go home, to Dunlairig Castle. We will need a little time to prepare ourselves, and to gather everyone who can fight. Is there any reason we cannot do this tonight?"

"There will be no moon tonight," he said. "'Twill be good for getting everyone into position, but not for fighting. 'Twould be good to surprise them under cover of darkness, but not if we cannot see who we fight."

"Then we prepare this night, and take back our home come first light," Rowan declared, giving Nicholas a smacking kiss and a huge smile.

Duncan struggled to his feet and with his good arm swept Scotia into a fierce embrace. "You did it, Scotia." He kissed her and was rewarded when she threw her arms around him. "You hold the key to our success. You hold the key to the Highland Targe!"

CHAPTER TWENTY-FOUR

THE REST OF THE DAY PASSED IN A FLURRY OF ACTIVITY. REPORTS came in quickly that the English were at the castle, but most remained outside the wall. They were finishing the temporary curtain wall that the MacAlpins had begun, cutting down trees and setting the trunks in place, though they had not gotten far enough with it yet to prevent the MacAlpins from entering the castle from the north, where the wall was little more than a pile of rubble.

The Guardians had retreated to a quieter part of the tiny hidden glen, where Jeanette had taught them the blessing that should allow them to create the Highland Targe, though it did nothing more than make a simple barrier, as they had crafted at their bower, easier to maintain.

"Are you sure of what the blessing means?" Jeanette asked for the hundredth time.

"I am. We each know what we must do. We have learned the blessing. All that we lack is the power to create the Targe, and that, as far as any of us know, is only available within the bailey." Scotia looked at her sister and her cousin. "We are as prepared as we can be, and there is little use in delaying our plan just because we are not certain this will work."

"Are you ready?" Kenneth asked as he neared them.

"Aye, Da, we are," Jeanette said, stepping into her father's arms. Scotia joined her, and Rowan did, too, all of them drawing strength from this man who had raised them, protected them, loved them, and who now had no choice but to follow them into battle.

"'Tis time we leave," he said, his voice thick as he let them go. "We want to move as close as we can while there is still light. Tomorrow we all go to war for control of our home and of the Highlands."

Hours later everyone able to fight, including some of the women dressed like men to make their numbers look greater than they were, were in position. Scotia, Rowan, and Jeanette, along with Malcolm, Duncan, and five other warriors, waited within the inky bolt-hole tunnel they had used to leave the castle not long ago, though it seemed like a year had passed since then.

Nicholas had another task before he would join them in the bailey . . . if he survived that long. Rowan had been furious with him, but he had taken her aside, and after a few moments of heated debate they returned to the council, Rowan silent but no longer arguing against her husband's plans. Nicholas had held his wife's hand until 'twas time for them all to take their places.

Jeanette and Malcolm sat not far down the tunnel, whispering low enough that Scotia could not make out their words, while Scotia murmured a prayer that the MacAlpin clan and their allies would prevail in the coming war and that they would all be returned safely to their true homes. And then she turned her attention away from what had been and toward what she meant to reclaim.

"It is right to be nervous, love," Duncan said quietly from where he sat beside her.

"I ken that." She immediately regretted the snap in her voice and reached for his hand. "I still wish that you had returned to the caves. You are not well enough for battle yet."

"I am well enough for my role in it, but I cannot lie and say it does not warm my heart that you are concerned for me." He squeezed her hand.

"You are as sappy as a lass sometimes." She looked at him, and though she could not make out any of his features in the darkness, she knew if he could see the stupidly happy smile on her face it would tell him just how deep her feelings for him ran. "You must promise me," she said, turning serious once more, "that you will stay by my side, no matter what happens. I almost lost you once. I do not ken what I would do if you were taken from me now when we've only found our way to each other."

"I promise. I will stay by your side, but I do not promise that I will sit by quietly, especially if the barrier does not work—"

"It will work."

"—or is breached."

"That will not happen either," she said, "but if it does"— she reached down and reassured herself that her sword was still attached to her belt—"we will all be fighting for our lives."

"And you must let me protect you if it comes to that, you and the other Guardians, of course. Nothing must happen to the three of you. If this battle goes badly, you three must live to continue the fight."

She wished, and not for the first time, that Jeanette's gift of vision had revealed something of the coming battle, but she had not been able to see anything of it. Scotia thought perhaps it was Jeanette's fear of what she might see that blocked her gift, and could only hope that in the midst of the battle she could wrest Jeanette's vision from her and wield it as she had done at the Story Stone when the need arose.

"Let us focus on what we must do, Duncan," she said, trying to get the thought of all that could go wrong out of her mind. 'Twas bad enough that even if they won this battle, they still had to erect the Highland Targe and keep it in place long enough to repel the inevitable next wave of soldiers sent by King Edward to capture Nicholas, the Guardians, the Targe, and this route into and through the Highlands, without the specter of losing more of the people she loved. She was not denying that she would most certainly lose people in the coming day, but she refused to dwell on it.

Duncan went silent beside her but did not release her hand.

NICHOLAS, DRESSED IN THE BLOODY CLOTHES AND DENTED helm of one of the soldiers who had been killed earlier that day, made his way through the moonless night quickly and quietly to the English camp sheltered in the lee of the castle wall. He lost no time in assessing the defenses of the camp. As he expected, those in plain sight were alert, and several of those hidden by the forest that grew thickly almost to the edge of the camp on the west were as well, but there were always one or two guards who attended to their posts with a lax attention. Once he found those he finalized his plans to infiltrate the camp, learn what he could from Lord Sherwood before killing him, and, if all went as he hoped, lure some of the soldiers into the trap awaiting them, evening the numbers for the coming battle.

When the time was right, he slipped past the guards and made his way into the camp, nodding to the few men who sat next to flickering fires, as if he knew them, while taking count of as many men as he could see, both awake and asleep in their blankets. No one questioned his appearance in the camp.

Before he arrived outside what was clearly Lord Sherwood's tent, the only one in the camp, he took advantage of the dark and adjusted his posture. He bent over a little and wrapped one arm over his stomach where the worst of the bloodstains were, and then shuffled up to the guard, who seemed to be drowsing on his feet.

"I need to speak to his lordship," Nicholas said in his best Nottinghamshire accent, taking care to slur his words as an injured soldier would. "My scouting party was attacked. I have information the lord will want."

The guard looked him up and down. "Do not bleed on his carpet," the man said. "He cannot stand that."

Nicholas nodded and made as if to part the tent flaps, but instead he brought the stone he had hidden in his hand down on the back of the man's head hard enough to drop him with only a quiet *oof*. Nicholas pulled him into the deeper shadow beside the tent and quickly arranged him so anyone who might see him would think him sleeping.

As he slipped inside the tent he was confronted with a space that should have been lavishly appointed, but then he remembered that the carts of goods and supplies had been left behind on the road and were surely in the care of the Scots at this point. The few things that some poor soul had no doubt hauled into the glen on his back—the carpet, thick and ornately decorated, a silver cup that sat on the ground next to an empty bottle of wine, and the leader of this band of soldiers wrapped in a fur-lined cloak, asleep on that carpet—reminded him of all he had left behind when he had chosen to remain in the Highlands with Rowan. It pleased him that he did not miss any of the trappings he had once coveted.

"My lord?" Nicholas said, drawing his dagger and covering the man's mouth with his hand. "I think 'tis time you awoke."

"You will never get away with this." Lord Sherwood glared up at Nicholas, who had him pinned where he'd slept, his dagger at the man's throat. "I know exactly who you are, spy. I know there is a price on your head, and I intend to deliver it to King Edward."

"That might be a wee bit difficult, as I intend to keep it where it is." Nicholas covered the man's mouth again as he listened to a rustling outside. "It appears you've lost at least ten men, Sherwood, and you'll lose the rest soon. The MacAlpins dinna look kindly on the English."

"Then why are you still here, fitz Hugh?"

"Ah, see, that is the problem, you think I am English, when the truth is I am the MacAlpin. Nicholas MacAlpin, chief of the MacAlpins of Dunlairig."

"I care not what you call yourself," Lord Sherwood hissed, as he glared up at Nicholas. "We will take you and the red-haired witch, as well as the hunk of rock that seems to be what started all of this, for the king. And when that is accomplished, we will rid the world of each and every savage who claims to be a MacAlpin. This glen, and that castle, will belong to King Edward before this day is through."

Nicholas made to slice the man's neck open when Sherwood managed to grab his hand and pull the blade away from his skin.

"Guards! Guards!" he shouted, but before anyone could come to his aid, Nicholas tried to twist free of the man's grasp. Sherwood's grip was far stronger than Nicholas had imagined. They grappled for control of the dagger, rolling back and forth over the carpet as each worked to stab the other. Nicholas heard the pounding of several men running toward the tent and knew he would have to take Sherwood another time. He rolled with Sherwood toward the back side of the tent, ending up on top of the Englishman, then used every bit of strength he had to raise the dagger. Instead of plunging it into the other man's chest, he twisted it so it ripped into the canvas, then he pushed it down enough to open a tear big enough for him to get through, but Sherwood was still gripping his wrist and had a hand at Nicholas's throat as three men rushed into the tent.

"Guards, take him!" Sherwood shouted.

Nicholas took a deep breath and managed to throw the dagger out through the tear in the tent. Then he called on every bit of strength he had and launched himself off Sherwood and dove out through the same tear, rolling as he hit the ground, then racing through the camp, knocking over anything and everything he could as he passed. He grabbed a torch and tossed it into the midst of soldiers sleeping near the cold remains of a fire, then made sure as many soldiers as possible saw him as he dashed out of the camp and headed up the ben as fast as his legs could take him.

"Do you think they will follow you?" Jock asked from behind a tree when Nicholas arrived at their rendezvous.

"I did my best to grab everyone's attention, so I expect they will. Is everything prepared?"

"Aye, Nicholas," Uilliam said, "we but need those daft English to take the bait. Did you learn what you needed to?"

"Aye, he knows naught of any Guardians except my Rowan, and he does not seem to ken what she can do. Our secret weapon is still secret from the king. Unfortunately, Sherwood still lives."

The three of them waited, and Nicholas took advantage of the calm before the storm to steady his breath and prepare for the next part of the plan.

Torches flared in the distance, but it quickly became apparent that no one followed him.

"Damnation."

"You need to get to the castle," Uilliam said to Nicholas. "The sun will be rising soon. Look, the sky is growing lighter already. You have riled the wasp nest, leave the rest to us."

"I had hoped we'd cull a few more soldiers before we had to face them in daylight. Do what you can, Uilliam, Jock. I will see you in the bailey ere long." Nicholas took off at a run, heading for the bolt-hole tunnel and the next stage of the plan.

THE OWL CALL QUIETLY FLEW DOWN THE TUNNEL, AND SCOTIA could hear Rowan sigh.

"He is here," Rowan said. "Nicholas is here."

"Malcolm, Jeanette, go now!" Scotia said, hating the necessity for the Guardians to split up, even for a short time.

"We will be back as soon as we can," Malcolm said as he lit a lantern and handed it to Jeanette. "Lead the way, angel."

JEANETTE LED MALCOLM UP THE STEEP, NARROW STAIR THAT wrapped around the tower between the inner and the outer wall. It had only one door at the bottom of the tower and one at the top. She and Rowan had discovered it once when they were children. She had not been down the stairs ever since. But she had used the small landing at the top to store the Chronicles of the Guardians, for that landing was just inside the secret door in her mother's solar.

"It should not be much further," Jeanette whispered, holding the lantern high so at least a little of the light fell behind her for Malcolm. She shook her head and pulled away a spider's web from her face. It was not the first she had run into, and she was certain it would not be the last.

"If you let me lead, I could clear those for you," Malcolm said. She could hear the hint of laughter in his voice and could not help but smile. It was one of the things she loved the most about her new husband—even when she could see only the worst in a situation, he found the humor in it, lifting her spirits as no one else could.

Once they arrived at the landing, it took only a moment for Jeanette to find the hidden latch. As soon as the door swung inward on silent hinges that Jeanette had oiled herself before they ever thought they might need to use the hidden stair, Malcolm pulled her aside and stepped up to the door. He listened carefully before pulling the door open enough for them to pass through it.

The heavy tapestry still hung over the doorway, obscuring it from the room, so Jeanette knew 'twas unlikely it had been found by the English.

"Leave the lantern there," Malcolm said. "We dinna want the light seen from the bailey."

Jeanette did as he said, then they both pushed past the tapestry and entered Elspet's solar, the chamber where she had been killed. Jeanette looked about in the dark, letting her eyes adjust after the light of the lantern, and slowly the room revealed itself to her. Almost nothing had changed since that day. The bed was stripped of the bloody bedding, but other than that, the destruction caused by the man who had killed her mum, Archie, the other spy who had come here with Nicholas, remained.

"Dinna look at it, angel," Malcolm said, taking her hand and pulling her to the window that looked out into the bailey. He opened it slowly, in the hopes that they would not draw attention to it from those few guards who were stationed along the top of the remaining parts of the curtain wall, and then they took up their post. Standing on either side of the open window, they watched for the first signs of the MacAlpin warriors attacking the English camp.

"Do you think Nicholas was able to kill Lord Sherwood?" Jeanette asked, keeping her voice as quiet as possible.

"I dinna ken," Malcolm replied just as quietly. "He is alive, and I was not sure he could accomplish that much. But the man survived as the king's favorite spy for years, so I have to believe he has skills he has not shared with any of us. When we return to the tunnel we shall find out soon enough exactly what we are up against this day."

Jeanette stared out over the bailey and nodded her head.

"No matter what, I will protect you." He reached out and took her hand again.

"I ken that, husband of mine." She smiled over at him and kept his hand clasped in hers as they watched the black sky of night turn the leaden grey that heralded the coming of the dawn. Suddenly, an arrow aflame arced out of the forest then sank below the level of the curtain wall, just where the English camp was set up. The war whoops of the MacAlpins and the MacKenzies came to them on the morning breeze.

"The attack has begun," Jeanette said, rushing to the hidden door.

Malcolm beat her to the tapestry, holding it out for her, then following her back into the hidden stairway. She closed the door and made sure 'twas latched securely, then he picked up the lantern and led the way as fast as they could manage the stairs.

"Are you ready, Jeanette?" he asked as they neared the bottom. "Are the Guardians ready?"

"As ready as we can be. 'Tis time to take back our home. 'Tis time to rid ourselves of these Sassenachs once and for all."

SCOTIA TOOK A DEEP BREATH AS NICHOLAS SLOWLY OPENED the cleverly disguised door that sat just where the tower butted up against the curtain wall. The two Protectors, Duncan, and one of the other warriors led the way into the still-dim bailey. The other four warriors would come behind the Guardians.

Her heart was beating hard, and her hands were damp. She wiped them on her trews, checked that her sword hung by her side, and wished she still had her shield, though she knew her task in this was not to fight with these expected weapons.

When everyone was out of the tunnel and standing against the curtain wall, hoping to conceal their presence in the bailey for just a little longer, Jeanette secured the door once more.

Nicholas whispered, "Ready? Now!" and the Protectors led the way to the well in the very center of the bailey at a run.

A cry went out from the wall walk, and Scotia knew they only had a few short moments to get a barrier up to protect the Guardians while they worked.

The three of them huddled on the north side of the well, not sure if it mattered if they were in exactly the right spot to draw the power of the Targe stone, but Malcolm had argued, and Duncan had agreed, that at least on the north side they would not have anyone standing on a curtain wall behind them, and the stone wall of the well might afford them some protection.

Rowan had the ermine sack on the ground and open already with the symbols facing the correct Guardian. The Targe stone was cradled in her hands. Jeanette had left the tunnel with her cup in one hand and a waterskin in the other, already unstoppered, so she had her cup filled and settled almost as quickly. It struck Scotia suddenly that she had nothing to prepare.

A frisson of fear ran over her skin, but she refused to give into it. She had touched the Story Stone when she became a Guardian, but she had not had it when they practiced what they were here to do. Was that why they had not been able to create the Highland Targe then and there? Doubt joined fear, dancing a raucous reel in her stomach.

The sound of swords clashing nearby startled all three of them, but Scotia refused to look.

"Say the blessing, Jeanette," Scotia said, her voice sharp with worry. "Quickly!"

Jeanette made the blessing faster than she ever had before, her hands flying through the air, and then the three of them touched the Targe stone while Jeanette intoned another blessing. The prickle of energy that passed over Scotia's skin loosened the tightness in her chest. The barrier was up.

"Duncan." She turned to where he was supposed to be, just behind her where the barrier would surround him, too, only to find him pelting toward the steps that led up to the curtain wall where the soldiers who had been on the wall walk had descended to engage in battle with the MacAlpins.

The fear almost took over.

"Does he not understand he is injured?" It took all her will to stay where she was, but her heart took up an even faster beat.

"Scotia, you cannot worry over Duncan right now," Rowan said. "None of us can worry about anything except creating the Highland Targe."

"I ken that," Scotia snapped. "Sorry," she said immediately, knowing that Rowan was right. 'Twas exactly what Duncan had taught her: in battle you had to do the task assigned you, no matter what. She was a warrior and a Guardian, and her task was clear.

"Are you sure the protective barrier will hold if we are not concentrating on it?" she asked her sister.

"Aye. This is one thing that Rowan and I have had plenty of time to prepare for."

"Then let us begin," Rowan said, holding the stone heart high between them.

Jeanette placed one hand on the stone and one on the lip of her cup so her fingertips met the surface of the water. Scotia placed one hand on the stone but did not know what to do with her other hand, so she rested it on the hilt of her sword.

They each took a moment to call forth their gifts. Scotia closed her eyes, letting her *knowing* roam freely, finding each of those men she loved, Duncan first, her da, Uilliam, the Protectors, but there was nothing in the *knowings* that caused her to focus on any of them directly.

She could hear the wind pick up outside the barrier and knew that Rowan was ready. She shifted her attention to her sister, and *knew* that she, too, was filled with her gift.

Slowly, carefully, for this was still very new to Scotia, she focused her attention on the Targe stone, and through it pulled Jeanette's gift of visions to meld with her own *knowing*. Next, and even more carefully, she reached for Rowan's gift. Her gift was volatile, and the slightest change in Rowan's emotions could increase or decrease the strength of it.

When she had all three gifts joined through the focus of the Targe stone she sent a bit of *knowing* into each of the others, and they began the blessing, a prayer really, that Jeanette had remembered and Scotia had understood. The words twined the gifts together even tighter than Scotia was able to do and began to weave the power that Rowan drew from the earth into a tiny round shield that glowed against her closed eyelids, growing with each repetition of the prayer.

She did not know how long they had been working when a *knowing* slammed into her. "Da!" she cried out, just as Jeanette and Rowan did. Without hesitation Scotia redirected the focus of their work, calling on Jeanette's vision to show them what her *knowing* told them.

Kenneth and Uilliam were fighting back to back, surrounded by too many soldiers. Kenneth had a gash on his forehead that showed white with bone, and the blood flowed into his eyes, and the Guardians knew he could not see because of it. Uilliam fought hard for both of them, but 'twas a losing battle. Before Scotia could act, Rowan's gift surged, surrounding the two beloved men with a wind so fierce it knocked the soldiers backward. She fed it more and more of the Targe stone's power, forcing the soldiers back further and further. Several turned and fled. Scotia searched with her *knowing* for someone she could find, and found Conall, but she did not know how to warn him that the deserters were heading directly for him.

Frustration burned in her, but then she felt Jeanette use Scotia's gift as a guide to push a vision of the soldiers fleeing to him. Together they used their joined gifts to force the *knowing* and vision upon him.

The sound of shouting close to the Guardians pulled all of their attention back to the bailey, but they did not open their eyes, using instead their gifts to understand that Lord Sherwood had ridden his horse through the gate, confronting the eight warriors with a score of soldiers.

"The Highland Targe," she said out loud. "We need it now!" And with that she felt Rowan pull viciously on the power that came from beneath their feet, feeding it through the Targe stone and into their woven gifts so fast it almost burned in Scotia's mind. As one, they took up the prayer where they had left off, repeating it faster and faster until it was more song than prayer, their voices filling the air around them as the Highland Targe took form, growing bigger and bigger.

Scotia's *knowing* told them all that their warriors were fighting a valiant fight, but they would not hold long.

DUNCAN STAGGERED AS LORD SHERWOOD SWUNG HIS SWORD down upon his upraised shield, sending pain deep into his shoulder. He could feel the trickle of blood from where Jeanette had stitched him up, and his head pounded, but he cared not. He had promised to keep Scotia and the other Guardians safe. He managed to duck Sherwood's next blow, then slashed at the man's leg, but somehow the English bastard got his own shield in the way, and swung for Duncan's head.

NICHOLAS SHOUTED AT SHERWOOD AS HE THREW HIS DAGGER at the man where his raised arm exposed a gap in his chain mail, leaving him vulnerable.

MALCOLM HACKED HIS WAY TO NICHOLAS'S SIDE JUST AS Sherwood roared in surprised pain, and the war cries of MacAlpins and their allies ricocheted off the walls as Kenneth, Uilliam, and more warriors poured over the downed part of the curtain wall.

For a moment it was almost as if the battle stopped as they all seemed to notice for the first time the glow that surrounded the Guardians in the middle of the bailey and the ethereal song that charged the air.

Sherwood roared, a sound of pain and rage, as he pulled the dagger free, leaned low over his horse's neck, and rode for the Guardians.

SCOTIA FOUGHT HARD TO KEEP HER FOCUS ON THE POWER THAT surged through the three of them and the stone. She fought to keep the words of the prayer racing from her lips, keeping pace with the other two, until she trembled with the effort. The *knowing* battered at her, telling her Duncan was down, her father was injured badly but was in the bailey now, Uilliam still at his side, and that Nicholas and Malcolm were alive, but she kept pushing all of that away lest she lose her focus and pull them all away from what they created again.

Words poured from them all, rising higher and higher until it sounded more like a keening than the prayer they had started with. Power pulled at her, harder and harder until she gave up any attempt to protect herself from whatever used her in this endeavor, and just when she thought she had no more to give there was a loud bang, like a thunderclap breaking right overhead, and she fell to the ground.

DUNCAN WAS PUSHING HIMSELF OFF THE GROUND WHEN A loud bang echoed through the bailey. All the air was sucked out of his lungs, and he was thrown down again with a force that was stronger than any he had ever felt before. But it was gone as quickly as it had hit. He lifted his head and was shocked to see everyone had been flattened as he had been. As he pushed up and made it to his feet this time, he looked around in shock. Everyone had been flattened, but only the Highlanders, and Sherwood's horse, were getting up. All around the bailey lay the English soldiers, splayed out as if they had all been knocked away from the source of the explosion, laying however they had fallen, and not a one of them was left alive.

Nicholas and Malcolm stood not far away from him, as stunned as he by what they saw. All three of them turned at the same time to where the Guardians had taken shelter by the well.

Sherwood's horse stood in their way, snorting and shaking his head as he nosed at his master, who lay on his back, his blank eyes open to the sky.

"Scotia!" Duncan moved as fast as he could. Nicholas and Malcolm went around the other side of the horse, and they arrived to find the three Guardians just pushing themselves up from the ground. Duncan passed through their protective barrier and only then realized that what had hit him, and everyone else, had felt like passing through a barrier, but so much more.

"You did it," he said, kneeling next to Scotia and pulling her into as fierce an embrace as he could with only one arm doing as he wished. She was trembling.

"Did we hurt you?" she asked, pulling back enough to look at him. Her brow furrowed when she saw the blood staining his shoulder again. "You were to stay with us," she said. "You were supposed to stay out of the fight."

"Love, you know I could not do that."

"But you promised me."

"Nay, I never promised that. I said I would stand by you in the battle, not that I would stay inside your barrier and watch the battle from there."

"You play with words."

He kissed her and only then noticed the other two couples were also whispering together, touching, kissing.

"That boom that flattened all of us, that was the Highland Targe, aye?"

She grinned. "Aye. Rowan has sent it to rest across the path of any who might wish to pass into the Highlands from this direction. Any who are of ill intent will—"

"Will find the death they deserve," Nicholas said as he pulled Rowan to her feet.

Scotia sucked in a loud breath as she stood and looked at the destruction the Guardians had wrought upon the English. "All of them?" she asked.

"Aye, it would appear that all of ill intent did not survive the passing of the Highland Targe over them."

She looked about, taking in the many bodies that lay where they had fallen, weapons still in their hands, eyes open to the sky. It was only then that Scotia noticed that the incomplete palisade wall of tree trunks had also been blown down by the blast of power from the Targe stone.

"Rowan, look!" she said, pointing to where the north side of the curtain wall had once stood, the tree trunks scattered over the remaining rubble as if a great wind had toppled them, pushing them outward, toward the loch, just as the curtain wall had fallen.

"The Targe?" Jeanette asked, but the timbre of her voice told Scotia she was busy sorting through all the Targe and Guardian lore she kept in her mind, looking for an answer. "The two of you were below the wall when it fell . . . arguing . . . strong emotion, the trigger for Scotia's gift, which can join with our gifts . . . with your gift, Rowan . . ." Jeanette squinted her eyes as if she were trying to see something in dim light. She turned around, looking at what they had wrought. "If Scotia's gift called to the power of the Targe, then took control of the gift Rowan did not even know she had yet . . . the north wall was between the two of you and this place where we have drawn the full power of the Targe stone this day . . ."

"We did this," Rowan said, her eyes on Scotia. "We did this, cousin."

"And you protected the two of you, Rowan, and Nicholas, just as you did as a wee lass when you protected yourself when your mum destroyed your cottage," Jeanette said quietly, awe in her voice. "I suspect we will find ourselves far stronger in our gifts as we learn to use them, if this is what the two of you could do before you were even chosen to be Guardians."

Scotia looked at the remains of the wall, then let herself take in the full measure of what they had done, what the Guardians had done. "I will not feel any guilt over this," she said, squaring her shoulders and looking up at Duncan. "I will not."

"And you should not," Duncan said at the same time Nicholas and Malcolm did.

"We are Guardians of the Highland Targe," Rowan said quietly, but with a new strength in her voice. "We are charged with protecting the Highlands from the greed of invaders, from the avarice of King Edward, who is no king of ours."

The moment she said *King Edward* a *knowing* gripped Scotia.

"Sister, I need your sight," she said, reaching for Jeanette's hand. Rowan stepped close enough to join hands with them. And just that easily their gifts were united. Scotia followed the *knowing*, the other gifts twined with it, and when she "arrived" they were at the bedside of a man far gone in illness. His grey hair was flecked with ginger, and his breath rattled loudly, once, twice, and then it ceased. His eyes stared blankly at nothing. Armor-clad soldiers, as well as a priest, stood round the massive bed, shifting uneasily as they held vigil.

King Edward was dead. The *knowing* floated among the joined gifts.

CHAPTER TWENTY-FIVE

THE DAWN BATTLE HAD BEEN ONLY THE BEGINNING OF A LONG and arduous day. The Guardians had spent most of the morning making sure the Highland Targe was stable as they learned how to feed it with the energy Rowan pulled through the Targe stone, directed at such a great distance by Scotia's *knowing*, and Jeanette's visions.

The warriors who were not badly injured collected the bodies of the dead. The Scots were buried in the meadow just east of the castle, a stone cairn marking each grave. The English were loaded into carts to be taken to the place Rowan had dropped a ledge on the soldiers who had accompanied Archie into their glen. Once they were all there the Guardians would pull down the rest of the outcropping and bury them all in the stone.

Jeanette had wanted to tend the injured, but Malcolm convinced her that the warriors could tend their own until the Guardians were done with their work. As soon as they were, she had tirelessly stitched and bound wounds until she had run out of supplies.

Once all the English had been moved, the Guardians returned to their place by the well, and as if they had been working together for years instead of less than a day, they quickly finished the job of burying their enemies.

More than enough food and blankets had been found in the English camp, so the MacAlpins and their allies gathered round the fires for the night.

Scotia had not left Duncan's side since they had found their way out of the castle sometime in the late afternoon, following their noses and growling stomachs to where Rowan had managed to put two large pots of stew over a fire.

Jeanette had restitched Duncan's previous injury and marveled that his many others were nothing more than scratches and a couple of shallow cuts that had already stopped bleeding.

Now Scotia lay near a fire wrapped in a plaid and cradled against Duncan's chest. One of his arms stretched out beneath her head while the other one was tucked tightly around her waist, as if even in his exhausted sleep he would not let her wander away from him. Not that she had any intention of doing so.

She had watched the sky all through the short summer night, unable to sleep though she had never been so tired in all her days. Was King Edward, the Hammer of the Scots, well and truly dead? And if so, would his son take up his father's crusade against them? At least they would not be able to harry the MacAlpins again, and for that she could not give enough thanks. As dawn began to lighten the sky she could lie still no longer and slowly, carefully sat up, letting Duncan's arm drape over her lap so he would know, even in his sleep, that she had not left him.

Conall sat nearby. He had a long cut along the left side of his face, and his blond hair was tangled with dried blood on that side.

"That will scar," she said to him.

"Aye. Perhaps now Uilliam will stop calling me a wee daft laddie?"

Scotia smiled. "Perhaps, though he kens it bothers you, so probably not."

A silence fell between them, and Scotia thought there was more Conall wanted to say.

"What?" she asked.

"You love him," he said, and she noted it was not a question. "You have always loved him, have you not?"

She looked down at Duncan and ran her fingers through his soft curly hair, still amazed that she had the right to touch him this way, and knew the honesty she had embraced of late must continue with Conall.

"Aye." She looked back at Conall. "Though in truth I did not realize it until very recently. I did not mean to dally with your heart, Conall, and I ask your forgiveness and understanding if I have hurt you through my own denial of my true feelings."

He said nothing, but she could see him struggling with her words in the stiffness of his shoulders and the set of his jaw. She had hurt him, and for that she was truly sorry. It would seem her penance for past behavior was not finished with today's victory. She took a deep breath and rubbed the night's grit from her eyes.

"I understand if you cannot forgive me," she said, hoping her voice conveyed the sincerity of her words. "I am ashamed of my past behavior and any pain it may cause you, but I cannot lie to myself, or anyone else anymore."

He stood as if to leave her, then stopped. "I kent it all along." He hooked his thumbs into his belt, and looked away from her. "I was so proud when you chose me that I did not want to believe your heart was given elsewhere, though 'twas clear to everyone but you. If you are guilty of lying to yourself, so am I, and I cannot hold you solely responsible for what happened between us."

Scotia realized in that moment that Conall truly was no longer the lovesick lad she had dallied with, any more than she was the same lass. They had both grown up, and now they were both taking responsibility for their actions. "I thank you for that understanding. It is more than I dared hope for."

He gave her a curt nod, looking down at Duncan once more. "Do not hurt him, Scotia. He does not deserve that."

She tried to swallow, but the lump in her throat made that difficult as she looked down at the man who had stolen her heart before she even knew it. "I will never hurt him on purpose again," she finally said. Conall seemed content with that answer and left them by the fire alone.

"That was well done." Duncan's voice was raspy and quiet, as if he did not have the energy to push it fully into the air. "Do you really love me?" He opened his eyes enough to peer up at her.

"I do. Can you forgive me for all the trouble I have caused you and the clan? I truly did not see how my actions hurt so many others."

"And now?" he asked, sitting up beside her and twining his fingers with hers.

"Can you ever see me as anything but a spoiled wean?"

"I already do, Scotia. Can you not tell? You have proved yourself changed over and over again in the past few days."

"I need you to know that I will do everything I can to be worthy of your love, your trust, and of my position as Guardian of the Targe. I need you by my side, Duncan. I am my best self when I am with you. I need you to be my friend, and my champion, as you have been my entire life." She looked down at their joined hands for a moment and let the multitude of emotions this man set off in her settle into one, the love for him that nearly overwhelmed her. She raised her gaze to his. "But I want more."

He said nothing, but she thought he was holding his breath.

"Duncan, I love you more than I can say, more than my heart can hold. I cannot imagine a day without you by my side . . . and in my bed." She waggled her eyebrows at him, teasing him even in this serious moment, but also telling the truth. She sobered. "If you feel even half of what I do, please say that you will be my Protector, my husband."

Now it was she who held her breath, but the grin that spread over his beloved face took away any doubt that he would not want her.

"You will be the death of me, my warrior lass. I love you with all my heart. I would be proud to be your Protector, and prouder still to call you wife." He pulled her close and kissed her, softly at first, and then more deeply, infusing the press of his lips, the slide of his tongue against hers, with so much longing, so much passion, a searing heat flashed through her, pooling low in her belly as a desire unlike any she had felt before nearly overwhelmed her.

"There is one condition, though," he said against her lips, as if he'd only just thought of it. He pulled away from her just far enough to look her in the eye, leaving her breathless and unsettled. His grin was gone, replaced by a familiar serious expression.

"What?"

"I dinna want to wait. Not a single day. I have waited a long time for you, Scotia." He ran his fingers over her cheek, then slid his hand down her neck and over her chest, letting his fingers lightly skim over her breast. Her breath hitched at his feathery touch. "I am done waiting." The rasp in his voice, as if he fought to hold himself in check even now when he knew she was his, opened her heart so wide it ached.

She laid her palm against his cheek and lightly kissed his lips, only now noting the scrape of his whiskers against her skin. "I am done waiting, as well, Duncan, and I would say our vows right here and now, but we need the entire clan to celebrate with us." She quirked one eyebrow at him. "I'll not have you backing out three days hence, saying vows were not said."

He smiled and sighed. "You are right. We need to do this before everyone. You are a Guardian, and if I am to be your Protector, we must be wed in front of the entire clan. So today, at the caves, before the sun sets again." He scrambled to his feet and pulled her up and into his arms for another searing kiss that had them both holding so fast to the other there was no room between them.

"Ahem."

Scotia heard the sound but did not think anything of it as she lost herself in the feel of his hard chest pressed against her breasts, the softness of Duncan's lips, the slip of his tongue over hers, and the heat of his desire that was oh so evident.

"Ye might want to stop what you are about to do with Kenneth's daughter, seeing as he is standing right here."

The kiss continued until the words finally filtered through. She stopped the kiss, and they looked at each other for a moment. Laughter danced in his eyes and threatened to bubble out of her, carried into the air on sheer joy.

"Duncan, ye might want to take a step away from the lassie," Uilliam said.

"Oh, nay," Scotia whispered against his lips. "You do not want to do that." She glanced down between them and laughed when Duncan's face turned pink. She kissed him quickly and spun in his arms, keeping him behind her. She laid her hands over his where they rested around her waist and faced her father and Uilliam with a smile she had no intention of hiding. The two men were scowling at the two of them, but ranged a little behind them were a grinning Nicholas and Rowan on one side, and a grinning Jeanette and Malcolm on the other.

"I think we are caught, Scotia," Duncan said, pulling her back so she leaned against him. "I'm afraid the only thing we can do to make this right is wed."

Kenneth started to speak but could only bluster and cough, his face going red. Uilliam pounded him on the back, shaking his head and laughing at his friend.

"I ken she is your wayward lassie, Kenneth, but she has always been his. It just took far longer than it should have for the two of them to realize their fate. A wedding is the only way to make sure she remains his trouble for as long as they live."

"Uncle," Rowan said, "Scotia is a Guardian and every Guardian must have a Protector." She leaned into Nicholas's side, their arms looped around each other's waist, and lay her head on his shoulder. She looked peaceful and relaxed as she had not in a very long time. "Can you think of a better, more experienced Protector for our Scotia? Indeed, I would say he has been training for the position Scotia's whole life."

Jeanette laughed. "Aye, that he has, but do you think Scotia will have him?"

Now it was Scotia's face that heated with the teasing.

"Aye, I will have him," she said, "and I shall wed with him this very day."

"This day?" Rowan asked.

"We will not wait any longer," Duncan said, smiling down at Scotia. "We cannot wait any longer."

Jeanette and Rowan grinned at each other.

"It seems we are to have another wedding, cousin," Rowan said.

"Aye, but if we are to have a wedding today," Jeanette replied, "we must return to the caves immediately. This may be quickly done, but 'twill be done well. Peigi will need a little time to prepare a wedding meal. Scotia, you cannot get wed in trews with a sword hanging from your belt. You can wear the gown I wore to wed with Malcolm, and this time I shall do your hair." She looked at her husband of just a few weeks. "I suppose we can give them our wee cave for the night." The wicked smile on her face told Scotia that Jeanette and Malcolm would retire to their favorite trysting place, the grotto where she had been chosen as Guardian.

"I suppose we can," Malcolm said with a grin that made him glow, turning him into the golden warrior Jeanette often called him.

Rowan closed the distance to Scotia and Duncan and gave her cousin a fierce hug. "You will continue to keep her out of trouble," she said to Duncan over Scotia's shoulder.

"I will," he said, "though I think the worst of her troublemaking is behind her."

Jeanette gave her a hug, too, but couldn't seem to say anything. She kissed them both on the cheek, then managed to say, "Take good care of each other."

"Nicholas, do you think there is any wine or whiskey in the English supplies?" Rowan asked.

"I know Sherwood had a bottle of wine last night. There is likely more."

"Good, we will take as much as we can with us so we can properly toast these two," she said. "I think we have all earned a celebration, and what better way to celebrate defeating the English than with the joining together of Scotia and Duncan!"

The three couples quickly gathered up the few things they had with them and headed for the caves, Nicholas and Malcolm leaving a trail of instructions behind them while Rowan and Jeanette invited everyone they passed to the wedding. Scotia and Duncan walked behind the others, arm in arm, unwilling to stop touching each other for even a moment.

Kenneth still stood mute behind them while Uilliam's deep laughter echoed off the castle wall.

IT TOOK ALL OF DUNCAN'S CONSIDERABLE PATIENCE TO ALLOW the women to postpone the ceremony long enough for everyone to arrive back at the caves from the castle, but when Scotia stepped out of the main cave and into the soft late-afternoon light he realized he had waited years for this woman, and the wait had been worth it.

Her raven hair was pulled back from her heart-shaped face simply, with a few yellow summer blooms tucked into it. Her pale green eyes were huge, as if she were unsure that he would still be waiting for her, but when their eyes met, all doubt fled and she glowed with happiness.

"Please tell me everyone is gathered," she said as she joined him. Taking his hand in hers, she leaned close. "I dinna ken how long I can wait before we are alone!"

He kissed her, gently, chastely, for he shared her impatience and dared not fan the flames of the passion that threatened to ignite between them, burning away all sense and propriety. "I dinna ken, either." He put a little more distance between them, but did not let her hand free of his. "But I promised myself a long time ago that I would not . . . not until . . ." He groaned and she laughed.

"It is not easy being a man of great conscience." She shook her head at him then looked around. "Jeanette, please God, tell me we are ready for the ceremony!"

"Come, sister, Duncan." She waved them over to a spot near the council circle where the trees would be a green background to their vows. They had no priest to bless them, so Nicholas and Rowan stood next to Malcolm and Jeanette in front of the couple, and the rest of the clan crowded around them, nearly filling the clearing.

"Duncan of Dunlairig, will you promise always to Protect this Guardian?" Rowan asked, her voice loud enough so all could hear.

"I do promise," he answered, giving Scotia's hand a squeeze. "I will put her life before mine, always."

"Will you take her to wife, keeping her safe, loving her well, all the rest of your days?" Jeanette asked.

Duncan turned to face Scotia, taking both of her hands in his and pulling her close enough so her spicy scent wrapped around him. "I promise all of that." He drew her hands to his mouth, placing one kiss on each. He thought he heard her groan as his lips pressed against her skin, and he could not help but grin. "I promise all of that," he repeated, just loud enough for Scotia to hear, "and so much more."

"Scotia MacAlpin, daughter of Kenneth and Elspet, Guardian of the Targe," Nicholas began, but Scotia did not let him get any further.

"I take this man, Duncan of Dunlairig, as my Protector, and as my husband. I promise to keep him safe and love him very, very well, all the rest of my days!"

There was a quiet whisper through the gathering as she promised to keep him safe, but Duncan's grin grew wider.

"She is a warrior-Guardian," he said loudly so all could hear him, but he never took his eyes off his bride, who grinned back at him, the light of her teasing adding heat to the desire that burned in her gaze. "I would have her no other way."

Laughter rippled through the clan, then shouts of "Kiss!" began to build.

"I am not one to do as people tell me to," Scotia said, stepping into his arms, "but just this once I think I will." She raised up onto her toes and sealed their vows with a kiss full of promises and passion.

CHAPTER TWENTY-SIX

"Do you not think we can slip away now?" Scotia sat so close to Duncan she did not even have to whisper in his ear. "I fear I will snap at someone soon if we do not!"

Duncan caught her lips with his, stoking the need within her, fanning it to a blaze. She swallowed the moan that tried to escape even as whoops and whistles wrapped around them from the gathering of their clan. Duncan grinned at her, his familiar brown eyes alight with a joy she'd never seen before. She grinned back and raised her eyebrows.

"I will snap," she promised.

"We cannot have that," he replied. "A bride should never snap at those celebrating her happiness." The grin faded. "You are happy, are you not?"

"Aye, Duncan." She cupped his cheek in her palm to the accompaniment of several happy female sighs from those sitting near them. "I am happier than I ever hoped to be. I still cannot believe that you love me after everything I have—"

He kissed her again, this time with care, as if it were another vow he made to her. "I have always loved you."

"I think I should like you to prove your love." She tried to keep the teasing out of her voice but was not successful.

"And I know I should like you to prove yours," he said, taking her hand that still rested against his face and placing a soft kiss in her palm.

"So we are agreed? 'Tis time to slip away from the celebration?"

"There will be no slipping away, you two," Peigi said.

They looked up to find the old woman standing behind them, her gnarled hands on her hips.

"'Tis not right to deprive the clan of their fun," she said, a rosy hue in her cheeks and a twinkle in her eyes.

Scotia rolled her eyes at the old woman and was rewarded with her wheezy cackle. Duncan drew Scotia up from their seat of honor on one of the logs by the cookfire, and everyone else went silent, all eyes on the two of them. Scotia was suddenly struck dumb by the genuine happiness she saw on every face directed at the two of them . . . not just at Duncan . . . and for the first time in a very long time she felt a beloved part of the clan.

"My bride is tired," Duncan said. Snorts and ribald retorts rattled through the crowd. "We shall take our leave—"

Kenneth stood, storm clouds in his eyes.

"Da," Scotia said, "I am wed now, and Duncan has always taken care of me."

"We will not leave the glen," Duncan said, "but we may not return here for a few days."

"Only a few days?" she teased, rousing the crowd to even louder retorts.

"Get ye away, lad!" Uilliam's voice rose over the others. "I dinna ken how much more of this Kenneth can take!" And then the jokes and whoops shifted to her da.

"'Tis time," she said to her husband, pulling him out of the clearing and into the forest.

SCOTIA LET DUNCAN LEAD HER QUICKLY AWAY FROM THE gathering to a small cave far enough away to give them privacy. Without words he drew her into his arms and kissed her, slowly, gently, as if he thought she might break. But that was not what she wanted. She tilted her head, threaded her fingers into his soft hair, and took control, her kiss turning greedy and demanding. He hesitated only a moment, then met her kiss for kiss, his hands roaming everywhere, pulling her tight against him. She fumbled with the broach that held his plaid at his shoulder, then went for his belt, dropping it and the plaid to the ground.

"'Tis not fair that you wear more than I," he whispered against her throat where he kissed and nipped and nuzzled. Her laces were undone before he stopped speaking. He pushed her gown down her arms to puddle at her feet, leaving her only in her kirtle, while he still wore his tunic. She stepped back, missing the heat of him, but wanting, needing to see her husband. She pulled the string at her neckline and let the kirtle slide off.

The look of hunger in Duncan's eyes made her smile. When he pulled his tunic over his head, her breath caught. Dark hair spread over his chest, narrowing down his stomach until . . .

He reached for her hand and pulled her a little deeper into the cave and down onto a pallet that she had not noticed. They were both breathing hard, and she found herself suddenly focused completely on the intensity of Duncan's stare, as if he could see nothing but her. He pressed her back and settled himself over her. The feel of his chest grazing her breasts with every gasping breath they took nearly overwhelmed her senses, leaving her exquisitely aware of every touch, every breath that feathered over her face, and the look of desire, and more, that filled his eyes. All at once Duncan groaned, though she had done nothing to hurt him, and covered her mouth with his greedy, urgent kiss.

Everything disappeared in Scotia's mind as her attention was overwhelmed by the feel of his lips against hers, the way his tongue swept into her mouth, tangling with her own, the way his fingers twined with hers, grasping her hands as if he could not bear to let them go, and the way his desire pressed against her belly, telling her more about his need of her than any words might.

And her own need answered his.

Rational thought fled, and sensation was all she knew. He rolled, settling her next to him, as he ran his hand down her arm, over her hip and waist, and up to cup her aching breast, all the while feasting on her lips. She reached down, running her own hand over his thigh, reaching around to cup his buttock, urging him closer to her, closer to her core, to her need. She moved her hand between them and trailed her fingers lightly up his length before she took him in her grip and began tormenting him with excruciatingly slow strokes. She hooked a leg over his hip, pressing him even closer with it. Need burned through her until she could think of nothing but Duncan, and the need to join completely with him.

And then he slid his hand between them, until he found the wetness between her legs and pressed a finger into her depths, drawing a groan of pleasure from both of them.

DUNCAN FOUGHT THE NEED SCREAMING THROUGH HIM TO complete the joining immediately. Instead he slowed his breath and slowly pulled his finger out of her slick folds, then even more slowly pressed it back inside her, again and again, achingly slow, until she was begging him with the undulations of her hips and the quick gasps of her breath to hurry his movements, to hurry her pleasure. But he did not. He reveled in the power he had to make her lose herself to the sensations he was creating within her body.

"You must cease tormenting me, Duncan." Desire made her voice smoky and low, thickly caressing him with the promise of pleasure, with the promise of . . .

"Now, Duncan. Come to me now."

He settled between her thighs, and then he stilled. "I love you, Scotia," he said, waiting for her to meet his gaze so she could see the depth and the truth of his words.

She cupped his cheek in her hand, as she had earlier. "And I love you, Duncan."

He held her gaze as he slowly buried himself within her. As he began to move within her she arched to meet him, urging him on with her hips, her hands, the sounds of pleasure that escaped her full lips.

The joining was not gentle, but then she did not seem to want it that way. She met him thrust for thrust, keening her pleasure, pulling him hard against her, into her, harder, faster, until they both leapt, their voices joining in the moment as their bodies pulsed against each other, complete and one at long last.

EPILOGUE

One year later . . .

DUNCAN STATIONED HIMSELF ON THE WALL WALK AS HE DID every morning, keeping watch over the three Guardians as they stood at a small round table near the well in the bailey below—auburn, pale yellow, and his own Scotia's raven-black heads bent over their work.

It had been a year since Duncan and Scotia had wed, and still he marveled at the woman he had married. She remained an imp at times, teasing him, and stirring up trouble here and there, but she did so with purpose, redirecting the squabbles of weans and the arguments of adults. She did so to bring a smile to the faces of her clan as she had when she was a lassie, and she did so to gain his attention, though that was not necessary. She was the center of his world, as she always had been.

Of course just this morning she had teased him that his love would have to be shared when their bairn was born in the early spring, but he knew in that moment his love would only multiply, if such a thing were possible.

"You are hopeless," Malcolm said as he joined Duncan, standing next to him, but his attention fixed on the Guardians below.

"Hopeless?"

"Every single morn you stand here gazing down upon your wife like a besotted lad."

Duncan shrugged. "'Tis true, I am besotted, but you are no better at hiding your feelings for your 'angel.'"

"And why should I hide them?" Malcolm grinned at Duncan. "Who could have known that being abandoned in battle by my kin and nearly losing the use of my sword hand would turn out to be what brought me to my destiny, to Jeanette?"

Nicholas joined them then, fresh from his morning inspection of the newly completed north section of the curtain wall. Bryn of Beaumaris had stayed with them after the defeat of the English force, preferring to build things for the MacAlpins rather than killing for the English. His skill had created a strong new wall for the clan, and now he was directing the building of a new great hall. This one would be larger than the last, the walls made of stone this time.

Malcolm and Duncan nodded at their chief, the three of them leaning against the wall as they watched in silence, as they did every morn, while the Guardians prepared to strengthen the Highland Targe, as *they* did every morn.

Rowan took a moment to settle her new bairn—Lilias, after the Guardian's mum—in the sling of plaid that Scotia had fashioned as a birthing gift for her. Jeanette arched her back and ran a hand over her huge belly. Her bairn, a lassie who would be named Elspet, as was revealed to the pale-haired Guardian in a vision, would be born any time now. 'Twas why they worked at a table instead of on the ground as they used to. Rowan had the table built when she was with child and could no longer sit upon the ground, nor rise from it without help.

Nicholas yawned, wide and not quietly.

Malcolm looked at their chief, his mouth cocked in a half grin as if he tried to suppress it but failed.

"How does the wee Lilias fare this morn?" Duncan asked Nicholas.

"She fares better than her mum and me," he replied. "She has a strong set of lungs, that one, and she uses them with gusto when she is hungry." He sighed. "Peigi says it may be a full year before she sleeps through the night." He shook his head, but the soft smile on his face betrayed the way the tiny girl had already burrowed into the man's heart.

As the Guardians began what Duncan thought of as the dance-of-hands that was part of the Highland Targe blessing, Malcolm nudged him with his shoulder. "Jeanette says you will have a son."

"She says what?" Nicholas asked, his attention suddenly on the two Protectors at his side.

"Scotia said she had told no one but me—" And then the rest of Malcolm's words sank in. "A son? Jeanette had a vision?"

"There are no secrets from my wife, Dunc," Malcolm said, slapping Duncan hard on the back on one side as Nicholas did on the other. "You should ken that well by now."

"'Twill be good to have a laddie to keep the lassies in check," Nicholas said with a grin on his face.

"If the lassies are anything like their parents," Duncan said, "there is no hope of keeping any of them in check."

"Especially if the laddie takes after his mum!" Malcolm said with a waggle of his tawny brows. "If he does he'll be leading our lassies into trouble by the time he can crawl."

Duncan gave a mock groan, and the three of them laughed, a deep joyful sound that drew eyes from everyone below, including their Guardian wives.

ACKNOWLEDGMENTS

PAMELA PALMER AND ANN SHAW MORAN—AS ALWAYS, YOUR insight, support, and friendship sustain me, inspire me, and keep me open to all possibilities.

Phyllis Hall Haislip and Kathy Huffman—your company each morning keeps me moving forward. I appreciate that more than you know!

The great women and men at Montlake Romance—it is such a pleasure to work with all of you! Thank you for all you do for me and my books!

My family, Dean, Samantha, and Alex—you are my strength, and my joy!

I also want to thank my amazing readers for buying my books, writing reviews, and seeking me out online. It is such a gift to know my stories touch your hearts!

ABOUT THE AUTHOR

Photo © 2012 Michael Taylor

LAURIN WITTIG WAS INDOCTRINATED INTO HER SCOTTISH heritage at birth when her parents chose her oddly spelled name from a plethora of Scottish family names. At ten, Laurin attended her first MacGregor clan gathering with her grandparents, and her first ceilidh (kay-lee), a Scottish party, where she danced to the bagpipes with the hereditary chieftain of the clan. At eleven, she visited Scotland for the first time, and it has inhabited her imagination ever since.

Laurin writes bestselling and award-winning Scottish medieval romances and lives in southeastern Virginia. For more information about all of Laurin's books, please visit her at http://LaurinWittig.com.